A Blunt Instrument

Author of over fifty books, Georgette Heyer is one of the best-known and best-loved of all historical novelists, making the Regency period her own. Her first novel, *The Black Moth*, published in 1921, was written at the age of fifteen to amuse her convalescent brother; her last was *My Lord John*. Although most famous for her historical fiction, she also wrote twelve mystery novels. Georgette Heyer died in 1974 at the age of seventy-one.

Praise for *A Blunt Instrument*

'Sharp, clear and witty' – *New Yorker*

GEORGETTE HEYER

A Blunt Instrument

arrow books

Published in the United Kingdom by Arrow Books in 2006

1 3 5 7 9 10 8 6 4 2

First published in the United Kingdom in 1938 by Hodder & Stoughton Ltd

First published in Great Britain in 1938 by
Hodder & Stoughton Ltd.
Random House, 20 Vauxhall Bridge Road,
London SW1V 2SA

www.rbooks.co.uk

Addresses for companies within The Random House Group Limited
can be found at: www.randomhouse.co.uk/offices.htm

The Random House Group Limited Reg. No. 954009

A CIP catalogue record for this book
is available from the British Library

ISBN 9780099550327

The Random House Group Limited supports The Forest Stewardship
Council (FSC), the leading international forest certification organisation.
All our titles that are printed on Greenpeace approved FSC certified paper
carry the FSC logo. Our paper procurement policy can be found at:
www.rbooks.co.uk/environment

Typeset by SX Composing DTP, Rayleigh, Essex
Printed and bound in Great Britain by
CPI Cox & Wyman, Reading, RG1 8EX

One

A breeze, hardly more than a whisper of wind, stirred the curtains that hung on either side of the long window, and wafted into the room the scent of the wisteria covering the wall of the house. The policeman turned his head as the curtains faintly rustled, his rather glassy blue eyes frowning and suspicious. Straightening himself, for he had been bending over the figure of a man seated behind the carved knee-hole desk in the middle of the room, he trod over to the window and looked out into the dusky garden. His torch explored the shadows cast by two flowering shrubs without, however, revealing anything but a nondescript cat, whose eyes caught and flung back the light for an instant before the animal glided into the recesses of the shrub. There was no other sign of life in the garden, and after a moment of keen scrutiny, the policeman turned back into the room, and went to the desk. The man behind it paid no heed, for he was dead, as the policeman had already ascertained. His head lay on the open blotter, with blood congealing in his sleek, pomaded hair.

The policeman drew a long breath. He was rather pale, and the hand which he stretched out towards the telephone shook a little. Mr Ernest Fletcher's head was not quite the right shape; there was a dent in it, under the coagulated blood.

The policeman's hand was arrested before it had grasped the telephone receiver. He drew it back, felt for a handkerchief, and with it wiped a smear of blood from his hand, and then picked up the receiver.

As he did so, he caught the sound of footsteps approaching the room. Still holding the instrument, he turned his head towards the door.

It opened, and a middle-aged butler came in, carrying a tray with a syphon and a whisky decanter and glasses upon it. At sight of the police constable he gave a perceptible start. His gaze next alighted on the figure of his master. The tumbler on the tray shuddered against the decanter, but Simmons did not drop the tray. He stood holding it mechanically, staring at Ernest Fletcher's back.

PC Glass spoke the number of the police station. His flat, unemotional voice brought Simmons's eyes back to his face. 'My God, is he dead?' he asked in a hushed voice.

A stern glance was directed towards him. 'Thou shalt not take the name of the Lord, thy God, in vain,' said Glass deeply.

This admonishment was more comprehensible to Simmons, who was a member of the same sect as PC Glass, than to the official at the Telephone Exchange, who took it in bad part. By the time the misunderstanding had been cleared up, and the number of the police station repeated, Simmons had set the tray down, and stepped fearfully up to his master's body. One look at the damaged skull was enough to drive him back a pace. He raised a sickly face, and demanded in an unsteady voice: 'Who did it?'

'That'll be for others to find out,' replied Glass. 'I shall be obliged to you, Mr Simmons, if you will shut that door.'

'If it's all the same to you, Mr Glass, I'll shut myself on the other side of it,' said the butler. 'This – this is a very upsetting sight, and I don't mind telling you it turns my stomach.'

'You'll stay till I've asked you a few questions, as is my duty,' replied Glass.

'But I can't tell you anything! I didn't have anything to do with it!'

Glass paid no heed, for he was connected at that moment with the police station. Simmons gulped, and went to shut the door, remaining beside it, so that only Ernest Fletcher's shoulders were visible to him.

PC Glass, having announced his name and whereabouts, was telling the Sergeant that he had a murder to report.

Policemen! thought Simmons, resentful of Glass's calm. You'd think corpses with their heads bashed in were as common as daisies. He wasn't human, Glass; he was downright callous, standing there so close to the body he could have touched it just by stretching out his hand, talking into the telephone as though he was saying his piece in the witness-box, and all the time staring at the dead man without a bit of feeling in his face, when anyone else would have turned sick at the sight.

Glass laid down the receiver, and restored his handkerchief to his pocket. 'Lo, this is the man that made

3

not God his strength, but trusted in his riches,' he said.

The sombre pronouncement recalled Simmons's thoughts. He gave a sympathetic groan. 'That's true, Mr Glass. Woe to the crown of pride! But how did it happen? How do you come to be here? Oh dear, oh dear, I never thought to be mixed up with a thing like this!'

'I came up that path,' said Glass, nodding towards the French windows. He drew a notebook from his pocket, and the stub of a pencil, and bent an official stare upon the butler. 'Now, Mr Simmons, if you please!'

'It's no use asking me: I don't know anything about it, I tell you!'

'You know when you last saw Mr Fletcher alive,' said Glass, unmoved by the butler's evident agitation.

'It would have been when I showed Mr Budd in,' replied Simmons, after a moment's hesitation.

'Time?'

'I don't know – not for certain, that is. It was about an hour ago.' He made an effort to collect his wits, and added: 'About nine o'clock. I was clearing the table in the dining-room, so it couldn't have been much later.'

Glass said, without raising his eyes from his notebook: 'This Mr Budd: known to you?'

'No. I never saw him before in my life – not to my knowledge.'

'Oh! When did he leave?'

'I don't know. I didn't know he had left till I came in just now. He must have gone by the garden-way, same as you came in, Mr Glass.'

'Was that usual?'

'It was – and it wasn't,' replied Simmons, 'if you know what I mean, Mr Glass.'

4

'No,' said Glass uncompromisingly.

'The master had friends who used to visit him that way.' Simmons heaved a sigh. 'Women, Mr Glass.'

'Thine habitation,' said Glass, with a condemnatory glance round the comfortable room, 'is in the midst of deceit.'

'That's true, Mr Glass. The times I've wrestled in prayer –'

The opening of the door interrupted him. Neither he nor Glass had heard footsteps approaching the study, and neither had time to prevent the entrance into the room of a willowy young man in an ill-fitting dinner-jacket suit, who paused on the threshold, blinked long-lashed eyelids at the sight of a policeman, and smiled deprecatingly.

'Oh, sorry!' said the newcomer. 'Fancy finding you here!'

His voice was low-pitched, and he spoke softly and rather quickly, so that it was difficult to catch what he said. A lock of lank dark hair fell over his brow; he wore a pleated shirt, and a deplorable tie, and looked, to PC Glass, like a poet.

His murmured exclamation puzzled Glass. He said suspiciously: 'Fancy meeting me, eh? So you know me, do you, sir?'

'Oh no!' said the young man. His fluttering glance went round the room and discovered the body of Ernest Fletcher. His hand left the door-knob; he walked forward to the desk, and turned rather pale. 'I should shame my manhood if I were sick, shouldn't I? I wonder what one does now?' His gaze asked inspiration of Glass, of Simmons, and encountered only blank stares. It found the tray Simmons had brought into the room. 'Yes, that's what one does,' he said, and went to the tray, and poured himself out a stiff, short drink of whisky-and-soda.

'The master's nephew – Mr Neville Fletcher,' said Simmons, answering the question in Glass's eye.

'You're staying in this house, sir?'

'Yes, but I don't like murders. So inartistic, don't you think? Besides, they don't happen.'

'This has happened, sir,' said Glass, a little puzzled.

'Yes, that's what upsets me. Murders only occur in other people's families. Not even in one's own circle. Ever noticed that? No, I suppose not. Nothing in one's experience – one had thought it so wide! – has taught one how to cope with such a bizarre situation.'

He ended on an uncertain laugh; it was plain that under his flippancy he was shaken. The butler looked at him curiously, and then at Glass, who, after staring at Neville Fletcher for a moment, licked his pencil-point, and asked: 'When did you see Mr Fletcher last, if you please, sir?'

'At dinner. In the dining-room, I mean. No, let us be exact; not the dining-room; the hall.'

'Make up your mind, sir,' recommended Glass stolidly.

'Yes, that's all right. After dinner he came here, and I wandered off to the billiard-room. We parted in the hall.'

'At what hour would that have been, sir?'

Neville shook his head. 'I don't know. After dinner. Do you know, Simmons?'

'I couldn't say, sir, not precisely. The master was usually out of the dining-room by ten to nine.'

'And after that you didn't see Mr Fletcher again?'

6

'No. Not till now. Anything you'd like to know, or can I withdraw?'

'It'll save time, sir, if you'll give an account of your movements between the time you and the deceased left the dining-room, and 10.05 p.m.'

'Well, I went to the billiard-room, and knocked the balls about a bit.'

'Alone, sir?'

'Yes, but my aunt came to find me, so I left.'

'Your aunt?'

'Miss Fletcher,' interpolated the butler. 'The master's sister, Mr Glass.'

'You left the billiard-room with your aunt, sir? Did you remain with her?'

'No. Which all goes to show that politeness always pays. I silently faded away, and now I'm sorry, because if I'd accompanied her to the drawing-room I should have had an alibi, which I haven't got. I went upstairs to my own room, and read a book. I wonder if I can have fallen asleep over it?' He looked doubtfully towards his uncle's chair, and gave a faint shudder. 'No, my God, I couldn't dream anything like this! It's fantastic.'

'If you'll excuse me, Mr Glass, I fancy that was the front-door bell,' interrupted Simmons, moving towards the door.

A few moments later a police-sergeant, with several satellites, was ushered into the study, and in the hall outside the voice of Miss Fletcher, urgently desiring to be told the meaning of this invasion, was upraised in some agitation. Neville slid out of the study, and took his aunt by the arm. 'I'll tell you. Come into the drawing-room.'

7

'But who are all those men?' demanded Miss Fletcher. 'They looked to me exactly like policemen!'

'Well they are,' said Neville. 'Most of them, anyway. Look here, Aunt Lucy –'

'We've been burgled!'

'No –' He stopped. 'I don't know. Yes, perhaps that was it. Sorry, aunt, but it's worse than that. Ernie has met with an accident.'

He stumbled a little over the words, looking anxiously at his aunt.

'Try not to *mumble* so, Neville dear. *What* did you say?'

'I said an accident, but I didn't mean it. Ernie's dead.'

'Dead? Ernie?' faltered Miss Fletcher. 'Oh no! You can't mean that! How could he be dead? Neville, you know I don't like that sort of joke. It isn't *kind*, dear, to say nothing of its being in very questionable taste.'

'It isn't a joke.'

She gave a gasp. '*Not?* Oh, Neville! Oh, let me go to him at once!'

'No use. Besides, you mustn't. Terribly sorry, but there it is. I'm a trifle knocked-up myself.'

'Neville, you're keeping something back!'

'Yes. He's been murdered.'

Her pale, rather prominent blue eyes stared at him. She opened her mouth, but no words passed her lips. Neville, acutely uncomfortable, made a vague gesture with his hands. 'Can I do anything? I should like to, only I don't know what. Do you feel faint? Yes, I know I'm being incompetent, but this isn't civilised, any of it. One has lost one's balance.'

She said: 'Ernie *murdered*? I don't believe it!'

8

'Oh, don't be silly,' he said, betraying ragged nerves. 'A man doesn't bash his own skull in.'

She gave a whimper, and groped her way to the nearest chair, and sank into it. Neville lit a cigarette with a hand that trembled, and said: 'Sorry, but you had to know sooner or later.'

She seemed to be trying to collect her wits. After a pause she exclaimed: 'But who would *want* to murder dear Ernie?'

'Search me.'

'There has been some dreadful mistake! Oh, Ernie, Ernie!'

She burst into tears. Neville, attempting no consolation, sat down in a large armchair opposite to her, and smoked.

Meanwhile, in the study, PC Glass was making his painstaking report to his superior. The doctor had gone; the cameramen had taken their photographs; and the body of Ernest Fletcher had been removed.

'I was on my beat, Sergeant, walking along Vale Avenue, the time being 10.02 p.m. When I came to the corner of Maple Grove, which, as you know, sir, is the lane running between Vale Avenue and the Arden Road, at the back of the house, my attention was attracted by a man coming out of the side gate of this house in what seemed to me a suspicious manner. He set off, walking very fast, towards the Arden Road.'

'Would you know him again?'

'No, Sergeant. It was nearly dark, and I never saw his face. He had turned the corner into Arden Road before I had time to do more than wonder what he was up to.' He hesitated, frowning a little. 'As near as I could make out, he was a man of average height, wearing a light-coloured soft hat. I don't know what gave me the idea there was something wrong about his coming out of Mr Fletcher's garden-gate, unless it was the hurry he seemed to be in. The Lord led my footsteps.'

'Yes, never mind about that!' said the Sergeant hastily. 'What did you do then?'

'I called out to him to stop, but he paid no heed, and the next instant had rounded the corner into the Arden Road. That circumstance led me to inspect these premises. I found the garden-gate standing open, and, seeing the light from this window, I came up the path with the intention of discovering whether anything was wrong. I saw the deceased, like you found him, Sergeant. The time, as verified by my watch and the clock there, was 10.05 p.m. My first action was to ascertain that Mr Fletcher was dead. Having assured myself that he was past mortal help, I effected a search of the room, and made sure no one was hiding in the bushes in the garden. I then called up the station on the telephone, the time being 10.10 p.m. While I was waiting to be connected, the butler, Joseph Simmons, entered the room, bearing the tray you see upon that table. I detained him, for interrogation. He states that at about 9 p.m. a person of the name of Abraham Budd came to see the deceased. He ushered same into this room. He states that he does not know when Abraham Budd left the house.'

'Description?'

'I hadn't got to that, sir. Mr Neville Fletcher came in at that moment. He states that he saw the deceased last at about 8.50 p.m., when they left the dining-room together.'

'All right; we'll see him in a minute. Anything else?'

'Nothing that I saw,' replied Glass, after a moment's scrupulous thought.

'We'll look around. Looks like an open-and-shut case against this man you saw making off. Friend Abraham Budd, eh?'

'Not to my way of thinking, Sergeant,' said Glass.

The Sergeant stared. 'Oh, it isn't, isn't it? Why not? The Lord been guiding you again?'

A flash of anger brought Glass's cold eyes to life. 'The scorner is an abomination to men!' he said.

'That's enough!' said the Sergeant. 'You remember you're speaking to your superior officer, if you please, my lad!'

'A scorner,' pursued Glass inexorably, 'loveth not one that reproveth him: neither will he go unto the wise. The man Budd came openly to the front door, making no secret of his name.'

The Sergeant grunted. 'It's a point, I grant you. May not have been a premeditated murder, though. Fetch the butler in.'

'Joseph Simmons is well known to me for a godly member,' said Glass, on his way to the door.

'All right, all right! Fetch him!'

The butler was discovered in the hall, still looking rather pale. When he entered the study he cast a nervous look towards the desk, and drew an audible sigh of relief when he saw the chair behind it unoccupied.

'Your name?' asked the Sergeant briskly.

'Joseph Simmons, Sergeant.'

'Occupation?'

'I am – I was employed as Mr Fletcher's butler.'

'How long have you been with him?'

'Six-and-a-half years, Sergeant.'

'And you state,' pursued the Sergeant, consulting Glass's notes, 'that you last saw your master alive at about 9 p.m., when you showed a Mr Abraham Budd into this room. Is that correct?'

'Yes, Sergeant. I have the person's card here,' said Simmons, holding out a piece of pasteboard.

The Sergeant took it, and read aloud: 'Mr Abraham Budd, 333c Bishopsgate, EC. Well, we know where he's to be found, that's one thing. You state that he wasn't known to you, I see.'

'I never laid eyes on the individual before in my life, Sergeant. He was not the type of person I have been in the habit of admitting to the house,' said Simmons haughtily.

Glass dispelled this pharisaical attitude with one devastating pronouncement. 'Though the Lord be high, yet hath he respect unto the lowly,' he said in minatory accents, 'but the proud he knoweth afar off.'

'My soul is humbled in me,' apologised Simmons.

'Never mind about your soul!' said the Sergeant impatiently. 'And don't take any notice of Glass! You listen to me! Can you describe this Budd's appearance?'

'Oh yes, Sergeant! A short, stout person in a suit which I should designate as on the loud side, and a bowler hat. I fancy he is of the Jewish persuasion.'

'Short and stout!' said the Sergeant, disappointed. 'Sounds to me like a tout. Did the deceased expect a visit from him?'

'I hardly think so. Mr Budd stated that his business was urgent, and I was constrained to take his card to Mr

12

Fletcher. My impression was that Mr Fletcher was considerably annoyed.'

'Do you mean scared?'

'Oh no, Sergeant! Mr Fletcher spoke of "damned impertinence", but after a moment he told me to show Mr Budd in, which I did.'

'And that was at 9 p.m., or thereabouts? Did you hear any sounds of altercation?'

The butler hesitated. 'I wouldn't say altercation, Sergeant. The *master*'s voice was upraised once or twice, but I didn't hear what he said, me being in the dining-room, across the hall, until I withdrew to my pantry.'

'You wouldn't say that a quarrel took place between them?'

'No, Sergeant. Mr Budd did not strike me as a quarrel-some person. In fact, the reverse. I got the impression he was afraid of the master.'

'Afraid of him, eh? Was Mr Fletcher a bad-tempered man?'

'Dear me, no, Sergeant! A very pleasant-spoken gentleman, usually. It was very seldom I saw him put-out.'

'But was he put-out tonight? By Mr Budd's call?'

The butler hesitated. 'Before that, I fancy, Sergeant. I believe Mr Fletcher had a – a slight difference with Mr Neville, just before dinner.'

'Mr Neville? That's the nephew? Does he live here?'

'No. Mr Neville arrived this afternoon to stay with his uncle for a few days, I understand.'

'Was he expected?'

'If he was, I was not apprised of it. I should mention,

in fairness to Mr Neville, that he is – if I may say so – a somewhat eccentric young gentleman. It is by no means an unusual occurrence for him to arrive here without warning.'

'And this difference with his uncle: was that usual?'

'I should not like to give a false impression, Sergeant: there wasn't any quarrel, if you understand me. All I know is that when I took sherry and cocktails to the drawing-room before dinner it seemed to me that I had interrupted an altercation. The master looked to be distinctly annoyed, which was a rare thing, in my experience, and I did hear him say, just as I came in, that he wanted to hear no more about it, and Mr Neville could go to hell.'

'Oh! And what about Mr Neville? Was he annoyed?'

'I shouldn't like to say, Sergeant. Mr Neville is a peculiar young gentleman, not given to showing what he feels, if he feels anything, which I sometimes doubt.'

'Well I do, frequently,' said Neville, who had come into the room in time to hear this remark.

The Sergeant, unaccustomed to young Mr Fletcher's noiseless way of entering rooms, was momentarily startled. Neville smiled in his deprecating fashion, and said softly: 'Good-evening. Isn't it shocking? I do hope you've arrived at something? My aunt would like to see you before you go. Do you know who killed my uncle?'

'It's early days to ask me that, sir,' replied the Sergeant guardedly.

'Your words hint at a prolonged period of suspense, which I find peculiarly depressing.'

'Very unpleasant for all concerned, sir,' agreed the

Sergeant. He turned to Simmons. 'That'll be all for the present,' he said.

Simmons withdrew, and the Sergeant, who had been eyeing Neville with a good deal of curiosity, invited him to sit down. Neville obligingly complied with this request, choosing a deep armchair by the fireplace. The Sergeant said politely: 'I'm hoping you may be able to help me, sir. I take it you were pretty intimate with the deceased?'

'Oh no!' said Neville, shocked. 'I shouldn't have liked that at all.'

'No, sir? Am I to understand you were not on good terms with Mr Fletcher?'

'But I was. I'm on good terms with everyone. Only I'm not intimate.'

'Well, but, what I mean, sir, is –'

'Yes, yes, I know what you mean. Did I know the secrets of my uncle's life? No, Sergeant: I hate secrets, and other people's troubles.'

He said this with an air of sweet affability. The Sergeant was a little taken aback, but rallied, and said: 'At all events, you knew him fairly well, sir?'

'We won't argue the point,' murmured Neville.

'Do you know if he had any enemies?'

'Well, obviously he had, hadn't he?'

'Yes, sir, but what I'm trying to establish –'

'I know, but you see I'm just as much at a loss as you are. You weren't acquainted with my uncle?'

'I can't say as I was, sir.'

Neville blew one smoke ring through another, and watched it dreamily. 'Everybody called him Ernie,' he sighed. 'Or Ernie dear, according to sex. You see?'

The Sergeant stared for a moment, and then said

slowly: 'I think I get you, sir. I've always heard him well spoken of, I'm bound to say. I take it you don't know of any person with a grudge against him?'

Neville shook his head. The Sergeant looked at him rather discontentedly, and consulted Glass's notebook. 'I see you state that after you left the dining-room you went into the billiard-room, where you remained until Miss Fletcher came to find you. At what hour would that have been?'

Neville smiled apologetically.

'You don't know, sir? No idea at all? Try and think!'

'Alas, time has hitherto meant practically nothing to me. Does it help if I say that my aunt mentioned that a most peculiar visitor was with my uncle? A fat little man, who carried his hat in his hand. She had seen him in the hall.'

'Did you see this man?' asked the Sergeant quickly.

'No.'

'You don't know whether he was still with your uncle when you went up to your room?'

'Sergeant, Sergeant, do you think I listen at keyholes?'

'Of course not, sir, but –'

'At least, not when I'm wholly incurious,' explained Neville, temporising.

'Well, sir, we'll say that some time between 9.00 and 10.00 you went up to your room.'

'At half-past nine,' said Neville.

'At – A moment ago, sir, you said you had no idea what time it was!'

'Oh, I hadn't, but I remember now one solitary cuckoo.'

The Sergeant shot a startled look towards Glass,

standing motionless and disapproving by the door. A suspicion that the eccentric Neville Fletcher was of unsound mind had darted into his brain. 'What might you mean by that, sir?'

'Only the clock on the landing,' said Neville.

'A cuckoo-clock! Well, really, sir, for a moment I thought – And it struck the half-hour?'

'Yes, but it's quite often wrong.'

'We'll go into that presently. Which way does your room face, sir?'

'North.'

'It's at the back of the house, then? Would it be possible for you to hear anyone coming up the side path?'

'I don't know. I *didn't* hear anyone, but I wasn't trying to.'

'Quite,' said the Sergeant. 'Well, I think that'll be all for the present, thank you, sir. Of course, you understand that you will not be able to leave this house for a day or two? Just a matter of routine, you know. We'll hope it won't be long before we get the whole thing cleared up.'

'Yes, let's,' agreed Neville. His gaze dwelt speculatively on a picture on the wall opposite the fireplace. 'It wouldn't be robbery, would it?'

'Hardly, sir, but of course we can't say definitely yet. It isn't likely a burglar would come when Mr Fletcher was still up, not to mention the rest of the household.'

'No. Only the safe is behind that picture – just in case you didn't know.'

'Yes, sir, so the butler informed me. We've been over it for finger-prints, and as soon as we can get Mr Fletcher's lawyer down we'll have it opened. Yes, Hepworth? Found anything?'

The last words were addressed to a constable who had stepped into the room through the window.

'Not much, Sergeant, but I'd like you to have a look at one thing.'

The Sergeant went at once; Neville uncoiled himself, got up, and wandered out of the room in his wake. 'Don't mind me coming, do you?' he murmured, as the Sergeant turned his head.

'I don't see as there's any objection, sir. The fact is, a man was seen sneaking out by the side gate just after 10 p.m., and unless I'm mistaken he's the chap we're after.'

'A – a fat man?' suggested Neville, blinking.

'Ah, that would be too easy, wouldn't it, sir?' said the Sergeant indulgently. 'No, just an ordinary looking chap in a soft hat. Well, Hepworth, what is it?'

The constable had led the way to the back of a flowering currant bush, which was planted in a bed close to the house. He directed the beam of his torch on to the ground. In the soft earth were the deep imprints of a pair of high-heeled shoes.

'They're freshly made, Sergeant,' said Hepworth. 'Someone's been hiding behind this bush.'

'The Women in the Case!' said Neville. 'Aren't we having fun?'

Two

By half-past eleven the police, with the exception of one constable, left behind to keep a watch over the house, had departed from Greystones. Miss Fletcher, gently interrogated by the Sergeant, had been unable to assist the course of justice. The news of the finding of the imprints of a woman's shoes did not seem either to shock or to surprise her. 'He was such an *attractive* man,' she confided to the Sergeant. 'Of course, I don't mean – but one has to remember that Men are not like Us, doesn't one?'

The Sergeant had found himself listening to a panegyric on the late Ernest Fletcher: how charming he was; how popular; what perfect manners he had; how kind he had always been to his sister; how gay; how dashing; how generous! Out of this turmoil of words certain facts had emerged. Neville was the son of Ernie's brother Ted, many years deceased, and certainly his heir. Neville was a dear boy, but you never knew what he would be up to next, and – yes, it *did* annoy poor Ernie when he got himself imprisoned in some horrid Balkan state – oh, nothing serious, but Neville was so hopelessly vague, and simply lost his passport. As for the Russian woman who had appeared at Neville's hotel with *all* her luggage before breakfast one morning in Budapest, saying he had invited her at some party the night before – well, one couldn't exactly approve, of course, but young men did get drunk sometimes, and anyway the woman was obviously no better than she should be, and really Neville was not like that at all. At the same time, one did rather feel for Ernie, having to buy the creature off. But it was quite, quite untrue to say that Ernie didn't like Neville: they hadn't much in common, but blood was thicker than water, and Ernie was always so understanding.

Questioned more closely, no, she knew of no one who nourished the least grudge against her brother. She thought the murderer must have been one of these dreadful maniacs one read about in the papers.

The Sergeant got away from her, not without difficulty, and very soon left the house. Aunt and nephew confronted one another in the drawing-room.

'I feel as though this were all a horrible nightmare!' said Miss Fletcher, putting a hand to her head. 'There's a policeman in the hall, and they've locked dear Ernie's study!'

'Does it worry you?' asked Neville. 'Was there anything there you wished to destroy?'

'That,' said Miss Fletcher, 'would be most dishonest. Not but what I feel sure Ernie would have preferred it to having strangers poking their noses into his affairs. Of course I wouldn't destroy anything important, but I'm sure there isn't anything. Only you know what men are, dear, even the best of them.'

'No, do tell me!'

'Well,' said Miss Fletcher, 'one shuts one's eyes to That Side of a Man's life, but I'm afraid, Neville, that there have been Women. And some of them, I think – though of course I don't *know* – not what I call Nice Women.'

'Men are funny like that,' said Neville dulcetly.

'Yes, dear, and naturally I was very thankful, because at one time I made sure Ernie would get caught.'

'Caught?'

'Marriage,' explained Miss Fletcher. 'That would have been a great blow to me. Only, luckily, he wasn't a very *constant* man.'

Neville looked at her in surprise. She smiled unhappily at him, apparently unaware of having said anything remarkable. She looked the acme of respectability; a plump, faded lady, with wispy grey hair and mild eyes, red-rimmed from crying, and a prim little mouth, innocent of lip-stick.

'I'm now definitely upset,' said Neville. 'I think I'll go to bed.'

She said distressfully: 'Oh dear, is it what I've told you? But it's bound to come out, so you had to know sooner or later.'

'Not my uncle; my aunt!' said Neville.

'You do say such odd things, dear,' she said. 'You're overwrought, and no wonder. Ought I to offer that policeman some refreshment?'

He left her engaged in conversation with the officer on duty in the hall, and went up to his own room. After a short interval his aunt tapped on his door, desiring to know whether he felt all right. He called out to her that he was quite all right, but sleepy, and so after exchanging good-nights with him, and promising not to disturb him again, Miss Fletcher went away to her own bedroom in the front of the house.

Neville Fletcher, having locked his door, climbed out of his window, and reached the ground by means of a stout drain-pipe, and the roof of the verandah outside the drawing-room.

The garden lay bathed in moonlight. In case a watch had been set over the side entrance, Neville made his way instead to the wall at the end of the garden, which separated it from the Arden Road. Espaliers trained up it made the scaling of it a simple matter. Neville reached the top, lowered himself on the other side, and let himself drop. He landed with the ease of the trained athlete, paused to light a cigarette, and began to walk westwards along the road. A hundred yards brought him to a cross-road running parallel to Maple Grove. He turned up it, and entered the first gateway he came to. A big, square house was sharply outlined by the moonshine, lights shining through the curtains of several of the windows. One of these, on the ground-floor to the left of the front door, stood open. Neville went to it, parted the curtains, and looked into the room.

A woman sat at an escritoire, writing, the light of a reading-lamp touching her gold hair with fire. She wore evening dress, and a brocade cloak hung over the back of her chair. Neville regarded her thoughtfully for a moment, and then stepped into the room.

She looked up quickly, and gave a sobbing gasp of shock. The fright of her eyes gave place almost immediately to an expression of relief. Colour rushed into her lovely face; she caught her hand to her breast, saying faintly: 'Neville! Oh, how you startled me!'

'That's nothing to what I've been through tonight,' replied Neville. '*Such* fun and games at Greystones, my dear: you wouldn't believe!'

She shut her blotter upon her half-finished letter. 'You haven't got them?' she asked, between eagerness and incredulity.

'All I've got is the jitters,' said Neville. He strolled over to her, and to her surprise went down on his knee.

'Neville, what on *earth* – ?'

His hand clasped her ankle. 'Let's have a look at your foot, my sweet.' He pulled it up and studied her silver kid shoe. 'O my prophetic soul! Now we are in a mess, aren't we? Just like your pretty little slippers.' He let her go, and stood up.

Swift alarm dilated her eyes. She glanced down at her shoes, and twitched the folds of her frock over them. 'What do you mean?'

'Can it, precious. You called on Ernie tonight, and hid behind a bush outside the study window.'

'How did you know?' she asked quickly.

'Intuition. You might have left it to me. What was the use of dragging me into it if you were going to muscle in? God knows I was unwilling enough.'

'That's just it. I didn't think you'd be any good. You're so unreliable, and I knew you hated doing it.'

'Oh, I did, and I am, and I wasn't any good, but all the same it was damned silly of you not to give me a run for my money. Did *you* get them, by the way?'

'No. He only – laughed, and – oh, you know!'

'Well isn't that nice!' said Neville. 'Did you happen to knock him on the head?'

'Oh, don't be silly!' she said impatiently.

'If that's acting, it's good,' said Neville, looking at her critically. 'Did you see who did?'

She was frowning. 'Did I see who did what?'

'Knocked Ernie on the head. My pretty ninny, Ernie's been murdered.'

A sound between a scream and a whimper broke from her. 'Neville! Oh no! *Neville*, you don't mean that!'

He looked at her with a smile lilting on his mouth. 'Didn't you know?'

Her eyes searched his, while the colour receded slowly from her face. 'I didn't do it!' she gasped.

'I shouldn't think you'd have the strength,' he agreed.

They were interrupted by the opening of the door. A slim young woman with a cluster of brown curls, a monocle screwed into her left eye, entered the room, saying calmly: 'Did you call, Helen?' Her gaze alighted on Neville; she said with every appearance of disgust: 'Oh, you're here, are you?'

'Yes, but I wouldn't have been if I'd known you were, hell-cat,' responded Neville sweetly.

Miss Drew gave a contemptuous snort, and looked critically at her sister. 'You look absolutely gangrenous,' she remarked. 'Anything the matter?'

Helen North's hands twisted nervously together. 'Ernie Fletcher's been murdered.'

'Good!' said Miss Drew, unperturbed. 'Neville come to tell you?'

Helen shuddered. 'Oh don't! It's awful, awful!'

'Personally,' said Miss Drew, taking a cigarette from the box on the table, and fitting it into a long holder, 'I regard it as definitely memorable. I hate men with super-polished manners, and charming smiles. Who killed him?'

'I don't know! You can't think I know!' Helen cried. 'Sally! – Neville! – oh, my God!' She looked wildly from one to the other, and sank down on to a sofa, burying her face in her hands.

'If it's an act, it's a good one,' said Neville. 'If not, it's mere waste of time. Do stop it, Helen! you're making me feel embarrassed.'

Sally regarded him with disfavour. 'You don't seem to be much upset,' she said.

'You didn't see me an hour ago,' replied Neville. 'I even lost my poise.'

She sniffed, but merely said: 'You'd better tell me all about it. It might be good copy.'

'What a lovely thought!' said Neville. 'Ernie has not died in vain.'

'I've always wanted to be in on a real murder,' remarked Sally thoughtfully. 'How was he killed?'

'He had his head smashed,' replied Neville.

Helen gave a moan, but her sister nodded with all the air of a connoisseur. 'A blow from a blunt instrument,' she said. 'Any idea who did it?'

'No, but Helen may have.'

Helen lifted her head. 'I tell you I wasn't there!'

'Your shoes belie you, sweet.'

'Yes, yes, but not when he was killed! I wasn't, I tell you, I wasn't!'

The monocle dropped out of Miss Drew's eye. She screwed it in again, bending a searching gaze upon her sister. 'What do you mean – "yes, but not when he was killed"? Have you been round to Greystones tonight?'

Helen seemed uncertain how to answer, but after a moment she said: 'Yes. Yes, I did go round to see Ernie. I – I got sick of the noise of your typewriter, for one thing, and, for another, I – I wanted particularly to see him.'

'Look here!' said Sally, 'you may as well spill it now as later! – what is there between you and Ernie Fletcher?'

'As a purist,' said Neville, 'I must take exception to your use of the present tense.'

She rounded on him. 'I suppose you're in on it, whatever it is? Then you'll dam' well tell me.'

'It isn't what you think!' Helen said quickly. 'Truly, it isn't, Sally! Oh, I admit I liked him, but not – not enough for that!'

'If you can tell Neville the truth you can tell it to me,' said Sally. 'And don't pull any stuff about going to see him because of my typewriter, because it won't wash.'

'Tell her,' advised Neville. 'She likes sordid stories.'

Helen flushed. 'Need you call it that?'

He sighed. 'Dear pet, I told you at the outset that I considered it too utterly trite and sordid to appeal to me. Why bring that up now?'

'You don't know what it is to be desperate,' she said bitterly.

'No, that's my divine detachment.'

'Well, I hope you get pinched for the murder,' struck in Sally. 'Then what price divine detachment?'

He looked pensive. 'It would be awfully interesting,' he agreed. 'Of course, I should preserve an outward calm, but should I quail beneath it? I hope not: if I did I shouldn't know myself any more, and that would be most uncomfortable.'

Helen struck the arm of the sofa with her clenched hand. 'Talk, talk, talk! What's the use of it?'

'There is nothing more sordid than the cult of utility,' replied Neville. 'You have a pedestrian mind, my dear.'

'Oh, do shut up!' begged Sally. She went to the sofa, and sat down beside Helen. 'Come on, old thing, you'd much better tell me the whole story! If you're in a jam, I'll try and get you out of it.'

'You can't,' Helen said wretchedly. 'Ernie's got IOUs of mine, and the police are bound to discover them, and there'll be a ghastly scandal.'

Sally frowned. 'IOUs? Why? I mean, how did he get them? What are they for, anyway?'

'Gambling debts. Neville thinks he probably bought them.'

'What on earth for?' demanded Sally, the monocle slipping out again.

Neville looked at her admiringly. 'The girl has a mind like a pure white lily!' he remarked. 'I am now taken-aback.'

Sally retorted hotly: 'I haven't got any such thing! But all this price-of-dishonour business is too utterly *vieux jeu*! Good Lord, I wouldn't put it in any book of mine!'

'Are you an escapist?' inquired Neville solicitously. 'Is that why you write improbable novels? Have you felt the banality of real life to be intolerable?'

'My novels aren't improbable! It may interest you to know that the critics consider me as one of the six most important crime novelists.'

'If you think that you're a bad judge of character,' said Neville.

Helen gave a strangled shriek of exasperation. 'Oh,

don't, don't! What does any of that matter at a time like this? What am I to *do*?'

Sally turned away from Neville. 'All right, let's get this thing straight,' she said. 'I don't feel I've got all the data. When did you start falling for Ernie Fletcher?'

'I didn't. Only he was so attractive, and – and he had a sort of sympathetic understanding. Almost a touch of the feminine, but not quite that, either. I can't explain. Ernie made you feel as though you were made of very brittle, precious porcelain.'

'That must have added excitement to your life,' said Neville reflectively.

'Shut up! Go on, Helen! When did it all begin?'

'Oh, I don't know! I suppose from the moment I first got to know him – to know him properly, I mean. You mustn't think that he – that he made love to me, because he didn't. It wasn't till just lately that I realised what he wanted. I thought – oh, I don't know what I thought!'

'You didn't think anything,' explained Neville kindly. 'You floated away on a sea of golden syrup.'

'That's probably true,' said Sally. 'You were obviously right under the ether. What did John think, if anything?'

Her sister coloured, and averted her face. 'I don't know. John and I – had drifted apart – before Ernie came into my life.'

Neville, apparently overcome, sank into a chair, and covered his face with his hands. 'Oh God, Oh God!' he moaned. 'I'm being dragged into this repulsive syrup! Dearest, let *us* drift apart – me out of your life, before I start mouthing clichés too. I know it's insidious.'

'I must say,' remarked Sally, fair-mindedly, 'that I rather bar "drifted apart" and "came into my life" myself. Helen, do try not to sentimentalise yourself; it all looks too darned serious to me. I thought you and John weren't hitting it off any too well. Some women don't know when they've struck ore. What went wrong between you? I should have thought John was the answer to any maiden's prayer.'

'Oh, it's so hard to explain!' Helen said, her eyes brimming with tears. 'I was so young when I married him, and I thought everything was going to be like my dreams. I'm not excusing myself: I know John's a fine man, but he didn't understand me, and he didn't want what I wanted – life, gaiety and excitement!'

'Didn't you love him?' asked Sally bluntly.

'I thought I did. Only everything went wrong. If only John had been different – but you know what he's like! If he'd shaken me, or even beaten me, I'd have pulled myself up. But he didn't. He simply retired into his shell. He was busy, too, and I was bored. I started going about without him. Sally, I tell you I don't know how it began, or how we got to this pitch, but we're utterly, utterly estranged!' The tears were running down her cheeks. She said with a catch in her voice: 'I'd give anything to have it all back again, but I can't, and there's a gulf between us which I can't bridge! Now *this* has happened, and I suppose that'll end it. I shall have dragged John's name in the mud, and the least I can do is to let him divorce me.'

'Don't be such an ass!' said Sally bracingly. 'John's much too decent to let you down when you're in trouble. You don't divorce people for getting into debt, and if your IOUs are found in Ernie Fletcher's possession it'll be obvious that you weren't a faithless wife.'

'If they're found, and it all comes out, I'll kill myself!'

Helen said. 'I couldn't face it. I could *not* face it! John doesn't know a thing about my gambling. It's the one thing that he detests above all others. Neville's a beast, but he's perfectly right when he says it's a sordid story. It wasn't Bridge, or the sort of gambling you have at parties, but a – a real hell!'

'Lummy!' said Miss Drew elegantly. 'Gilded vice, and haggard harpies, and suicides adjacent? All that sort of thing?'

'It wasn't gilded, and I don't know about any suicides, but it was a *bad* place, and yet – in a way – rather thrilling. If John knew of it – the people who belonged to it – Sally, no one would *believe* I wasn't a bad woman if it was known I went to that place!'

'Well, why did you go there?'

'Oh, for the thrill! Like one goes to Limehouse. And at first it sort of *got* me. I adored the excitement of the play. Then I lost rather a lot of money, and like a fool I thought I could win it back. I expect you know how one gets led on, and on.'

'Why not have sold your pearls?'

A wan smile touched Helen's lips. 'Because they aren't worth anything.'

'*What?*' Sally gasped.

'Copies,' said Helen bitterly. 'I sold the real ones ages ago. Other things, too. I've always been an extravagant little beast, and John warned me he wouldn't put up with it. So I sold things.'

'Helen!'

Neville, who had been reposing in a luxurious chair with his eyes shut, said sleepily: 'You said you wanted copy, didn't you?'

'Even if it didn't concern Helen I couldn't use this,' said Sally. 'Not my line of country at all. I shall have to concentrate on the murder. By the way, Helen, who introduced you to this hell? Dear Ernie?'

'Oh no, no!' Helen cried. 'He absolutely rescued me from it! I can't tell you how divine he was. He said everything would be all right, and I wasn't to worry any more, but just be a good child for the future.'

'Snake!' said Sally hotly.

'Yes, only – it didn't seem like that. He had such a way with him! He got hold of those ghastly IOUs, and at first I was so thankful!'

'Then he blackmailed you!'

'N – no, he didn't. Not quite. I can't tell you about that, but it wasn't exactly as you imagine. Of course, he did use the IOUs as a weapon, but perhaps he didn't really mean it! It was all done so – so *laughingly*, and he was very much in love with me. I expect I lost my head a bit, didn't handle him properly. But I got frightened, and I couldn't sleep for thinking of my IOUs in Ernie's possession. That's why I told Neville. I thought he might be able to do something.'

'Neville?' said Miss Drew, in accents of withering contempt. 'You might as well have applied to a village idiot!'

'I know, but there wasn't anyone else. And he is clever, in spite of being so hopeless.'

'As judged by village standards?' inquired Neville, mildly interested.

'He may have a kind of brain, but I've yet to hear of him putting himself out for anyone, or behaving like an ordinarily nice person. I can't think how you ever succeeded in persuading him to take it on.'

'The dripping of water on a stone,' murmured Neville.

'Well having taken it on, I do think you might have put your back into it. Did you even try?'

'Yes, it was a most painful scene.'

'Why? Was Ernie furious?'

'Not so much furious as astonished. So was I. You ought to have seen me giving my impersonation of a Nordic public-school man with a reverence for good form and the done-thing. I wouldn't like to swear I didn't beg him to play the game. Ernie ended up by being nauseated, and I'm sure I'm not surprised.'

'You know, you're not hard-hearted, you're just soulless,' Sally informed him. She glanced at her sister. 'Was I invited to stay to be a chaperon?'

'Yes, in a way. Besides, I wanted you.'

'Thanks a lot. What happened tonight?'

'Oh, nothing, Sally, nothing! It was silly of me, but I thought if only I could talk quietly to Ernie, and – and throw myself on his generosity, everything would be all right. You were busy with your book, so I got my cloak, and just slipped round by the back way to Greystones, on the off-chance of finding Ernie in his study.'

'It looks to me as though it wasn't the first time you've called on Ernie like that,' interpolated Sally shrewdly.

Helen coloured. 'Well, no, I – I have been once or twice before, but not after I realised he had fallen in love with me. Honestly, I used to look on him as an exciting sort of uncle.'

'More fool you. Carry on! When did you set out on this silly expedition?'

'At half-past nine, when I knew you'd had time to get absorbed in your silly book,' retorted Helen, with a flash of spirit. 'And I knew that Ernie was in his study, because when I turned up into Maple Grove from the Arden Road, I saw a man come out of the Greystones side gate, and walk off towards Vale Avenue.'

'Abraham,' said Neville. 'Well, that settles him, at all events. Pity: the name had possibilities.'

'I don't know what you're talking about. I let myself into the garden, and walked up the path to Ernie's study. Ernie was there, but I soon saw I'd made a mistake to come. He was – almost horrid – as horrid as a person with charm like his could be.'

'That's what comes of getting me to become a pukka sahib,' said Neville. 'You can't blame Ernie.'

'How long did you stay with him?' demanded Sally. 'Think! it's probably important.'

'I don't have to think: I know,' said Helen. 'Ernie said something about my being found with him at a compromising hour, and I looked at the clock, and said if he thought a quarter to ten a compromising hour he must be actually a Victorian, though I'd thought him merely Edwardian.'

'Good!' approved Sally.

'Yes, I was in a rage,' admitted Helen. 'And I walked straight out, the way I'd come.'

'Straight home?'

Helen hesitated, her eyes on Neville, who was regarding her with an expression of sleepy enjoyment. 'No,' she said, after a pause. 'Not quite. I heard the gate open, and naturally I didn't want to be seen, so I dived behind a bush beside the house.'

'Who was it?' asked Sally quickly.

'I don't know. I couldn't see. A man, that's all I can tell you.'

Sally looked at her rather searchingly, and then said: 'All right, go on!'

'He went into the study. I think he closed the window behind him; I didn't hear anything except a sort of murmur of voices.'

'Oh! Did you beat it while you had the chance?'

Helen nodded. 'Yes, of course.'

'And no one but Ernie saw you?'

'No.'

'And you didn't go dropping handkerchiefs about, or anything like that?'

'Of course I didn't.'

'Then there's nothing except the IOUs to connect you with the murder!' Sally declared. 'We've got to get hold of them before the police do.'

Helen said: 'Oh, Sally, if only I could! But *how*? They aren't in his desk –'

'How do you know?' asked Sally swiftly.

'Why, I – something Ernie said,' faltered Helen.

'I shouldn't set much store by anything he said. Of course, they may be in a safe, but we'll hope he didn't go in for safes. Neville, this is your job.'

Neville opened his eyes. Having surveyed both sisters in his peculiarly dreamy way, he dragged himself out of his chair, and wandered over to the table where the cigarette-box stood. He selected and lit one, produced his own empty case, and proceeded to fill it. 'All this excitement,' he said softly, 'has gone to your head.'

'Oh no, it hasn't! You're staying in the house; you said you'd help Helen. You can jolly well find those IOUs before Scotland Yard gets on to the case.'

'Scotland Yard!' gasped Helen.

'Yes, I should think almost certainly,' replied Sally. 'This is the Metropolitan area, you know. They'll probably send a man down to investigate. Neville, are you willing to take a chance?'

'No, darling,' he replied, fitting the last cigarette into his case.

'You would fast enough if they were your IOUs!'

He looked up. 'I daresay I should. But they aren't mine. I won't have anything to do with them.'

'If you had a grain of decency, or – or *chivalry* –'

'Do stop trying to cast me for this beastly Gunga Din rôle!' he implored. 'Find someone else for the job! You must know lots of whiter men than I am.'

'Very well!' said Sally. 'If you haven't the guts to do it, I have, and I will!'

'I don't want to blight your youthful ardour, sweet one, but I think I ought to tell you that there's a large, resolute policeman parked in the front hall.'

Her face fell. 'I never thought of that,' she said slowly. An idea occurred to her. 'Do you mean he's keeping a watch over the household?'

'Well, he's certainly not a paying-guest.'

She started up. 'You utter, abysmal idiot, what did you come here for if the house was being watched?'

'To get some cigarettes. We've run out.'

'Oh, don't be a fool! Don't you realise you'll have led them straight to Helen?'

'Oh no! No, really I haven't,' Neville replied, with his

35

apologetic smile. 'I climbed out of my window, and over the wall.'

'You – Did you really?' exclaimed Sally, her thunderous frown vanishing. 'I must say I should never have thought it of you.'

'Atavism,' he explained.

'Oh, Neville, how on earth did you manage it?' Helen asked, a note of admiration in her voice.

He looked alarmed. 'Please don't get misled! It wasn't a bit heroic, or daring, or even difficult.'

'It must have been. I can't think *how* you did it! I should never have had the nerve.'

'No nerve. Merely one of the advantages of a University education.'

'Well, I think it was fairly sporting of you,' said Sally. 'Only it doesn't help us to solve the problem of how to get those IOUs.'

'Don't strain yourself,' Neville recommended. 'You can't get them. They're probably in Ernie's safe, just like you suggested.'

'There are ways of opening safes,' said Sally darkly, cupping her chin in her hands. 'I suppose you don't happen to know the combination?'

'You're right for the first time tonight. God, how I hate women!'

'Sally, you don't really know how to open safes, do you?' asked Helen, forgetting her troubles in surprise.

'No, not offhand. I should have to look it up. Of course, I know about soup.'

'What sort of soup?' inquired Neville. 'If we're going to talk gastronomy I can be quite intelligent, though seldom inspired.'

'Ass. Not that kind of soup. The stuff you blow open safes with. I forget exactly what it's made of, but it's an explosive of sorts.'

'Is it really?' said Neville. 'What lovely fun! Won't it go big with the policeman in the hall?'

'I wasn't thinking of using it, even if I knew how to make it, which I don't.'

'That must be your weak woman's nature breaking through the crust, darling. Get the better of it, and don't stop at the safe. Blow the whole house up, thus eliminating the policeman.'

'Have a good laugh,' said Sally. 'After all, you aren't in this jam, are you?' She got up, and began to stride about the room. 'Well, let's face it! We can't open the safe, and we don't know how to get by the policeman. In fact, we're futile. But if I created this situation in a book I could think of something for the book-me to do. Why the devil can't I think of something now?'

Neville betrayed a faint interest. 'If we were in one of your books, we should all of us have much more nerve than we really have, to start with.'

'Not necessarily.'

'Oh yes! You always draw your characters rather more than life-size. We should have more brains, too. You, for instance, would know how to make your soup —'

'Any where to buy the — the ingredients, which actually one just *doesn't* know,' she interpolated.

'Exactly. Helen would go and scream blue murder outside the house, to draw the policeman off while you blew up the safe, and I should put up a great act to regale him with on his return, telling him I thought I heard someone in the study, and leading him there when you'd beaten it with the incriminating documents. And can you see any one of us doing any of it?'

'No, I can't. It's lousy, anyway. It would be brought home to us because of Helen's being an obvious decoy.'

'Helen would never be seen. She'd have merged into the night by the time the policeman got there.'

'Let's discuss possibilities!' begged Helen.

'I'll go further, and discuss inevitabilities. We shall all of us sit tight, and let the police do the worrying. Ernie's dead, and there isn't a thing we can do, except preserve our poise. In fact, we are quite definitely in the hands of Fate. Fascinating situation!'

'A dangerous situation!' Sally said.

'Of course. Have you never felt the fascination of fear? Helen has, in that gambling-hell of hers.'

'Not now!' Helen said. 'This is too awful. I only feel sick, and – and desperate!'

'Take some bicarbonate,' he advised. 'Meanwhile, I'm going home to bed. Oh, did I say thank you for the cigarettes? By the way, where is John supposed to be?'

'In Berlin,' replied Helen listlessly.

'Well, he isn't,' said Neville. 'I saw him in London today.'

She came to her feet in one swift movement, paper-white, staring at him. 'You couldn't have! I know he's in Berlin!'

'Yes, I saw him,' murmured Neville.

He was by the window, a hand on the curtain. Helen moved quickly to detain him. 'You thought you saw him!

Do you imagine I don't know where my own husband is?'

'Oh, no!' Neville said gently. 'I didn't say that, precious.'

Three

'Well, it doesn't look such a whale of a case to me,' said Sergeant Hemingway, handing the sheaf of typescript back to his superior. 'No one in it but the one man, on the face of it.'

'True,' agreed Hannasyde. 'Still, there are points.'

'That's right, Superintendent,' nodded Inspector True. 'That's what I said myself. What about them footprints? They weren't made by the old lady: she doesn't wear that kind of shoe.'

'Housemaid, saying good-night to her young man,' said the experienced Hemingway.

'Hardly,' said Hannasyde. 'She wouldn't choose a bush just outside her master's study.'

'No, nor there wasn't anything like that going on,' said the Inspector. 'The cook is a very respectable woman, married to Simmons, the butler, and the housemaid is her own niece, and this Mrs Simmons swears to it both she and the kitchen-maid never stirred outside the house the whole evening.'

'It's my belief those footprints'll be found to be highly irrelevant,' said Hemingway obstinately. 'All we want is this chap your man – what's-his-name? – Glass saw making off. Nothing to it.'

Hannasyde cocked an eyebrow at him. 'Liverish, Skipper?'

'I don't like the set-up. Ordinary, that's what it is. And I don't like the smashed skull. Just doesn't appeal to me. Give me something a bit recherché, and I'm right on to it.'

Hannasyde smiled a little. 'I repeat, there are points. The murdered man seems to have been universally liked. No motive for killing him even hinted at.'

'You wait till we've done half-an-hour's work on the case,' said Hemingway. 'I wouldn't mind betting we'll find scores of people all stiff with motives.'

'I thought you said all we had to do was to find the man PC Glass saw?'

'I daresay I did, Chief, and what's more I was probably right, but you mark my words, we shall find a whole lot of stuff just confusing the main issue. I've been on this kind of case before.'

'The way I look at it,' said the Inspector slowly, 'we want to find the instrument it was done with.'

'Yes, that's another of the points,' replied Hannasyde. 'Your man Glass seems quite certain that the fellow he saw wasn't carrying anything. What sort of a chap is he? Reliable?'

'Yes, sir, he is, very reliable. That's his conscience. He's a very religious man, Glass. I never can remember what sect he belongs to, but it's one of those where they all wrestle with the devil, and get moved by the Lord to stand up and testify. Well, I'm Church of England myself, but what I say is, it takes all sorts to make a world. As a matter of fact, I was thinking of detailing Glass to you, to give you any assistance you may need, Superintendent. I reckon he's one of my best men – not quick, you know, but not one to lose his head, or go flying off at a tangent. Seems only right to put him on to this case, seeing as it was him discovered the body.'

'All right,' said Hannasyde absently, his eyes running down the typescript in his hand.

The Inspector coughed. 'Only perhaps I'd better just warn you, sir, that he's got a tiresome habit of coming out with bits of the Bible. One of these blood-and-thunder merchants, if you know what I mean. You can't break him of it. He gets moved by the spirit.'

'I daresay Hemingway will be able to deal with him,' said Hannasyde, rather amused.

'I knew I wasn't going to like this case,' said Hemingway gloomily.

Half-an-hour later, having made a tour of the grounds of Greystones, inspected the footprints behind the flowering currant bush, and cast a jaundiced eye over the stalwart, rigid form of PC Glass, he reiterated this statement.

'If thou faint in the day of adversity, thy strength is small,' said Glass reprovingly.

The Sergeant surveyed him with acute dislike. 'If you get fresh with me, my lad, we're going to fall out,' he said.

'The words are none of mine, but set down in Holy Writ, Sergeant,' explained Glass.

'There's a time and a place for everything,' replied the Sergeant, 'and this isn't the place nor the time for the Holy Writ. You attend to me, now! When you saw that chap sneaking out of this gate last night, it was just after ten o'clock, wasn't it?'

'It was, Sergeant.'

'And getting dark?'

'As you say, Sergeant.'

'Too dark for you to see him very clearly?'

'Too dark for me to distinguish his features, but not too dark for me to take note of his build and raiment.'

'It's my belief it was too dark for you to see whether he was carrying anything or not,' said the Sergeant.

'His hands were empty,' replied Glass positively. 'I will not bear false witness against my neighbour.'

'All right, skip it!' said the Sergeant. 'Now, you've been in this district some time, haven't you?'

'For three years, Sergeant.'

'Well, what do you know about these Fletchers?'

'Their eyes stand out with fatness; they have more than heart could wish.'

'Yes, that's a lot of use, isn't it? What about the nephew?'

'I know nothing of him, either good or ill.'

'And the late Ernest?'

A sombre look came into Glass's face. 'He that pursueth evil pursueth it to his own death.'

The Sergeant pricked up his ears. 'What evil?'

Glass looked sternly down at him. 'I believe him to have been wholly given up to vain show, double of heart, a fornicator, a —'

'Here, that'll do!' said the Sergeant, startled. 'We're none of us saints. I understand the late Ernest was pretty well liked?'

'It is true. It is said that he was a man of pleasing

manners, filled with loving kindness. But the heart is deceitful above all things, and desperately wicked: who can know it?'

'Yes, that's all very well, but where do you get that fornication idea? From those footprints, eh?'

'No. Joseph Simmons, who is in the way of light, though a foolish man, knew some of the secrets of his master's life.'

'He did, did he? We'll see!' said the Sergeant briskly, and turned towards the house.

He entered it through the study window, and found his superior there, with Ernest Fletcher's solicitor, and Neville Fletcher, who was lounging bonelessly in an armchair, the inevitable cigarette drooping from the corner of his mouth.

'Then, if that is all, Superintendent,' the solicitor was saying, 'I will take my leave. Should you require my further services, there is my card.'

'Thank you,' said Hannasyde.

The solicitor picked up Ernest Fletcher's Will, and replaced it in his brief-case. He glanced rather severely over the top of his pince-nez at Neville, and said: 'You are a very fortunate young man, Neville. I hope you will prove yourself worthy of the benefits your poor uncle has conferred on you.'

Neville looked up with his fleeting smile. 'Oh, so do I! I shall try hard not to let all this vulgar wealth corrupt my soul.'

'It's a great responsibility,' said the lawyer gravely.

'I know, that's what depresses me. People will expect me to wear a hat, and look at tape-machines.'

'I hope you will do more than that,' replied the lawyer.

'Now, if you please, I should like to have a word with your aunt. Perhaps you could take me to her.'

Neville obligingly rose, and opened the door for him. They passed out of the room together, and Sergeant Hemingway, who had been standing silent in the window, said: 'Who's the bit of chewed string, Chief?'

'The heir,' answered Hannasyde. 'Neville Fletcher.'

'Oh! well, I don't grudge it him. He looks as though he hasn't got tuppence to rub together, let alone hardly having the strength to stand up without holding on to something.'

'You shouldn't go by appearances, Sergeant,' said Hannasyde, a twinkle in his eye. 'That weary young man holds the record for the high jump. Got a half-blue at Oxford, so the solicitor informed me.'

'You don't say! Well, I wouldn't have thought it, that's all. And he's the heir? What did I tell you? Motive Number One.'

'I'll remember it if I draw a blank on that unknown visitor,' promised Hannasyde. 'Meanwhile, we've found this little lot.'

The Sergeant came to the desk, and looked over Hannasyde's shoulder at three slips of paper, all signed by Helen North. 'IOUs,' he said. 'Well, well, well, she *did* splash money about, didn't she? Know what I think, Super? There's a nasty smell of blackmail hanging round these bits of paper. I believe friend Ichabod wasn't so far off the mark after all, with his pursuit-of-evil stuff.'

'My name is not Ichabod, Sergeant, but Malachi,' said Glass stiffly, from the window.

'It had to be,' said the Sergeant. 'What price those footprints, Chief?'

'The medical evidence goes to show that it is in the highest degree improbable that a woman could have struck the blow which killed Ernest Fletcher. Still, I agree that these notes will bear looking into.'

'Young Neville know anything about this Helen North?'

'I haven't asked him. In the event of those IOUs having no bearing on the case, I'm not anxious to stir up any mud.' He glanced up to see Glass staring at him with knit brows. 'Well? Does the name convey anything to you?'

'There's a man of that name living with his wife not five minutes' walk from this house,' replied Glass slowly.

The Sergeant pursed his lips in a soundless whistle. Hannasyde said: 'Know anything about them?'

'No, sir.'

'Address?'

'You will find the house in the road which runs parallel to Maple Grove. It is called the Chestnuts.'

Hannasyde jotted it down. The Sergeant, meanwhile, was turning over a collection of photographs and snapshots laid on the desk. 'Looks like you weren't so far out, Glass,' he remarked. 'I have to hand it to the late Ernest. He certainly knew how to pick 'em. Regular harem!' He picked up a large portrait of a dazzling blonde, dressed, apparently, in an ostrich-feather fan, and regarded it admiringly. That's Lily Logan, the dancer. What a figure!'

Glass averted his eyes with a shudder. 'Can a man take fire in his bosom, and his clothes not be burned? As a jewel of gold in a swine's snout, so is a fair woman which is without discretion!'

'That's what you think,' said Hemingway, laying Lily Logan down, and looking critically at another smiling beauty. 'Went the pace a bit, didn't he? Hullo!' His eyes had alighted on the portrait of a curly-headed brunette. He picked it up. 'Seems to me I've seen this dame before.'

'As his female acquaintance seems to have consisted largely of chorus girls, that's not surprising,' said Hannasyde dryly.

'Yours lovingly, Angela,' read out the Sergeant. 'Angela . . .' He scratched his chin meditatively. 'Got something at the back of my mind. Do you seem to know that face, Chief?'

Hannasyde studied the photograph for a moment. 'It does look a little familiar,' he admitted. 'Some actress, I daresay. We'll check up on them presently.'

Hemingway held the photograph at arm's length. 'No, I'm pretty sure I don't connect her with the stage. No use asking you, Glass, I suppose?'

'I do not wish to look upon the face of a lewd woman,' Glass said harshly. 'Her end is bitter as wormwood, sharp as a two-edged sword.'

'Look here, what's the matter with you?' demanded the Sergeant. 'Some actress given you the air, or what?'

'I have no dealings with actresses.'

'Well, then, stop panning them. How do you know anything about this poor girl's end, anyway?' He laid the portrait down.

'Anything else, Chief?'

'Nothing so far.'

At this moment the door opened and Miss Fletcher came in. She was dressed in deep mourning, and her

47

plump cheeks were rather pale, but she smiled sweetly at Hannasyde. 'Oh, Superintendent – you are a Superintendent, aren't you?'

He had risen to his feet, and unobtrusively slid the big blotter over the heap of photographs. 'Yes, that's right, madam.'

She looked at the mass of papers on the desk. 'Oh dear, what a lot you must have to do! Now, tell me, *would* you like a little refreshment?'

He declined it, which seemed to disappoint her, and asked her civilly if she wished to speak to him.

'Well, yes,' she admitted. 'Only *any* time will do. You're busy now, and I mustn't disturb you.'

'I'm quite at your disposal, Miss Fletcher. Won't you sit down? All right, Glass: you can wait outside.'

'You have such a kind face,' Miss Fletcher told him. 'Quite unlike what one expected. I feel I can *talk* to you. Are you *sure* you won't have something? A little coffee and a sandwich?'

'No, really, thank you. What was it you wanted to say to me, Miss Fletcher?'

'I'm afraid you'll say I'm wasting your time. So silly of me not to have asked dear Mr Lawrence while he was here! We have known him for so many years that I always say he is more like a friend than a solicitor, though of course there is no reason why he shouldn't be *both*, as indeed I hope he feels he is. It was particularly foolish of me, because it is just the sort of thing he would know.'

'What is it, Miss Fletcher?' asked Hannasyde, breaking into the gentle flow of words.

'Well, it's the reporters,' she confided. 'Poor things, one knows they have their living to earn, and it must be very disagreeable work, when one comes to think of it, and one doesn't want to be unkind –'

'Are they worrying you?' interrupted Hannasyde. 'All you have to do is to tell your butler to say that you have no statement to make.'

'It seems so very disobliging,' she said doubtfully. 'And one of them looks dreadfully under-nourished. At the same time, I should very much dislike to see my photograph in the papers.'

'Of course. The less you say to them the better, Miss Fletcher.'

'Well, that's what I thought,' she said. 'Only my nephew is so naughty about it. It's only his fun, but you never know how much people will believe, do you? I suppose you wouldn't just *hint* to him that he oughtn't to do it? I feel that what *you* said would carry more *weight* than what I say.'

'What's he been up to?' asked Hannasyde.

'Well, he's told one of the reporters that he's employed here as the Boots, and when the man asked him his name he said it was Crippen, only he didn't want it to be known.'

Hannasyde chuckled. 'I don't think I should worry very much about that, Miss Fletcher.'

'Yes, but he told another of them that he came from Yugoslavia, and was here on very secret business. In fact, he's in the front garden now, telling three of them a ridiculous story about international intrigue, and my brother at the back of it. And they're taking it down in their notebooks. Neville's such a *marvellous* actor, and of course he speaks Serbian, from having travelled in the Balkans. But I don't think he ought to deceive those poor men, do you?'

'No, I don't,' said Hannasyde. 'It's most unwise to play jokes on the gentlemen of the Press. Hemingway, go and ask Mr Fletcher if I can have a word with him, will you?'

'Thank you *so* much!' said Miss Fletcher gratefully. 'Poor Neville, one always has to remember that he hasn't known a mother's love. I feel that accounts for so much, don't you? Not that he isn't a dear boy, of course, and I'm very fond of him, but he is like so many of the young people nowadays, so strangely *heartless*! Nothing seems to matter to him, not even a thing like this.' Her lips trembled; she groped for her handkerchief, and dabbed her eyes with it. 'You must forgive me: I was very much attached to my dear brother. It doesn't seem to me as though any of this can really have happened.'

'It must have been a terrible shock to you,' said Hannasyde sympathetically.

'Yes. You see, my brother was such a charming man. Everyone liked him!'

'So I understand, Miss Fletcher. Yet it seems that he had one enemy at least. Have you no idea who that might be?'

'Oh, no, no! I can't think of anyone. But – I didn't know all his – friends, Superintendent.' She looked up anxiously, but Hannasyde said nothing. 'That was one of the things I came to talk to you about,' she ventured. 'I'm afraid you will think it rather odd of me to mention such things, but I have made up my mind that I ought to.'

'You may be perfectly frank with me, Miss Fletcher,' he said encouragingly.

She fixed her eyes upon a point beyond his shoulder. My brother,' she said in a faint voice, 'had affairs with – with women.'

Hannasyde nodded.

'I never inquired into them, and of course he never spoke of them to me, but naturally I knew. In my young days, Superintendent, ladies did not discuss such matters. Nowadays things are different, and young people seem to talk of everything, which I can't help feeling is a pity. It is much better to shut one's eyes to some things, don't you agree? But it has occurred to me – I thought it all over during the night – that whoever killed my brother may – may have done so from jealousy.'

'Yes, that is a possibility,' Hannasyde said.

'Yes. Of course, if it *was* so, it will have to come out. I quite realise that. But if you find it wasn't, or – or fail to discover the man who did it – do you think my brother's – private affairs – need be known?'

'Certainly not,' Hannasyde replied. 'I quite understand your feelings in the matter, Miss Fletcher, and I can assure you that I shall respect them as much as I possibly can.'

'*So* kind!' she sighed. 'I have such a dread of the papers printing horrid things about my poor brother – perhaps getting hold of letters. You know the sort of thing I mean, I expect.'

'You need not be afraid of that,' he assured her. 'There are no such letters as you refer to.'

'Oh, how *thankful* I am!' she breathed. 'You have taken a load off my mind!'

She got up, as Sergeant Hemingway ushered her nephew into the room, and bestowed a tremulous smile upon the Superintendent. Neville came in talking in his soft, rapid way, and it was plain from Hemingway's strained, appreciative expression that his discourse was of an entertaining nature. When he saw his aunt he broke off in mid-sentence, and recommended her to make no statement to the police except in the presence of her lawyer. Miss Fletcher explained to Hannasyde that this was only his fun, and made her way to the door.

Neville closed it behind her, saying plaintively: 'Of course, I know one has to obey the summons of the Law, but you interrupted me at a most delicate moment, Superintendent.'

'I'm sorry,' replied Hannasyde, adding with a gleam of humour in his eye: 'International complications?'

'Yes, I had just worked in a Montenegrin patriot with a knife. The whole story was unfolding itself beautifully, but I've lost the thread now.'

'Take my advice, and don't try to fool the Press. Suppose – though it's improbable – that your International story did get published?'

'Oh, but I do hope it will!' Neville said. 'Really, it's a lovely story, and I've taken pains with it. I don't usually, but old Lawrence seems to think I ought to try to become more earnest. Did you want me for anything in particular? Because if not I'm in the middle of telling your Sergeant about an experience which befell me in Skopje. It isn't exactly a polite story, but I find he has a lovely dirty mind. In fact, we're practically affinities.'

The reminiscent grin which still lingered on the Sergeant's face vanished. A dusky blush mounted into his cheeks, and he gave an imploring cough.

'I daresay,' replied Hannasyde. 'But this is hardly the time to indulge in smutty anecdotes, do you think?'

'Oh, I don't agree with you!' said Neville engagingly.

'Given the right company, there's no real close season for dirty stories.'

'Tell me, Mr Fletcher, did you know your uncle well?'

'I expect it'll save time if I say no,' answered Neville. 'I can see we are on the verge of talking at cross-purposes.'

'Why?' Hannasyde asked bluntly.

'Oh, one doesn't know people. Mothers say they know their children through and through. Fallacy. Rather disgusting, too. Indecency inherent in over-probing, and results misleading, and probably disquieting.'

'Oh!' said Hannasyde, who had followed this rapid and telegraphic speech with some difficulty. 'I see what you mean, but it doesn't answer my question. As well as one person may know another, did you know your uncle?'

'No. Interest being the natural forerunner to understanding.'

'You'd none in him?'

'Nor anyone, 'cept objectively. An' I'm not sure of that either. Do you like people?'

'Don't you?'

Neville spread his hands out, slightly hunching his thin shoulders. 'Oh, some – a little – at a distance.'

'You seem to be an ascetic,' said Hannasyde dryly.

'Hedonist. Personal contacts pleasant at first, but leading to discomfort.'

Hannasyde regarded him frowningly. 'You have peculiar ideas, Mr Fletcher. They're not getting us anywhere.'

A smile flickered in Neville's eyes. 'Eschew my company. You see, I don't want to get anywhere. Prolonged intercourse with me bad for your temper.'

'You are probably right,' returned Hannasyde with a touch of asperity: 'I won't detain you any longer.'

'Oh, can I go back to my entrancing reporters?'

'If you think it wise – or desirable.'

'Like feeding goldfish,' said Neville, drifting out by way of the window.

The Sergeant watched him go, and drew a long breath. 'What I call a turn in himself,' he said. 'He's certainly a new one on me.'

Hannasyde grunted. The Sergeant cocked an intelligent eye at him. 'You didn't take to him, did you, Chief?'

'No. Or believe him.'

'I'm bound to say I don't entirely follow his talk – what I can hear of it, which isn't much.'

'I think he knows more than he pretends, and doesn't want to be questioned. However, he'll keep. I've nothing on him – so far.' He looked at his wrist-watch, and got up. 'Take charge of those papers, and the photographs, will you? I'm going now to call on Mrs North. I'll leave Abraham Budd to you. Find out from Headquarters, while you're in town, if they've got anything out of the finger-prints.'

He had no difficulty in finding his way to the Chestnuts, and, upon sending in his card, was ushered presently into a pleasant morning-room at the back of the house. There he found not only Helen North, but Miss Drew also, who was seated at a table in the window with a portable typewriter in front of her.

Helen came forward a few steps, saying nervously: 'Good-morning. I'm Mrs North. I understand you want to see me?'

'Yes,' Hannasyde replied. He glanced towards the window, and added: 'Perhaps if I might have a word with you alone it would be best.'

'Oh no! I mean, I would like my sister to remain. Won't you sit down? I – I've never entertained a detective before!'

'I should explain, Mrs North, that I am investigating the murder of Ernest Fletcher, who I believe was an acquaintance of yours.'

'Yes. Yes, I quite understand. Please go on!'

'You knew that Mr Fletcher had been murdered?' he asked.

Before she could answer, Sally cut in. 'In common with the butcher, the baker, the milkman, all the servants, the postman, and the paper-boy.'

He looked at her appraisingly, but did not answer, merely inclining his head slightly.

'News gets round so frightfully quickly in the suburbs,' Helen said, again with her uneasy, artificial laugh.

'Yes,' he agreed. 'I expect it does. When did you last see Mr Fletcher, Mrs North?'

'What's your reason for asking that question?' demanded Sally.

'I am investigating a murder, Miss –'

'I'm Sally Drew. You can hardly think that my sister knows anything about a murder.'

'I'm quite ready to believe that she doesn't,' he replied, with a good-humoured inflexion in his voice which surprised her. 'But I have a reason for asking Mrs North certain questions, and a right to do so.'

'Oh, of course!' Helen said quickly. 'Only it's rather difficult to say when I saw Ernie Fletcher last. Let me see now . . . it was probably in town. Oh yes, we were both at a party last week!'

'Are you quite sure that you haven't seen him since then?'

He kept his eyes on her face, taking note of the fluctuating colour in her cheeks, the frightened, wary look in her eyes that told plainly of indecision.

'Why, no, I – I don't think so!'

'You did not, by any chance, see him last night?'

'Last night?' Helen repeated. 'Of course not! Whatever made you think I might have?'

'I have reason to think that some woman visited him yesterday evening.'

'Good gracious, why should it be me, I wonder!'

He said in his quiet way: 'Please don't misunderstand me, Mrs North. I am quite prepared to find that the woman was not you. Indeed, I'm sorry to be obliged to worry you with these questions. But I'm sure you'll realise that the presence of a woman at Greystones last night must be investigated, for it is just possible that she, whoever she is, may be able to throw a little light on the murder.'

'How?' she said quickly.

'She may, quite unwittingly, have seen the murderer.'

'Oh!' she exclaimed, shuddering. 'But it's preposterous to suppose that I –'

He interrupted, saying in a matter-of-fact way: 'Well, Mrs North, the question can be settled quite easily. What size in shoes do you wear?'

A quiver ran over her face; she threw a glance towards her sister, who stepped promptly into the breach. 'Five-and-a-half, don't you, like me?'

'Yes,' she admitted. 'Yes, I do. I think most women of our height do.'

'Thank you,' said Hannasyde. 'I wonder if you would lend me the shoes you were wearing last night?'

'Lend you my shoes! Really, Superintendent, that's quite impossible!'

'Why, Mrs North?'

'Well, you must *see* – Oh, this is idiotic! *I* had nothing to do with Ernie Fletcher's death!'

'Then you can have no possible objection to lending me your shoes for half-an-hour,' said Hannasyde.

'Of course she hasn't,' said Sally. 'What's more, you shall have mine as well. I knew Ernest Fletcher too, so presumably there is just as much reason to suspect me of having been at Greystones last night as my sister.'

'Not quite,' he replied.

Helen sat down suddenly on the sofa. 'I can't stand this!' she said in a choking voice. 'There's no reason why you should come and badger me! Simply because I happened to know Ernie Fletcher –'

'Not entirely,' he said. 'Are not these yours, Mrs North?'

She looked at the slips of paper which he had taken from his pocket-book. The colour rushed into her face, but some of her strained rigidity left her. 'Yes. They're mine,' she answered. 'What of it?'

'They call for some kind of explanation, as I think you'll agree,' he said. 'Did you owe these various sums of money to Mr Fletcher?'

'No. That is, not in the way you seem to think. He bought up those debts, to get me out of a – a hole, and I was – I was repaying him bit by bit.' She glanced up fleetingly, and added, twisting her handkerchief between her fingers: 'I did not wish my – my husband to know. He – I – oh, this is impossible!'

'I quite appreciate your reluctance to discuss your affairs, Mrs North. It may make it easier for you to be frank with me if you can bring yourself to believe that except in so far as they may relate to the case I am at work on I have no interest in them, and certainly no desire to create any unnecessary – er – scandal.'

'There's nothing to make a scandal about!' she said. 'Mr Fletcher was just a friend. The whole arrangement was perfectly amicable. I don't know what you are imagining, but –'

'You can put an end to any imaginings of mine by being open with me, Mrs North. I have told you that I appreciate your point of view, but you must see that the discovery of these notes of yours in Ernest Fletcher's safe is a circumstance which must be fully inquired into. If you can satisfy me that you did not visit Greystones last night I shall have no further need to worry you with interrogations which you must naturally find unpleasant. But if you can bring no proof forward in support of your denial, and persist in refusing to let me compare your shoes with the footprints we have found in the garden at Greystones, I can have no alternative to pursuing my inquiries further. In which event, I fear there will be little hope of your evading the sort of publicity you must wish to avoid.'

Sally got up from her seat by the table, and walked forward. 'That,' she said, 'sounds remarkably like a threat, Superintendent.'

'I expect it does,' he agreed equably. 'It isn't, though.

I am only trying to point out to your sister that her wisest course is to be entirely frank with me. If I have to question her servants as to her whereabouts last night –'

'I get it,' said Sally, grimacing. She took a cigarette from the box on the table, and fitted it into her holder. She glanced speculatively at Hannasyde, and took a lighter from her pocket. The little flame spurted up; she lit her cigarette, once more looked at Hannasyde, and then said tersely: 'He's right, Helen. And what he says about having no interest in your affairs is true. He's got nothing on you, but obviously you've got to be eliminated.'

Helen looked frightened, but after a pause said: 'I did call on Ernie Fletcher last night. I've explained that he was a – a great friend, though *years* older than me. I looked on him as a sort of uncle.'

'Quite,' said Hannasyde. 'Had you any particular purpose in paying this call?'

'No, not exactly. My sister was busy, and I was bored. It was quite early, and I thought I'd just look in on Ernie.'

In spite of herself she coloured, but Hannasyde merely asked: 'At what hour did you arrive at Greystones?'

'It must have been at about five-and-twenty to ten. I know I left this house at half-past nine.'

'Just tell me everything that happened, Mrs North.'

'Really, there's so little to tell. I went by way of the Arden Road, because for one thing it's quicker than going all the way up this road, and along Vale Avenue, and for another – I expect this seems odd to you, but it isn't really – I didn't much want to see Miss Fletcher, so I thought I'd go in by the garden-entrance, on the chance of finding Ern – Mr Fletcher in his study.' She broke off, and exclaimed wretchedly: 'Oh, this is too impossible! It sounds as though I had some horrid assignation! But I hadn't, I hadn't!'

'Don't go over at the knees,' recommended her sister. 'It's obvious you hadn't, or you'd have thought up some convincing reason for calling on Ernie.'

'Oh, don't! Do you suppose I can't see what a false impression anyone must get, not – not knowing the terms I was on with Ernie?'

'The only impression the Superintendent's got is that you're a paralytic ass,' responded Sally cheerfully. 'Why you chose to enter by the garden-gate has got nothing to do with him, so get on with your story!'

'I don't know where I was. Oh yes! Well, Mr Fletcher was in his study – oh, I forgot to tell you that I saw a man coming out of the gate, just as I turned up into Maple Grove. I – I don't know whether that's any use to you?'

'Can you describe him, Mrs North?'

'No, except that he was rather stout and short. You see, it was dusk, and I didn't see his face. He walked off towards Vale Avenue. Well, I found Mr Fletcher in his study, as I said.'

'Was he alone?'

'Oh yes!'

'And then?'

'Well – well, nothing, really. We had a – a talk, and then I said I mustn't be late, and – and just left.'

'Do you know what the time was then?'

'Yes, it was a quarter to ten.'

'A quarter to ten?' he repeated, raising his head from his notebook.

'Yes. There was a clock on the mantelpiece, and I happened to notice the time.'

'Then you were only with Mr Fletcher for ten minutes?'

'I suppose so. Yes, it must have been about that.'

'A very short call, Mrs North, was it not?'

'I don't see why – What do you mean?'

'Merely that it strikes me as odd that having, as you yourself state, gone to see Mr Fletcher because you were bored, you stayed so short a time with him. Did anything happen to make you anxious to leave at once?'

'No. No, of course not. Only I could see he was busy, and I didn't want to be a nuisance.'

He made a note in his book. 'I see. So you left the study at 9.45. Did you return home by the way you had come?'

'Yes. But not immediately. I heard the garden-gate open, and – and it occurred to me that it would look rather odd – my being there at that hour. I didn't want anyone to see me, so I hid behind a bush.'

'Mr Fletcher, then, did not accompany you to the gate?'

'No,' she faltered. 'There was no reason why he should.'

'Oh!' said Hannasyde. 'Very well, Mrs North: you hid behind a bush. Did you see who it was that entered the garden?'

'No, I didn't. I mean, in the dusk, and – and only being able to peer through the bush, I couldn't get a clear view. I only know it was a man. He looked quite ordinary, but he had a hat on, and I didn't see his face.'

'What sort of hat, Mrs North?'

'A Homburg, I think.'

'Light or dark?'

She hesitated. 'I think it was a light one.'

'Did you happen to notice whether he carried a walking-stick?'

'No. No, I'm sure he didn't.'

'Did he go up to the house?'

'Yes, he went into Mr Fletcher's study.'

'Did you hear what happened then?'

'No. As soon as it was safe to do so I went away, of course. I don't know anything more.'

Hannasyde shut his notebook, and, looking straight across at Helen, said bluntly: 'Mrs North, are you prepared to state that your visit to Mr Fletcher was not in connection with these notes of yours?'

'I don't understand. I've told you –'

'I don't think you've told me the whole truth.'

'I don't know why you should say that, or what you may choose to suspect, but –'

'I suspect that Mr Fletcher was threatening to use these notes against you, Mrs North.'

'That's absurd! I tell you he was a friend of mine!'

'Yes, you have told me that, but I find it difficult to reconcile that statement with the presence of the IOUs in his safe. If his motives in obtaining possession of them were as chivalrous as you say they were, it would surely have been more natural for him either to have destroyed them, or to have given them back to you?'

'Are you suggesting that he was trying to blackmail me? It isn't true! Good heavens, what could he possibly want to blackmail me for?'

'Perhaps he wanted something from you which you were unwilling to give, Mrs North.'

She flushed. 'Oh – ! You've no right to say that! Besides, how could he blackmail me? It isn't a sin to get into debt!'

'He might have threatened to lay your IOUs before your husband, might he not?'

'He wouldn't – he wasn't like that!' she said faintly.

'Where is your husband, Mrs North?'

'He's in Berlin. He went last week, and won't be back till next Wednesday.'

Even as the words left her lips he saw her face change. The click of an opening door had sounded. Hannasyde turned quickly. A man had entered the room, and was standing on the threshold, his hand resting on the door-knob, his cool, rather stern grey eyes surveying the group in the middle of the room.

Four

Hannasyde heard the frightened gasp that came from Helen, and glanced once towards her. She was very white, gazing as though benumbed at the newcomer. It was Sally who spoke.

'Hullo, John!' she said nonchalantly. 'Where did you spring from?'

John North closed the door, and walked forward. 'How do you do, Sally?' he responded. His voice was a deep one, and he spoke with a certain deliberation. He was a well-built man of average height, good-looking, and with a manner quietly assured. Having shaken hands with his sister-in-law, he nodded at his wife, saying: 'Well, Helen? Sally keeping you company?'

'Yes, she's staying here,' Helen answered breathlessly. 'John, what are you doing here? I thought you were in Berlin!'

'I got through my business there more quickly than I expected.' He looked at Hannasyde in a measuring way, and said: 'Will you introduce me, Helen?'

She threw an imploring look at Hannasyde, but said: 'Yes, of course. It is Superintendent – oh dear, I'm afraid I have forgotten your name, Superintendent!'

'Hannasyde,' he supplied.

'Yes, from Scotland Yard, John. Rather a dreadful thing has happened – well, a *ghastly* thing! Ernest Fletcher has been murdered.'

'That doesn't seem to me to explain the presence of the Superintendent in my house,' he said calmly. 'May I know what you are doing here, Superintendent?'

Before Hannasyde could reply Helen had hurried into speech. 'Oh, but don't you see, John? The Superintendent is trying to discover someone who might be able to throw any light on the mystery, and hearing that I knew Ernie, he came to see if I could help. Only of course I can't. The whole thing seems absolutely incredible to me.'

His brows rose a little. 'Are you making a house-to-house visitation of all Fletcher's acquaintances, Superintendent? Or do you suspect my wife of having knocked him on the head? I hardly think she possesses the necessary strength.'

'You are well informed, Mr North. Where did you learn that he had been knocked on the head?'

John North looked at him with a faint smile in his eyes. He drew a folded newspaper from under his arm, and handed it to Hannasyde. 'You may study the source of my information if you wish,' he said politely.

Hannasyde glanced down the columns of the evening paper. 'Quick work,' he remarked, folding the paper again, and giving it back. 'Were you acquainted with the deceased, Mr North?'

'I knew him, certainly. I should not describe my acquaintance with him as very close. But if you are interrogating everyone who knew him, perhaps you would like to come into the library, and interrogate me?' He moved to the door as he spoke, and opened it. 'Or have you not yet finished questioning my wife?'

'Yes, I think so.' Hannasyde turned to Helen, meeting her anguished look with the flicker of a reassuring smile. 'Thank you, Mrs North: I won't take up any more of your time. Good-morning, Miss Drew.'

'You haven't seen the last of me by a long chalk,' Sally told him. 'I don't think my name conveys anything to you, which is rather levelling, but I'm a writer of crime novels, and I have never before had the opportunity of studying a crime at close quarters. What is of particular interest to me is your handling of the case. One is always apt to go wrong on police procedure.'

'I suppose so,' answered Hannasyde, looking rather appalled.

She gave him a sudden, swift smile. 'You've taught me one thing at least: I've always made my detectives a bit on the noisome side up till now.'

He laughed. 'Thank you!' He bowed slightly to Helen, and went out of the room before John North, who was still holding the door for him.

'This way, Superintendent,' North said, leading the way across the hall. 'Now what is it you would like to ask me? You have established the fact that I was acquainted with Fletcher.'

'But not, I think you said, very well acquainted with him?'

'Not so well acquainted with him as my wife was,' replied North. 'You will probably find that his closest friends were all of them women.'

'You did not like him, in fact, Mr North?'

'I can't say I was drawn to him,' admitted North. 'I should describe him as a ladies' man. The type has never appealed to me.'

'Did you consider him a dangerous man – with ladies?'

'Dangerous? Oh no, I shouldn't imagine so!' North said, a suggestion of boredom in his voice. 'My wife, for instance, regarded him, I believe, somewhat in the light of a tame cat.'

'I see. So, speaking as a husband, you would not consider it worth while to be – let us say – jealous of him?'

'I cannot pretend to speak for anyone but myself. But I take it that you do not want me to. I was not jealous of him. Is there anything else you wish to ask me?'

'Yes, I should like to know when you returned from the Continent, Mr North?'

'I arrived in London yesterday afternoon.'

'But you did not come down to Marley until this morning?'

'No, Superintendent, I did not.'

'Where did you go, Mr North?'

'To my flat, Superintendent.'

'Where is that, if you please?'

'In Portland Place.'

'Was that usual?'

'Quite.'

'You will have to forgive my bluntness, Mr North, but I must ask you to explain yourself a little more fully. Do you and Mrs North inhabit separate establishments?'

'Not in the sense which you appear to mean,' replied North. 'I may be wrong, but you seem to attach a sinister importance to my having chosen to remain in London for the night. My wife and I have been married for five years, Superintendent: we are long past the stage of living in one another's pockets.'

There was an edge to the deliberate voice, which Hannasyde was quick to hear. As though aware of it himself, North added lightly: 'I am often kept late in town. I find the flat convenient.'

'I see. Did you dine there?'

'No, I dined at my club.'

'And after dinner?'

'After dinner I returned to the flat, and went to bed.'

'You were alone there? Or are there any servants?'

'Oh, I was quite alone! It is a service flat, and I had given my valet leave to go out for the evening. I'm afraid I cannot – at the moment – bring forward any corroborative evidence, Superintendent. Perhaps you would like to take my finger-prints?'

'No, not at present, thank you,' returned Hannasyde. 'In fact, I hardly think I need detain you any longer.'

North walked over to the door. 'Well, you know where you can find me if you should want to ask me any further questions. My business and flat addresses are both in the London Telephone Directory.'

He led the way into the hall, and across it to the front door. A pale grey Homburg lay on the gate-leg table, beside a pair of wash-leather gloves. Hannasyde's eyes rested on it for a moment, but he made no comment, merely picking up his own hat from the chair whereon he had laid it.

Having seen him off the premises, North returned unhurriedly to the morning-room, entering it in time to hear his sister-in-law say trenchantly: 'You must be suffering from mental paralysis! You can't possibly hope to keep it from –'

She saw who was coming into the room, and snapped the sentence off in mid-air. North closed the door, tossed the newspaper he was still carrying on to the table, and said suavely: 'What can't she possibly hope to keep from me?'

'Did I say from you?' demanded Sally.

'It was sufficiently obvious.' He began methodically to fill a pipe. An uncomfortable silence fell. Helen was sitting with her gaze fixed on North's face, and her hands tightly clasped in her lap. As he restored his pouch to his pocket he raised his eyes, and for a moment looked steadily into hers. 'Well? Isn't it so?'

She evaded the question. 'What brought you home so unexpectedly, John?'

'Does that really interest you?' he inquired.

She said in a low, unsteady voice: 'You came back to spy on me!'

A hard look came into his face. He said nothing, however, but felt in his pocket for matches, and began to light his pipe.

A less intense note was introduced by Miss Drew, who said brightly: 'Would you by any chance like me to withdraw tactfully? I should hate to think I was cramping either of your styles.'

'No, don't go!' Helen said. 'John and I have nothing private to discuss.' She glanced up at North, and added with an attempt at nonchalance: 'It would be interesting to know why you elected to come home in the middle of the morning. You can't have felt an overwhelming desire for my company, or you'd have come last night.'

'No,' he replied imperturbably. 'We are rather beyond that, aren't we? I came when I read about Fletcher's murder.'

'There! What did I tell you?' said Sally. 'The answer to the maiden's prayer! Not that I'm fond of the protective type myself, but I should be if I were a pretty ninny like you, Helen.'

'Oh, don't be absurd!' Helen said, a catch in her voice. 'So you thought I might be mixed up in the murder, did you, John?'

He did not answer for a moment, but after a pause he said in his cool way: 'No, I don't think I suspected that seriously until I found a Superintendent from Scotland Yard in the house.'

She stiffened. 'Surely you understand the reason for that! He came simply –'

'Yes, I understood.' For the first time a harsh note sounded in his voice. 'The Superintendent came to discover whether the woman's footprint in the garden was yours. Was it?'

'Count ten before you answer,' recommended Sally, her eyes on North's grim face. Golly, she thought, this isn't going to be such plain sailing as I'd imagined.

'Oh, why can't you be quiet?' Helen cried sharply. 'What are you trying to do?'

'Stop you telling useless lies. You may be all washed-up, you two, but I don't see John letting you get pinched for murder if he can help it.'

'I didn't murder him! I didn't! You can't think that!'

'Were the footprints yours?' North asked.

She got up jerkily. 'Yes! They were mine!' she flung at him.

Sally gave a groan. 'How not to break the news!' she said. 'For God's sake, try to stop looking like something carved out of the solid rock, John! Holy mackerel, to think I've written books about people like you, and never believed a word of it!'

North disregarded her, addressing his wife. 'No doubt I shall seem to you unwarrantably intrusive, but I should like to know why you visited Fletcher in this apparently clandestine fashion?'

'I went to see him because he's – he was – a friend of mine. There was nothing clandestine about our relations. I don't expect you to believe that, but it's true!'

Sally polished her eyeglass. 'Questioned, Miss Sally Drew, an eminent writer of detective fiction, corroborated that statement.'

'You are a somewhat partial witness, Sally,' North said dryly. 'Oh, don't look so belligerent, Helen! I merely asked out of curiosity. It's really quite beside the point. What seems to me to be more important is what, if anything, you know about the murder?'

'Nothing, nothing!'

'When were you with Fletcher?' he asked.

'Oh, early, quite early! I left his study at a quarter to ten. John, I know it sounds strange, but I went to see him on a perfectly trivial matter. I – I wanted to know if he'd go with me to the Dimberleys' affair next week, that's all.'

He paid no heed to this, but picked up the newspaper and studied the front page. 'I see that Fletcher's body was discovered at 10.05 p.m.,' he remarked. He looked steadily across at his wife. 'And you know nothing?'

'I saw a man come up the path,' she said in a low voice. 'That's why I hid behind the bush.'

He folded the newspaper very exactly. 'You saw a man come up the path? Well? Who was it?'

'I don't know.'

'Do you mean you didn't recognise him?'

'Yes – that is, I couldn't see him distinctly. I – I only know that he went into the study, through the window.'

'Have you told the police this?'

'Yes, I – I told them.'

'Did the Superintendent ask you if you would be able to recognise this mysterious man if you saw him again?'

'No. I told him that I couldn't see at all clearly, and only had a vague impression of an ordinary sort of man in a light hat.'

There was a slight pause. 'In a light hat? Oh! And would you recognise him again?'

'No, I tell you! I haven't the least idea who it was!'

'I hope the Superintendent believed you,' he remarked.

'Why?' demanded Sally, who had been watching him closely.

He glanced indifferently down at her. 'Why? Because I have no desire to see my wife in the witness-box, of course.'

'Oh, my God, I shan't have to give evidence, shall I?' gasped Helen. 'I couldn't. I'd rather die! Oh, what a ghastly *mess* it all is!'

'It is indeed,' he said.

Sally, who had been rhythmically swinging her monocle on the end of its cord, suddenly screwed it into her eye, and asked: 'Does the Superintendent suspect you of having had anything to do with it, John?'

'I've no idea what he suspects. Helen's connection

with the crime has evidently given him food for thought. He probably suffers from old-fashioned ideas about jealous husbands.'

She cocked her head on one side. 'I should have thought you were capable of being a trifle primitive. What's more, your somewhat unexpected appearance on the scene must look a bit fishy to him.'

'Why should it? If I'd murdered Fletcher I should hardly have come down here today.'

She considered this dispassionately. 'Dunno. It's a point, of course, but it would have looked bad if you'd lain low, and he'd found out that you weren't in Berlin at all.'

'Give me credit for a little common sense, Sally. When I commit a murder I can assure you I shall take good care to cover my tracks.' He glanced at his wrist-watch. 'Ask them to put lunch forward, will you, Helen? I've got to go back to town.'

'I'll go and tell Evans,' offered Sally, and went out, firmly shutting the door behind her.

Helen mechanically straightened an ornament on the mantelpiece. 'Are you – are you coming back?' she asked.

'Certainly I'm coming back,' he replied.

She hesitated, then said in a low voice: 'You're very angry about this . . .'

'We won't discuss that. The mischief is done, and I imagine my possible anger is unlikely to make you regret it more than you are already doing.'

She lifted her hand to her cheek. 'You don't believe me, but I wasn't having an affair with Ernie.'

'Oh yes, I believe you!' he returned.

Her hand fell. 'You do believe me? You didn't think I was in love with him – ever? I thought –'

'You thought because I personally disliked the man, and your intimacy with him, that I was jealous,' he said sardonically. 'You were wrong. I always knew he was not the type you fall for, my dear.'

She winced. 'It is not fair to say I fall for anyone. It sounds – rather Victorian, but I've been perfectly faithful to you.'

'I am aware of that.'

'You have made it your business to be sure of that!'

'It was my business,' he replied hardly.

'Why did you behave as you did over my friendship with Ernie, then? You knew you could at least trust me not to indulge in a vulgar intrigue!'

'It wasn't you, but Fletcher whom I mistrusted,' he said. 'I warned you that I wouldn't stand for that particular friendship, didn't I?'

'What right had you to expect me to drop him or any other of my friends? You allowed me to go my own road, and you went yours –'

'This is a singularly unprofitable discussion,' he interrupted. 'You chose to go your own road, but if I remember rightly I made it clear to you two years ago that I would not tolerate either your debts or your indiscretions. Six months ago I requested you to keep Ernest Fletcher at arm's length. You have been almost continuously in his company ever since.'

'I liked him. I didn't love him!'

'You can hardly have expected the world to know that.'

'But you knew it!'

74

He looked at her with narrowed eyes. 'I knew that Fletcher had a peculiar fascination for women.'

'Yes! That's true, and I did feel that fascination. But love – ! Oh, no, no, no!' She turned away in some agitation, and walked rather blindly towards the window. With her back to the room, she said after a moment: 'Why did you come down here today? You suspected I was – mixed up in this, didn't you?'

'Yes,' he said. 'I did.'

'I wonder you came, then,' she said bitterly.

He did not answer at once, but presently he said in a gentler voice: 'That's silly, Helen. Whatever our differences we are man and wife, and if there's trouble brewing we're both in it. I hope, however, that it'll blow over. Try not to worry about it – and don't say more than you need if Superintendent Hannasyde questions you any further.'

'No. I'll be very careful,' she replied.

Miss Drew reappeared at that moment, with the tidings that luncheon would be ready in five minutes.

'Thanks. I'll go and wash,' North said, and went out.

Sally eyed her sister's back speculatively. 'Tell him the truth?'

'No.'

'Fool.'

'I couldn't. It's no use arguing: you just don't understand.'

'He'd prefer the true story to the obvious alternative.'

'You're wrong. He knows there was nothing between Ernie and me.'

'*Does* he?' said Sally.

Helen wheeled round. 'What do you mean?'

'I'm not sure. But somehow he didn't give me that impression. If he knew there was nothing between you and Ernie, I don't quite see the reason for the very definite animus against Ernie.'

'He never cared much for him. But as for animus, that's absurd!'

'Oh no, it isn't, and you know it isn't, my girl! John's wasting no tears over Ernie's death. Moreover, it wouldn't altogether surprise me to learn that he knows more than you think he does.'

'Once a novelist always a novelist!' said Helen, with a little laugh.

'Too true! And that being so, I think I'll wander round to take a look at the scene of the crime after lunch.'

'You can't possibly do that!'

'What's to stop me?'

'It isn't decent!'

'Decent be blowed! I shall go and rout that poor worm Neville out. He's another person who conceivably knows more than he chooses to admit. I hope the police aren't underrating him; immense potentialities in Neville.'

'Potentialities for what?'

'You have me there, sister,' replied Sally. 'I'm damned if I know, but I'm going to have a shot at finding out.'

Luncheon was announced a moment later, and the subject of Ernest Fletcher's death was abandoned. Throughout the meal, Helen said little, and ate less. Miss Drew maintained a cheerful flow of small talk, and North, having eaten a hurried meal, left the table early, informing his wife that he would be back to dinner.

After the ladies had finished their coffee, Sally gave it as her considered opinion that Helen would be the better

76

for a rest. Somewhat to her surprise Helen fell in with this suggestion, and allowed herself to be escorted upstairs. When Sally lowered the window-blinds she said: 'You aren't really going round to Greystones, are you?'

'Yes, I am. Taking a message of condolence from you to poor old Miss Fletcher. I shall say you are writing to her, of course.'

A faint voice from amongst the banked-up pillows said: 'Oh! I ought to have done that!'

'Time enough when you've had a nap,' said Sally, and withdrew.

Half-an-hour later, when she presented herself at the front door at Greystones, it was to be met by the intelligence that Miss Fletcher, like Helen, was resting. She was spared the necessity of inquiring for Neville by that willowy young gentleman's strolling out of the drawing-room into the hall, and inviting her to enter and solace his boredom.

Simmons made it plain by his cough and general air of pious gloom that he considered the invitation unseasonable, but as neither Sally nor Neville paid the slightest heed to him, there was nothing for him to do but to retire to his own domain, on the far side of a baize door leading out of the hall, and draw, for his wife's edification, an unpleasing picture of the fate awaiting the hard-hearted and the irreligious.

Meanwhile, Neville had escorted his visitor into the drawing-room. 'Come to see the sights, darling?' he inquired. 'You're too late to see the dragging of the lily-pool.'

'Ah!' she said. 'So they're after the weapon, are they?'

'Yes, but there's no pleasing them. I offered them

Aunt Lucy's Indian clubs, a mallet, and the bronze paper-weight on Ernie's desk, but they didn't seem to like any of them.'

'So there was a bronze paper-weight on his desk, was there? H'm!'

'Well, no,' said Neville softly, 'there wasn't. I put it there.'

'What on earth for?'

'Oh, just to occupy their minds!' said Neville, seraphically smiling.

'It'll serve you right if you get pinched for the murder,' Sally told him.

'Yes, but I shan't. I was right about Honest John, wasn't I?'

'Yes. How did you know he was back?'

'News does get about so, doesn't it?'

'Rot!'

'All right, precious. I saw him drive past the house on the way to the station. Flying the country?'

'Not he. John's not that sort. Besides, why should he?'

Neville regarded her with sleepy shrewdness. 'Do not bother to put on the frills with me, sweet maid. It *is* worrying for you, isn't it?'

'Not in the least. My interest in the murder is purely academic. Why do they think the instrument is still on the premises? Because of what Helen said?'

'They don't confide in me as much as you'd think they would,' replied Neville. 'What did Helen say?'

'Oh, that she was sure the man she saw wasn't carrying anything!'

'Bless her little heart, did she? Isn't she fertile? First, she didn't see the man at all; now she knows he wasn't carrying anything. Give her time and she'll remember that he had bandy legs and a squint.'

'You poisonous reptile, just because it wasn't light enough for her to recognise the man –'

'Oh, do you think it wasn't?' asked Neville. 'You've a kind heart, and no Norman blood.'

'Oh! So you think she did recognise the man, and that it was John, do you?'

'Yes, but I have a low mind,' he explained.

'You've taken the words out of my mouth.'

'I know.'

'Well, I've got the same kind of low mind, and the thought that crosses it is that you're probably the heir to Ernie's money. Correct?'

'Yes, rather,' said Neville cordially. 'I'm practically a plutocrat.'

'Yes?' said Sally. 'Then it'll be a nice change for you, Mr Neville Fletcher, after having been up to your eyes in debt!'

Five

This suggestion, hurled at his head like a challenge, was received by Neville with unruffled placidity. He appeared to consider the matter dispassionately, remarking at length: 'Well, I don't know that I altogether agree with you.'

'What?' said Sally scornfully. 'You don't agree that a fortune is better than debt?'

'Depends what you're accustomed to,' said Neville.

'Don't be a fool! You don't imagine I'm going to swallow that, do you?'

'No.'

'Then what on earth's the use of saying it?'

'I mean I haven't speculated on the processes of your mind,' explained Neville. 'Unprofitable occupation, quite without point.'

'Look here, Neville, are you sticking to it that you've no objection to being snowed under by debts?' demanded Sally.

'Yes, why not?'

'It doesn't add up, that's why not. There's nothing more uncomfortable than not having any money, and being dunned by tradesmen. Receiving To Account

Rendered by every post, with a veiled threat attached, and totting up the ghastly totals –'

'Oh, but I don't do anything like that!' Neville assured her. 'I never open bills.'

'Then you get County Courted.'

'You soon get used to that. Besides, Ernie hated it, so he got into the way of paying my outstanding debts. Really, the whole thing worked out very well. Now I've got his money I shall never have a moment's peace. People will badger me.'

'Well, you can employ a secretary.'

'I shouldn't like that at all. I should have to have a house to put him in, and servants to run it, and before I knew what had happened I should find myself shackled by respectability.'

This point of view struck Sally quite forcibly. 'I must say, I hadn't looked at it like that,' she admitted. 'It does sound rather lousy. What do you want to do?'

'Nothing, at the moment. But I may easily want to wander off to Bulgaria next week. It's a place I hardly know.'

'You'll still be able to, won't you?'

'First class ticket to Sofia, and a suite at the best hotel? Not if I know it!'

Sally was so much interested that she was beguiled into pursuing the subject of foreign travel. Neville's disjointed yet picturesque account of incredible adventures encountered during the course of aimless and impecunious wanderings held her entranced, and drew from her at length a rather wistful exclamation of: 'Golly, what fun you must have had! I wish I were a man. Why haven't you written a book about all this?'

'That,' said Neville incorrigibly, 'would have invested my travels with a purpose, and spoilt them for me.'

'You're definitely sub-human,' said Sally. She eyed him curiously. 'Does anything ever worry you?'

'Yes. Problem of how to escape worry.'

She grinned, but said: 'I hate paradox. Does this little situation worry you?'

'What, Ernie's murder? No, why should it?'

'Does it strike you that you've got a pretty good motive for having killed Ernie?'

'Naturally not.'

'The police will think so.'

'Too busy chasing after the unknown man seen by Helen and Malachi.'

'Who?'

'Haven't you met Malachi?' said Neville, roused to sudden interest. 'Oh, I must introduce you at once! Come on!'

'Yes, but who is he?' demanded Sally.

He took her wrist and led her out into the garden through the long window. 'He's the bobby who discovered the crime.'

'Good Lord, did he see Helen's man too? That wasn't in the paper John brought home!'

'Oh, here we live at the hub of the crime!' said Neville.

'Just a moment,' interposed Sally, pulling her hand away. 'I want to take a look at the general lay-out. Anyone mounting guard over the study?'

'Not now. Nothing to be seen.'

'I might get an idea,' Sally said darkly.

'Morbid mind, professional interest, or family feeling?'

She ignored the implication of this last alternative. 'Professional interest.'

They had rounded the corner of the house, and come in sight of the path leading to a gate set in the fence separating the garden from Maple Grove. A thick bed of shrubs concealed the fence from view, and was being subjected to a rigorous search by two hot and rather dishevelled policemen. Sally cast them a cursory glance, and transferred her attention to the house. 'Which is Helen's bush?'

He pointed it out to her, and she went to it, inspected the footprints, and would have concealed herself behind it had it not been for the prompt action of PC Glass, who, having observed her arrival with some disapproval, now abandoned his search in the shrubbery to admonish her.

'It's all right,' said Sally. 'I'm not going to obliterate the prints, or anything like that. I only want to get an idea of what anyone hidden here, in the dark, could actually see. I'm interested in crime.'

'Remove thy foot from evil,' recommended Glass severely. 'These things are in the hands of the police.'

'Don't you bother your head about me: I've made a study of murder. I may be able to help,' said Sally.

'Like me,' murmured Neville. 'I tried to help, but no one was grateful.'

A cold eye was bent upon him. 'Bread of deceit is sweet to a man,' said Glass. 'But afterwards,' he added forebodingly, 'his mouth shall be filled with gravel.'

Sally, having by this time satisfied herself that very little could be seen from behind the currant bush, emerged. 'Is that out of the Bible?' she inquired. 'Nearly all the best things are, except those that come out of Shakespeare. Can I go into the study, Neville?'

'Do!' he said cordially.

'What is your business here?' demanded Glass. 'Why do you desire to enter that room?'

'I'm a novelist,' explained Sally. 'Crime stories.'

'You were better at home,' he said sombrely, but made no further attempt to stop her.

Followed by Neville, who had produced a Bible from his pocket, and was swiftly flicking the pages over, Sally entered the study, and stood just inside the window, looking round. Neville sat down on the edge of the desk, absorbed in his search through the Proverbs.

'Where was he found?' Sally said abruptly.

Neville jerked his head in the direction of the chair behind the desk.

'Facing the window?'

'Yes. Don't bother me!'

'Actually seated in his chair?'

'Mm. I've got a goodish bit here about the lips of the strange woman, but that's not the one I want.'

'And the murderer is supposed to have entered by way of the window, which Ernie was directly facing?'

'Flattery is the tongue of the strange woman . . . no, that's not it.'

'Oh, do take your head out of that! Don't you see that if the murderer entered by way of the window Ernie must have been entirely unsuspicious? He apparently didn't even get up from his chair!'

'Got it!' said Neville triumphantly. '*She is loud and stubborn; her feet abide not in her house.* That's you. I'm going to tell Glass.' He slid off the edge of the table, and departed in search of the policeman.

Left alone, Sally sat down in an armchair, dropped her chin in her cupped hands, and frowned upon her surroundings. Neville soon reappeared, saying: 'He reproved me. Seemed to know the context.'

'What was that?' asked Sally absently.

'Not polite. Only two kinds of women in the OT. This was the other kind. Solved the whole mystery?'

'No, but as I see it one fact stands out a mile. It wasn't John.'

'All right; have it your own way.'

'Yes, but don't you see?' she insisted. 'Ernie wasn't expecting to be murdered. If John had walked in, wouldn't he – No, I suppose it doesn't absolutely follow. One doesn't expect even jealous husbands to murder one.'

'Oh, is John jealous?' said Neville. 'I thought he was quite complaisant.'

'That's what a great many people think, but –' She stopped. 'Forget it!'

'Crediting me with an earnest desire to incriminate Honest John?' inquired Neville. 'Non-existent, believe me.'

'Nevertheless I should probably be wise not to say too much to you,' said Sally bluntly.

'That's all right with me too,' he assured her. 'As a subject for conversation, I find that Ernie's murder palls on one.'

She looked at him. 'You're a cold-blooded fish, Neville. I didn't like Ernie, but gosh, I'm sorry for him!'

'What a waste of emotion!' he remarked. 'What's the use of being sorry for a dead man?'

'There's something in that,' she admitted. 'But it's hardly decent to say so. Oh, damn it all, this is a rotten mess! Why the dickens couldn't you have got hold of those IOUs before it all happened?'

'Oh, have they been found?' said Neville.

'Of course they have!'

'John pleased?'

'He doesn't know anything about them. Helen won't tell him.'

He blinked. 'Let me get this straight, just in case of accidents. What is Helen's story?'

'That she went round to see Ernie on some trivial matter. Yes, I know it's insane, but she probably knows her own business best. John wasn't particularly encouraging, and as he's apparently rabid on the subject of gambling and debts, I daresay she's right not to tell him. If you run into John, you'd better know nothing about it.'

'You go home and tell Helen about the bread of deceit,' said Neville. 'I don't think she's being very clever.'

'No, poor darling, but she's all in. I've left her on her bed, and I hope she'll be feeling a bit better by the time I get back – more able to cope. I don't think she slept much last night.'

'Well, let's hope she doesn't do anything silly,' said Neville. 'She probably will, but with any luck she'll merely confuse the issue.'

'She happens to be my sister,' said Sally frigidly.

'Yes, it's the best thing I know of her,' agreed Neville.

Sally, taken by surprise, showed signs of being over-come.

'And the worst thing I know of you,' added Neville dulcetly.

Sally cast him a withering look, and left the study to exercise her charm on the younger of the two policemen still searching the shrubbery.

Helen, meanwhile, was not, as her sister had supposed, upon her bed, but closeted with Superintendent Hannasyde at the police station.

Upon Sally's leaving the house, she had lain for some few minutes, thinking. After glancing once or twice at the telephone she had at last sat up in bed, with the sudden energy of one who has come to a difficult decision, and lifted the receiver off its rest. 'I want to be put through to the police station,' she told the operator calmly.

She was connected almost immediately, and asked for Superintendent Hannasyde. The voice at the other end of the wire desired her, somewhat suspiciously, to divulge her identity. She hesitated, and then said: 'I am Mrs John North. If Superintendent Hannasyde –'

' *'Old* on a minute!' said the voice.

She waited. Presently a fresh voice addressed her, and she recognised the Superintendent's even tones.

She hurried into speech. 'Superintendent, this is Mrs North speaking. I wonder if I could see you? There's something I wish to tell you.'

'Certainly,' he replied. 'I'll come up to your house.'

She glanced at her watch. 'No, don't do that. I have to go into town and I can quite easily call in at the police station, if that would be convenient to you?'

'Quite convenient,' he said.

'Thank you. I'll be there in about twenty minutes, then. Goodbye!'

She laid the receiver down and, flinging back the eiderdown, slid off the bed on to the floor. She pulled up the blinds which Sally had so thoughtfully lowered, and in the relentless glare of sunlight sat down at her dressing-table, and studied her face in the mirror. It was pale, with shadowed eyes. 'Heavens! What a guilty-looking sight!' she said under her breath, and with quick, nervous hands, pulled open a drawer and exposed an array of face-creams, lotions, and cosmetics.

Ten minutes later she was pulling on her gloves, her eyes resting critically on her own reflection. Her make-up had been delicately achieved; the face that confronted her from under the brim of a shady hat was faintly tinged with colour, the corn-coloured curls neatly arranged in a cluster in her neck, the eyebrows lightly pencilled, the lovely mouth a glow of red.

On her way down the stairs she encountered her maid, who exclaimed at her, bemoaning the fact that Madam was not resting after all.

'No, I've got to go out,' Helen answered. 'If Miss Drew should get back before me, tell her I've gone into the town, will you, but shall be back for tea.'

She drove herself to the police station, and was taken at once to the somewhat comfortless office where Hannasyde was going through a pile of documents.

He got up as she came in, and favoured her with a rather keen look. 'Good-afternoon, Mrs North. Will you sit down?'

She took a chair on the side of the desk opposite to him. 'Thank you. Do you know, the only time I've ever been to a police station before was about a dog I once lost?'

'Indeed?' he said. 'What is it you wish to say to me, Mrs North?'

She raised her eyes to his face. 'I want to tell you something which I ought to have told you this morning,' she said frankly.

'Yes?'

His voice betrayed nothing but a kind of polite interest. She found it a little disconcerting, and stumbled over her next words. 'It was silly of me, but you know how it is when one is suddenly confronted – or no, perhaps you don't. It's always you who – who asks the questions, isn't it?'

'I have had plenty of experience of people who either concealed the truth, or told me only a part of it, if that is what you mean, Mrs North.'

'I suppose it is,' she admitted. 'Perhaps you can understand, though, how awkward it was for me, when you – well, exposed my – my indiscretions this morning. I won't attempt to deny that I was badly rattled, not because of the murder, because I had nothing to do with that, but because I'm not the sort of woman my dealings with Mr Fletcher might have led you to suppose, and – and there could be nothing worse from my point of view than to have an indiscretion – like that – made public. The only idea in my head this morning was to admit as little as I need. You – you *do* understand that, don't you?'

He nodded. 'Perfectly, Mrs North. Please go on!'

'Yes. Well, since I saw you I've had time to think it over, and of course I realise that when it's a question of murder it would be terribly wrong of me to keep anything back. Moreover –' she smiled shyly across at him – 'you were so very nice about it, not – not giving me away to my husband, that I feel sure I can trust you.'

'I had better make it clear, Mrs North, that while I have not the smallest desire to create any unnecessary unpleasantness in connection with this case, my consideration for your feelings cannot interfere with the execution of what I may decide to be my duty.'

'Of course not; I quite appreciate that.'

He looked at her. A few hours earlier she had been nervous to the point of distraction, but she had herself well in hand now. She met his eyes deprecatingly, but quite squarely, and was sure enough of herself to employ little feminine tricks to beguile him. She was a lovely woman; he wondered what the brain behind her soft blue eyes was evolving. She was probably playing a part, but so well that he could not be sure of it. It was easy to believe that she had concealed some of the truth earlier in the day; the reasons she put forward for having done so were quite credible; but it would not be so easy to know how much of whatever revelations were to come was to be believed.

He said impersonally: 'Well, Mrs North? What is it that you are going to tell me?'

'It is about what happened after I hid behind that bush, outside Mr Fletcher's study. I said that as soon as the man who came up the path had entered the house I went away. Actually, I didn't go away.'

His keen eyes narrowed slightly. 'Indeed! Why not?'

She began to fidget a little with the clasp of her handbag. 'You see, what I originally said about my interview with Mr Fletcher wasn't true. It – it wasn't amicable. At least, not on my part. Mr Fletcher, as you suggested this morning, Superintendent, did want something from me which I – which I was more than unwilling to give. I don't want to give you a false impression. Looking back, I feel sure I lost my head over the whole affair, and – and perhaps exaggerated things. Mr Fletcher *was* using my IOUs against me, but in a playful sort of way. I expect it was only a bluff, for really he wasn't a bit like that. Only I was frightened, and behaved stupidly. I went round to his house that evening to try to persuade him to give me back my notes. Something he said made me lose my temper, and I walked out of the house in a rage. But while I was hiding behind the bush I realised that losing my temper wasn't going to help me. I thought perhaps I ought to have another shot at coaxing the notes out of Mr Fletcher, though at the same time I rather dreaded the idea of going back into that room.'

'Just a moment!' Hannasyde interrupted. 'What happened in the study while you were hiding behind the bush?'

'I don't know. You remember I told you that I thought the man I saw closed the window? Well, that was true. I only heard a confused murmur of voices. I don't think he was in the room for more than six or seven minutes. It seemed longer to me, but it can't have been, because the clock in the hall began to strike ten when I finally left the house. But I haven't got to that yet. While I was still waiting, and not knowing quite what I ought to do next, the window of the study was pushed open, and both Mr Fletcher and the other man came out. Mr Fletcher had a light, carrying voice, and I distinctly heard him say: "A little mistake on your part. Permit me to show you the way out!"'

'And the other? Did he speak?'

'Not in my hearing. Mr Fletcher said something else, but I couldn't catch what it was.'

'Did he appear to be at all put-out?'

'No, but he was the sort of man who never showed when he was annoyed. He sounded rather mocking, I thought. I don't think there can have been a quarrel, because he just strolled down the path with the other man quite casually, not hurrying, or anything. In fact, I rather thought that perhaps the man had walked in by mistake.'

'Oh! And then?'

'Well, you know that the path to the gate twists past some bushes? As soon as they had reached the bend, I slipped from behind the bush, and ran back to the study. I – I had a wild sort of hope that my notes might be in Mr Fletcher's desk, and it seemed to me that here was my chance to get hold of them. Most of the drawers were unlocked, and I didn't bother about them. But the centre drawer had its key in it, and I happened to know that Mr Fletcher used to keep it locked. I've seen him take the key out of his pocket to open it. I pulled it out, but I couldn't see my notes. Then I heard Mr Fletcher coming up the path: he was whistling. I got a sudden panic, and instead of staying where I was I shut the drawer, and whisked myself over to the door. I just had time to open it very gingerly to make sure that no one was in the hall, before escaping that way. There wasn't anyone in sight, and I slipped into the hall before Mr Fletcher had reached the study. That was when the clock began to strike. As a matter of fact, it gave me a dreadful start, because it's one of those tall-case clocks that make a whirring noise before they begin striking. I walked down the hall to the front door, let myself out as quietly as I could, and went home by way of Vale Avenue, which, I expect you know, cuts across the top of my own road.'

There was a short silence after she had finished speaking. Hannasyde moved a paper slightly on his desk. 'Mrs North, why have you told me this?' he asked.

'But – but isn't it obvious?' she said. 'I couldn't let you think that a perfectly innocent man might have murdered Mr Fletcher! You see, I *know* that Mr Fletcher was alive when that man left the house.'

'How long were you in the study, the second time?' he asked.

'I don't know, but not more than three minutes. Oh, less! I had only time to look hurriedly through that drawer before I heard Mr Fletcher coming back.'

'I see.'

Something in his voice made her stiffen. 'You don't believe me? But it's true: I can prove it's true!'

'Can you? How?'

She spread out her hands. 'I wasn't wearing gloves. My finger-prints must have been on the door. Look, I'll show you!' She got up, and moved to the door, clasping the handle in her right hand, and laying her left hand on the panel above it. 'You know how one eases a door open, if one's afraid of its making any noise? I remember putting my left hand on it, just like this.'

'Have you any objection to having your finger-prints taken, Mrs North?'

'No, none,' she answered promptly. 'I want you to have them taken. That's partly why I chose to see you here.'

'Very well, but there are one or two questions I should like to ask you first.'

She came back to her chair. 'Why, certainly!' she said.

'You have said that Mr Fletcher was using your IOUs against you. Does that mean that he was pressing for payment, or that he was threatening to lay them before you husband?'

'He did hint that my husband might be interested in them.'

'Are you on good terms with your husband, Mrs North?'

She gave an embarrassed little laugh. 'Yes, of course. Perfectly.'

'He had no cause to suspect you of any form of intimacy with Mr Fletcher?'

'No. Oh no! I have always had my own friends, and my husband never interfered.'

'He was not, then, jealous of your friendships with other men?'

'How old-fashioned of you, Superintendent! Of course not.'

'That implies great confidence in you, Mrs North.'

'Well, naturally . . . !'

'Yet in spite of this perfect understanding which you tell me existed between you, you were ready to steal your IOUs from Mr Fletcher rather than allow the knowledge of your gambling debts to come to your husband's ears?'

She took a moment or two to answer, but replied at length quite composedly: 'My husband very much dislikes gambling. I have always been rather extravagant, and I shrank from telling him about those debts.'

'You were afraid of the consequences?'

'In a way, yes. It was lack of moral courage, really. If I had foreseen all that was going to happen –'

'You would have told him?'

'Yes,' she said hesitantly.

'Have you told him, Mrs North?'

'No. No, I –'

'Why not?'

'But you must see!' she exclaimed. 'The whole thing has – has become so distorted! Now that Mr Fletcher is dead there would be only my word that everything happened as it did. I mean, his getting hold of my IOUs, and my not having till then the least suspicion of his – well, of his wanting me to become his mistress! I know very well how incredible it sounds, and I've no doubt I was a perfect fool, but I *didn't* guess! But anyone just hearing my account would be bound to think there must have been more between Mr Fletcher and me than there actually was. If I'd had the sense to tell my husband at once – as soon as I knew Mr Fletcher had got possession of my IOUs – But I hadn't! I tried to get them back myself, which makes it look as though I were afraid of something coming out about me and Mr Fletcher. Oh, can't you understand?'

'I think so,' he replied. 'The fact of the matter is that you were not speaking the truth when you told me that your husband did not object to your friendship with Mr Fletcher. Isn't that so?'

'You are trying to make me say that he was jealous, but he wasn't! He certainly did not like Mr Fletcher much: he thought he had rather a bad reputation with women. But –' Her throat contracted; she lifted her head and said with difficulty: 'My husband does not care enough for me to be jealous of me, Superintendent.'

His eyes dropped to the papers under his hand. He said quite gently: 'He might perhaps be jealous of your good name, Mrs North.'

'I don't know.'

'That is not consistent with the rest of your evidence,' he pointed out. 'You ask me to believe in a state of confidence existing between you and your husband that was unaccompanied by any great depth of affection, yet at the same time you wish me to believe that it is impossible for you to make a clean breast of the whole story to him.'

She swallowed and said: 'I do not wish to be dragged through the Divorce Courts, Superintendent.'

He raised his eyes. 'There is, then, so little confidence between you that you were afraid your husband might do that?'

'Yes,' she said, doggedly returning his look.

'You had no fear that he might, instead, be – very angry – with the man who had put you in this unpleasant position?'

'None,' she said flatly.

He allowed a pause to follow. When he spoke again, it was with an abruptness that startled her. 'A few minutes ago you repeated words to me which you heard Mr Fletcher utter when he passed down the garden-path with his visitor. How was it that you were able to hear these so clearly, and yet distinguish nothing that his companion said?'

'I have told you that Mr Fletcher had a light, rather high-pitched voice. If you have ever been with a deaf person you must know that such a voice has a far greater carrying power than a low one.'

Apparently he accepted this explanation, for he nodded, and got up. 'Very well, Mrs North. And now, if you are willing, your finger-prints.'

A quarter of an hour later, when Helen had left the police station, he sat down again at his desk, and meditatively studied certain notes which he had jotted down on a slip of paper.

Evidence of PC Glass: At 10.02, man seen coming out of garden-gate. Evidence of Helen North: At 9.58, approximately, unknown man escorted to garden-gate by Fletcher.

He was still looking pensively at these scribblings when PC Glass entered the office to report that no trace of any weapon had been found in the garden at Greystones.

Hannasyde gave a grunt, but said as Glass turned towards the door: 'Just a moment. Are you certain that the time when you saw a man come out of the garden-gate was two minutes after ten?'

'Yes, sir.'

'It could not, for instance, have been two or three minutes *before* ten?'

'No, sir. The time, by my watch and the clock in the room, was 10.05 p.m. when I entered the study. Therefore I am doubly certain, for to reach that room from the point where I was standing was a matter of three minutes, not of seven.'

Hannasyde nodded. 'All right; that's all. Report to Sergeant Hemingway in the morning.'

'Yes, sir,' Glass replied, but added darkly: 'He that hath a froward heart findeth no good.'

'I daresay,' said Hannasyde discouragingly.

'And he that hath a perverse tongue falleth into mischief,' said Glass with a good deal of severity.

Whether this pessimistic utterance referred to himself or to the absent Sergeant, Hannasyde did not inquire. As Glass walked towards the door, the telephone-bell rang, and the voice of the constable on duty informed the Superintendent that Sergeant Hemingway was on the line.

The Sergeant sounded less gloomy than when Hannasyde had parted from him. 'That you, sir?' he asked briskly. 'Well, I've got something, though where it's going to lead us I *don't* see. Shall I come down?'

'No, I'm coming back to town; I'll see you there. Any luck with those prints?'

'Depends what you call luck, Super. Some of 'em belong to a bloke by the name of Charlie Carpenter.'

'Carpenter?' repeated Hannasyde. 'Who the dickens is he?'

'It's a long story – what you might call highly involved,' replied the Sergeant.

'All right: reserve it. I'll be up in about half-an-hour.'

'Right you are, Chief. Give my love to Ichabod!' said the Sergeant.

Hannasyde grinned as he laid down the receiver, but refrained from delivering a message which, judging by Glass's forbidding countenance, would not be well received. He said kindly: 'Well, Glass, you've been doing a lot of work on this case. You'll be glad to hear that some of the finger-prints have been identified.'

Apparently he was wrong. 'I hear, but I behold trouble

and darkness,' said Glass.

'The same might be said of all murder cases,' replied Hannasyde tartly, and closed the interview.

Six

Hannasyde found his subordinate awaiting him in a cheerful mood. 'Any luck your end, Chief?' he inquired. 'I've had a fullish sort of a day myself.'

'Yes, I got hold of a certain amount,' Hannasyde replied. 'Glass could find no trace of the weapon at Greystones, though, which is disappointing.'

'He was probably too busy holding prayer meetings with himself to have time to look for the weapon,' said the Sergeant. 'How's he doing? I can see he's going to be my cross all right.'

'As far as I can gather, you're likely to be his,' said Hannasyde, with the ghost of a smile. 'He made a somewhat obscure reference to forward hearts and perverse tongues which I took to mean you.'

'He did, did he? Ah well, the only wonder to me is he didn't call me a hissing and an abomination. I daresay he will yet. I don't mind him reciting his pieces, though it isn't strictly in accordance with discipline, as long as he doesn't take it into his silly head I've got to be saved. I've been saved once, and that's enough for me. Too much!' he added, remembering certain features of this event. 'Nasty little tracts about Lost Sheep, and the Evils of

Drink,' he explained. 'It's a funny thing, but whenever you come up against any of these reforming chaps they always have it fixed in their minds you must be a walking lump of vice. You can't persuade 'em otherwise either. What you might call a Fixation.'

Hannasyde, who knew that the Sergeant's study of his favourite subject had led his adventurous feet into a strange realm of bastard words and lurid theories, intervened hastily, and asked for an account of his day's labours.

'Well, it's been interesting, but like what Glass said about me: obscure,' said the Sergeant. 'Taking our friend Abraham Budd first, we come to the first unexpected feature of the case. When I got up to Headquarters this morning, what should I find but his lordship waiting for me on the mat.'

'Budd?' said Hannasyde. 'Do you mean he came here?'

'That's right, Chief. Came along as soon as he'd read the news in the evening paper. They'll start getting the evening editions out before breakfast soon, if you ask me. Anyway, Mr Budd had his copy tucked under his arm, and was just oozing helpfulness.'

'Do get on!' said Hannasyde. 'Does he know something, or what?'

'Not so as you'd notice,' responded the Sergeant. 'According to him, he left the house by way of the garden-gate at about 9.35 p.m.'

'That tallies with Mrs North's account, at all events!' said Hannasyde.

'Oh, so you got something there, did you, Super?'

'Yes, but go on with your report. If Budd left at 9.35

he can't have seen anything, I suppose. What did he come to Scotland Yard for?'

'Funk,' said the Sergeant tersely. 'I've been reading a whole lot about causations, and that naturally made it as plain as a pikestaff to me –'

'Cut out the causations! What's Budd got to be frightened of? And don't hand me anything about Early Frustrations or Inhibitions, because I'm not interested! If you knew what you were talking about I could bear it, but you don't.'

The Sergeant, accustomed to this lack of sympathy, merely sighed, and said with unimpaired good humour: 'Well, I haven't, so far, got to the bottom of Mr Budd's trouble. He calls himself an outside broker, and, by what I can make out, the late Ernest was in the habit of using him as a kind of cover-man every time he wanted to put through any deals which, strictly speaking, he oughtn't to have put through. At least, that's the way it looked to me, putting two and two together, and making allowances for a bit of coyness on friend Budd's part.'

'I'd gathered that he was a broker. There are one or two copies of letters to him amongst Fletcher's papers, and a few of his replies. I haven't had time yet to go through them carefully. What took him down to see Fletcher at nine o'clock at night?'

'That's where the narrative got what you might call abstruse,' replied the Sergeant. 'Nor, if you was to ask me, should I say that I actually believed all that Budd told me. Sweating very freely, he was. But then, it's been a hot day, and he's a fleshy man. However, the gist of it was that owing to the difficulty of hearing very well over the telephone there was some sort of misunderstanding about some highly confidential instructions issued by the late Ernest in – er – a still more highly confidential deal. Our Mr Budd, not wishing to entrust any more of this hush-hush business to the telephone, went off to see the late Ernest in person.'

'It sounds very fishy,' said Hannasyde.

'That's nothing to what it smelt like,' said the Sergeant. 'I had to open the window. But bearing in mind that the man we're after isn't Budd, I didn't press the matter much. What I did see fit to ask him, though, was whether the aforesaid misunderstanding had led to any unpleasantness with the late Ernest.'

Hannasyde nodded. 'Quite right. What did he say?'

'Oh, he behaved as though I was his Father Confessor!' said the Sergeant. That may have been on account of my nice, kind personality, or, on the other hand, it may not. But he opened right out like a poppy in the sun.'

'I can do without these poetical flights,' said Hannasyde.

'Just as you say, Chief. Anyway, he took me right to his bosom. Fairly oozed natural oil, and what I took to be highly unnatural frankness. He didn't keep a thing from me – nothing I'd already got wind of, at any rate. There was a little unpleasantness, due to the late Ernest's having assumed that certain of his instructions had been acted on, which, owing to the telephone and one thing and another, they hadn't been. However, once the late Ernest had got over his naughty temper, all became jake again, and they parted like brothers.'

'Oh!' said Hannasyde. 'Quite plausible. It might be true.'

'Yes, but I'll tell you a funny thing,' said the Sergeant. 'I've been swotting flies all day, but the whole time little Abraham was with me I never saw a fly settle on him, not once.'

'Oh!' said Hannasyde again. 'Like that, is he?'

'Yes,' replied the Sergeant. 'He is. What's more, Super, though you and I may not see eye to eye about Psychology, I know when a man's got the wind up. Little Abraham was having quite a job to keep his feet down on the ground. But I'm bound to say he did it. He answered all my questions before I'd even had time to ask them, too. Gave me a word-picture of his state of mind when he read about the late Ernest's death that was a master-piece. First you could have knocked him down with a feather; then he thought, why, it must have happened not half-an-hour after he had left the late Ernest. After that he hoped he wouldn't get mixed up in it, and from there it was only a matter of seconds before he remembered handing the late Ernest's butler his card; and, on top of that, having Ernest address him in a loud and angry voice. Finally, it struck him like a thunder-clap that the late Ernest had shown him out by the side gate, so that no other person had witnessed his departure. Having assembled all these facts, he perceived that he was in a very compromising situation, and the only thing to be done was to come straight round to the kind police, whom he was brought up to look upon as his best friends.'

Hannasyde was frowning. 'It's almost too plausible. What did you do?'

'Gave him a piece of toffee, and sent him home to his mother,' answered the Sergeant promptly.

Hannasyde, who knew his Sergeant, apparently approved of this somewhat unorthodox conduct, for he said: 'Yes, about the best thing you could do. He'll keep. Now, what about this Charlie Carpenter you spoke of over the telephone?'

The Sergeant abandoned flippancy for the moment. 'A packet!' he said. 'That's where we come on the second unexpected feature of this case. As a matter of fact, I thought we were going to draw a blank on those finger-prints. But this is what we've got.' He picked up a folder from the desk as he spoke, and handed it to his superior. It contained a portrait of a young man, two sets of photographed finger-prints, and a brief, unsentimental record of the latter career of one Charlie Carpenter, aged twenty-nine years, measuring five feet nine inches, weighing eleven stone six pounds, having light-brown hair, grey eyes, and no distinguishing birth-marks.

Hannasyde's brows went up as he read, for the record was one of petty rogueries, culminating in a sentence of eighteen months' imprisonment for false pretences. 'This is certainly unexpected,' he said.

'Doesn't fit at all, does he?' agreed the Sergeant. 'That's what I thought.'

Hannasyde was studying the portrait. 'Flashy-looking fellow. Hair probably artificially waved. All right, Sergeant: I can see you're bursting with news. Let's have it.'

'Newton handled his case,' said the Sergeant. 'He doesn't know much about him, beyond his little lapses. Young waster with no background, and a taste for hitting the high spots. Dances and sings a bit; been on the stage, but not what you'd call noticeably; at one time did the gigolo act at a cheap dance-hall in the East End; seems to have gone pretty big with the ladies: you know the type. Not in the late Ernest's walk of life at all. In fact, I was just thinking I'd hit on the greatest discovery of the age, which was that Bertillon had made a mistake after all, when Newton said something that opened out a whole new vista before me.'

'Well?'

'He said that at the time of his arrest, which took place, as you'll notice, in November of 1934, Charlie was living with an actress – that means front row of the Beauty Chorus – of the name of Angela Angel!'

Hannasyde looked up. 'Angela Angel? Wasn't there a case about a year ago to do with a girl called Angela Angel? Suicide, wasn't it?'

'It was,' said the Sergeant. 'Sixteen months ago, to be precise.' He opened the case in which he had borne Ernest Fletcher's papers away from Greystones, and picked up a photograph that was lying on the top of a pile of documents. 'And that, Super, is Angela Angel!'

Hannasyde took the photograph, and recognised it at once as the one which had struck an elusive chord of memory in the Sergeant's brain earlier in the day.

'As soon as Newton mentioned the name, which he only did because of the girl having been a case herself, poor kid, I remembered,' said the Sergeant. 'Jimmy Gale was in charge of her little affair, which was how I came to hear a bit about it at the time. Did herself in for no particular reason that anyone ever discovered. She wasn't in trouble, she'd got a job in the chorus of the cabaret show at Duke's, and quite a bit of money put by in the bank. All the same, she stuck her head in a gas oven one night. Well, looked at as a case, there was nothing to it. But there were points which interested Gale in a mild sort of a way. For one thing, she didn't leave any letter behind, explaining why she'd done it, which, in Gale's experience, was unusual. Nine times out of ten a suicide'll leave a letter behind which'll make some poor devil feel like a murderer for the rest of his life, whether he deserves to or not. She didn't. What's more, they never found out what her real name was. She even opened her bank account under the name of Angela Angel. She didn't seem to have any relations, or if she had they never came forward to claim her; and she wasn't, by all accounts, one of those who tell their girl-friends the whole story of their lives. None of the rest of the chorus knew much about her when it came to the point. But what they did know was that about seven or eight months before she killed herself she got off with a very nice gentleman, who set her up in style in a smart flat with the usual trimmings.'

'Fletcher?'

'Taking one thing with another, and adding up a few simple figures, that's what it looks like, Chief. Not that I've got his name yet, for I haven't. There are two girls still dancing at Duke's who were there in Angela's time, but they neither of them seem to think they ever heard what her boy-friend's real name was. All they could think of was Boo-Boo, which was what she called him, but which doesn't sound to me the sort of name any self-respecting man would put up with except from a girl he happened to have gone nuts over. So that's not much help.'

'Any description?'

'Yes, he was middle-aged, dark, thin, and natty. The late Ernest to the life. A lot of other people to the life too, if you come to think of it, but it'll do to go on with. Well, as I say, he set Angela up in the best of style, and she chucked dancing for a life of gilded leisure. That was a matter of six months after friend Charlie had gone to gaol. Nothing more was heard of Angela at Duke's for the next six months, which brings us to the end of December 1935, when she turned up again, wanting her old job back.'

'Cast off?'

'That,' said the Sergeant guardedly, 'is the inference, but the fair Lily –'

'Who?'

'One of the chorus. She stated at the time, and today, when I saw her, that Angela was as close as an oyster about the whole business. Sifting the grain from the chaff, which isn't as easy as you might think when Lily starts talking, I came to the conclusion that the late Ernest (or substitute) was by way of being the great passion of Angela's life. Only he'd cooled off. But taking into account the fact that she wasn't in trouble, and had quite a bit of money put by, I'm bound to say it looks to me as though he didn't treat her so badly. However, the fair Lily sticks to it that she'd got a broken heart, and couldn't seem to fancy any of the other fellows who were floating around. After a couple of months she decided she couldn't live without the late Ernest, so she put her head in a gas oven, and that was the end of her.'

'Poor girl! The more I discover about Fletcher the less I like him.'

'Now, be fair, Chief!' begged Hemingway. 'This isn't

one of your seduction rackets. If Angela didn't know what was likely to happen she ought to have. But that's neither here nor there. What I want to know is, where and how does Charlie Carpenter fit into the scenario?'

'Have you been able to discover anything about his movements since he was released from prison? When exactly was that?' He consulted the dossier on the desk. 'June 1936! A year ago, in fact. What's he been up to all this time?'

'You can search me,' said the Sergeant. 'He hasn't got pinched for anything, that's all I can tell you. Funny, isn't it? If he was out to pull a big revenge act, what's he want to wait a year for?'

Hannasyde looked at the photograph again. 'Revenge? Does he give you that impression?'

'No, he doesn't. Silly, weak kind of face, and by all accounts he was a selfish young bounder, not given to putting himself out for anyone *but* himself. No, what it looks like to me, at first glance, is an attempt to put the black on the late Ernest. Not much of an attempt either, which is about what you'd expect, judging from his record.'

'Yes,' Hannasyde agreed. 'And then we come up against the murder.'

'Slap up against it,' nodded the Sergeant. 'And it doesn't fit.'

'Several loose ends somewhere. He fits the description given by Glass and Mrs North, though – but I admit they were too vague to be of much use.'

'Oh, so Mrs North was there, was she?'

'She was there, and unless I am much mistaken she thinks it was her husband who killed Fletcher.'

The Sergeant opened his eyes at that. 'You do see life in the suburbs, don't you? Nice goings-on! Whatever does Ichabod say about it?'

'As I haven't told him anything about it, he hasn't yet favoured me with his opinion.'

'You wait till he gets wind of it. He'll learn a whole new piece to say to us. But this line on Mrs North's husband is very confusing. What's been happening your end, Chief?'

Hannasyde gave him a brief account of his two interviews with Helen North. The Sergeant listened in silence, his bright, penetrating eyes fixed on his superior's face with an expression in them of gradually deepening disgust.

'What did I tell you?' he said, when Hannasyde had finished. 'The whole stage is getting cluttered up with supers. I'll tell you something else, too; by the time we're through we shall have had just about all we can stand of this North woman. I wouldn't mind betting she thinks we've got nothing better to do than run round in circles while she gets on with this three-act problem play of hers. I'm surprised at you, Chief, letting yourself get dragged into her differences with her husband. What's more, where's the sense of her hiding all this IOU business from him? He's bound to find out in the end.'

'I daresay, but I can't see that it's any part of my job to tell him.'

The Sergeant sniffed. 'What's the husband like? Give any reason for coming home a week before he was expected?'

'None. He's a good-looking chap. Got a bit of a chin, and thinks more than he says. Determined fellow, I should imagine; not easily rattled, and by no means a fool.'

'I hope we bring it home to him,' said the Sergeant uncharitably. 'From the sound of it, he's going to be as big a nuisance as his wife. No alibi?'

'So he said. In fact, he made me a present of that piece of information.'

The Sergeant cocked an eye at him. 'He did, did he? Did it strike you he might be fancying himself in the part of a red herring?'

'It's a possibility, of course. He may suspect his wife of having killed Fletcher. It depends how much he knows about her dealings with the man.'

The Sergeant groaned. 'I get it. A nice game of battledore and shuttlecock, with you and me cast for the shuttlecocks. Of course, our heads won't really start aching till Mrs North gets on to it that the man she saw may have been Charlie Carpenter. We'll have her eating all that evidence of hers about the late Ernest showing him off the premises then. Probably boloney, anyway.'

'It may be, but she spoke the truth about her finger-prints being on the door. I verified that before I left Marley. The real discrepancy is in the time. At 9.35 p.m. Budd left Greystones by the garden-gate. I think we can take that as being true. Mrs North was walking up Maple Grove at that time, and states that she saw a fat man come out of Greystones.'

The Sergeant jotted it down on a piece of paper. 'That checks up with his own story: 9.35 p.m. Budd leaves; the North dame arrives.'

'Next we have Mrs North leaving the study at 9.45.'

'Short visit,' commented the Sergeant.

'She and Fletcher had a row. She admitted to that the second time I saw her. Also at 9.45 we have the unknown man entering the garden by the side gate.'

'X,' said the Sergeant. 'That's when Mrs North hid behind the bush?'

'Yes. X entered the study, we suppose, a minute later. That isn't important. Now, according to her first story, Mrs North then left by way of the garden-gate. According to her second version, she remained where she was, until about 9.58, when X, accompanied by Fletcher, came out of the study, and walked down the path to the gate. She then slipped back into the study to search for her IOUs, heard Fletcher returning, and escaped through the door into the hall. She was in the hall as the clock began to strike 10.00. At 10.02, Glass, on his beat, saw a man corresponding to Mrs North's description of X coming out of the garden-gate, and making off towards the Arden Road. He entered the garden and reached the study at 10.05 p.m., to find Fletcher dead, and no sign of his murderer to be seen. What do you make of it?'

'I don't,' said the Sergeant flatly. 'It's looked like a mess to me from the start. What I do say is that all this stuff of Mrs North's isn't to be trusted. In fact, there's only one thing we've got to hold on to, which is that at 10.05 p.m. Glass found the late Ernest with his head bashed in. That at least is certain, and what's more it makes Mrs North's evidence look a bit cock-eyed. Glass saw X leaving the premises at 10.02, which means that if he was the murderer he must have done Ernest in between 10.00 and 10.01, allowing him a minute to get out of the study and down the path to the gate.'

'All right: that's probably a fair estimate.'

'Well, it doesn't fit – not if you're accepting Mrs North's evidence. According to her, it was just on 10.00 when she heard Ernest coming back to the study. You think of it, Chief: Ernest has got to have time to get into his chair behind the desk again, and start to write the letter that was found under his head. It was obvious he was taken by surprise, which means that X didn't come stampeding up the path directly behind him. He waited till Ernest was in the house: it stands to reason he must have. Once Ernest has settled down he gets to work – enters, strikes Ernest with some kind of a blunt instrument, not once, mark you! but two or three times – and then makes off. Well, if you can cram all that into two minutes you're cleverer than I am, Super, that's all. Take it this way: if Ernest saw him off the premises, he pretended to walk away, didn't he?'

'You'd think so.'

'I'm dead sure of it. While Ernest is strolling back to the house, he comes back cautiously to the gate. If he'd made up his mind, as he must have, to kill Ernest, he didn't open that gate till Ernest had reached the house again, which was at 10.00 p.m. He wouldn't have run the risk of Ernest hearing him. No point in it. Does he stride up the path bold as brass, thus advertising his presence? Of course he doesn't! He creeps up, and if it takes a minute to reach the study from that gate, walking ordinarily, as we know it does, it's my belief it took X a sight longer to do it in the dark, treading warily. By the time he's in the study again it must be a couple of minutes after 10.00, at which time, mark you, Glass saw him coming out of the garden-gate.'

'I'm afraid you've got a fixation, Skipper,' said Hannasyde gently. 'We don't know that X was the murderer.'

The Sergeant swallowed this, replying with dignity: 'I was coming to that. It could have been Budd, come back secretly, and lying in wait in the garden till the coast was clear; or it could have been Mr North. But if X, whom Glass saw, was Charlie Carpenter, what was he doing while Ernest was being knocked on the head?'

'There's another possibility,' said Hannasyde. 'Suppose that North was the murderer –'

'Just a moment, Super! Is North X?' demanded Hemingway.

'Nobody is X. Assuming that North was the man Mrs North saw coming up the path, we have to consider the possibility of Fletcher's having been killed at any time between 9.45 and 10.01.'

The Sergeant blinked. 'Mrs North's revised version being so much eye-wash? Where does Carpenter come in?'

'After the murder,' replied Hannasyde.

There was a short pause. 'We've got to find Carpenter,' announced the Sergeant.

'Of course. Have you got anyone on to that?'

'I've got practically the whole Department hunting for him. But if he's kept out of trouble for the past year, it may be a bit of a job to locate him.'

'The other point that puzzles me is the weapon used. The doctors seem to be agreed that the blows were struck with a blunt instrument like a weighted stick. The skull was smashed right in, you know. Now, both Glass and Mrs North say that the man they saw was carrying nothing. You may rule Mrs North's evidence out of court if you like, but you can't rule out what Glass says. The natural thing would be for the murderer to get rid of the weapon at once, but I've had the garden searched with a toothcomb, and nothing has come to light.'

'Anything in the room? Bronze ornament, or paper-weight, which could have been stuffed into the murderer's pocket?'

'The butler states that nothing is missing from the room, and although there is a heavy paper-weight there, I understand that it was produced later by your playful little friend, Neville Fletcher – about whom I'm going to make a few inquiries, by the way.'

The Sergeant sat up. 'He produced it, did he? From what I've seen of him, Chief, that's just about what he would do – if he happened to have murdered his uncle with it! It would strike him as being a really high-class bit of humour.'

'Fairly cold-blooded.'

'Don't you fret, he's cold-blooded enough! Clever enough, too. But if he did it, Mrs North must have seen him on her way out of – Oh, now we're assuming Mrs North's first story was the true one, are we?'

'If we're considering Neville Fletcher as the possible murderer, it looks as though we should have to. But that brings us up against two difficult fences. The first is that her finger-prints *were* on the panel of the door, and I don't quite see how they came there if she didn't leave the room by that way. The second is that if her original story was true we know that a man entered the study at about 9.45, and left the premises again at 10.02 – for it seems a trifle far-fetched to suppose that more than one man visited Fletcher during those seventeen minutes. That being so, when did Neville find time to murder his uncle? In between Glass's seeing X depart and himself entering the study? Stretching the bounds of probability rather far, isn't it?'

'It is,' admitted the Sergeant, caressing his chin. 'But now you come to point it out to me I don't mind owning that the absence of the weapon wants a bit of explanation. I suppose the murderer could have shoved a heavy stick down his trouser leg, but it would have made him walk with a stiff leg, which Glass would have been bound to have noticed. I'm trying to think of something he could have had in his pocket – a spanner, for instance.'

'That's assuming the murder was premeditated. One doesn't carry heavy spanners in one's pockets. Somehow it doesn't look premeditated to me. I can't bring myself to believe in a murderer who plans to kill his victim by battering his skull in, midway through the evening, in his own study.'

'No, that's true,' said the Sergeant. 'And we went over the fire-irons. It looks as though the weapon, whatever it may have been, was got rid of pretty cleverly. It might be a good thing if I had a look round the place myself. A little quiet chat with that butler wouldn't do any harm. Surprising what you can pick up from servants – if you know the way to go about it.'

'By all means go down there,' said Hannasyde. 'I want the place kept under observation. Meanwhile, I've some inquiries to make about the state of Neville Fletcher's bank balance, Mr North's movements on the night of the murder, and the expansive Mr Budd's mysterious business with Fletcher.'

'You'll have a busy morning,' prophesied the Sergeant. 'Growing, isn't it? We started off with one man, and we've now got one lady, one jealous husband, one outside broker, one dead cabaret-girl, one criminal and one suspicious-looking nephew implicated in it. And we've only been at work on it since 9.00 this morning. If it goes on at this rate, we shan't be able to move for suspects in a couple of days' time. You know, I often wonder what made me join the Force.' He began to put his papers together. 'If it weren't for the fact that murder doesn't seem to fit in with what we know of Charlie Carpenter, my money would be on him. Do you suppose he's been hunting the late Ernest down ever since he came out of gaol?'

'I don't know, but considering that not even your fair Lily knew who Angela's protector was, it seems quite possible.'

'Or,' said the Sergeant musingly, 'he found out by accident, and thought he saw his way to putting the black on the late Ernest. Come to think of it, that theory goes nicely with Mrs North's revised version – the bit about Ernest saying the man X had made a mistake. Well, one thing's certain: we've got to get hold of Carpenter.'

'The Department can look after that. I'd like you to get down to Marley first thing tomorrow, and see what you can pick up.' Hannasyde rose, adding with a twinkle: 'By the way, if you should run across a forceful young woman with a monocle, God help you! She's Mrs North's sister, and interested in crime. Writes detective stories.'

'What?' said the Sergeant. 'You mean to tell me I'm going to have an authoress tagging round after me?'

'I should think it's quite probable,' replied Hannasyde gravely.

'Well, isn't that nice?' said the Sergeant with awful sarcasm. 'You'd have thought Ichabod was a big enough cross for anyone to bear, wouldn't you? It just shows you: when Fate's got it in for you there's no limit to what you may have to put up with.'

Hannasyde laughed. 'Go home and study Havelock Ellis, or Freud, or whoever it is you do study. Perhaps that'll help you to cope with the situation.'

'Study! I won't have time,' said the Sergeant, reaching for his hat. 'I'm going to be busy this evening.'

'You'd better relax. You've had a pretty strenuous day. What *are* you going to do?'

'Mug up the Bible,' said the Sergeant bitterly.

Seven

It was late when Hannasyde left his room at Scotland
Yard, and when at last he went home he had learnt
enough from his perusal of Ernest Fletcher's papers
to make him visit the offices of Mr Abraham Budd
shortly after nine o'clock the following morning.

Mr Budd did not keep him waiting. The typist
who had carried his card in to her employer returned
almost immediately, pop-eyed with curiosity, ready to
dramatise, as soon as a suitable audience should present
itself, this thrilling and sinister call, and invited him, in a
fluttering voice, to follow her.

Mr Budd, who rose from a swivel-chair behind his
desk as Hannasyde was ushered in, and came eagerly
forward to greet him, corresponded so exactly with
Sergeant Hemingway's description of him, that
Hannasyde had to bite back a smile. He was a short, fat
man, with a certain oiliness of skin, and an air of open
affability that was almost oppressive. He shook
Hannasyde by the hand, pressed him into a chair,
offered him a cigar, and said several times that he was
very glad to see him.

'Very glad, I am, Superintendent,' he said. 'What a

shocking tragedy! What a terrible affair! I have been most upset. As I told the Sergeant at Scotland Yard, it struck me all of a heap. All of a heap,' he repeated impressively. 'For I respected Mr Fletcher. Yes, sir, I respected him. He had a Brain. He had a Grasp of Finance. Over and over again I've said it: Mr Fletcher had a Flair. That's the word. And now he's gone.'

'Yes,' said Hannasyde unemotionally. 'As you say. You did a good deal of business with him, I understand?'

Mr Budd managed to convey by a glance out of his astute little eyes and a gesture of the hands which betrayed his race, an answer in which assent was mingled with deprecation.

'What kind of business?' said Hannasyde.

Mr Budd leaned forward, resting his arms upon his desk, and replied in a confidential tone: 'Strictly private, Mr Hannasyde!' He looked slyly at Hannasyde. 'You take my meaning? There isn't a soul in this world I'd discuss a client's affairs with, least of all Mr Fletcher's, but when a thing like this happens, I see it's different. I'm discreet. I have to be discreet. If I weren't, where do you think I'd be? *You* don't know; *I* don't know, but it wouldn't be where I am today. But I'm on the side of law and order. I realise it's my duty to assist the police where and how I can. My duty as a citizen. That's why I'm going to make an exception to my rule of silence. Now, you're a broad-minded man, Mr Hannasyde. You're a man of experience. You know that everything that goes on in the City doesn't get published in the *Financial News*.' He shook with amusement, and added: 'Not by a long chalk!'

'I am aware, certainly, that a not-over-scrupulous man

in Mr Fletcher's position – he was upon several boards, I think? – might find it convenient to employ an agent to buy on his behalf stocks which he would not like it to be known that he had bought,' replied Hannasyde.

Mr Budd's eyes twinkled at him. 'You know everything, don't you, Mr Hannasyde? But that's it. That's it in a nutshell. *You* may not approve of it, *I* may not approve of it, but what has it to do with us, after all?'

'It has this much to do with you, that Mr Fletcher was in the habit of employing you in that manner.'

Budd nodded. 'Quite right. I don't deny it. Where would be the sense in that? My business is to obey my clients' instructions, and that's what I do, Mr Hannasyde, asking no questions.'

'Not always, I think,' said Hannasyde.

Budd looked hurt. 'Why, what do you mean? Now, that's a thing that has never been said to me yet. I don't like it, Mr Hannasyde. No, I don't like it.'

'Surely you told Sergeant Hemingway yesterday that you had failed to obey certain of Mr Fletcher's instructions?'

The smile, which had vanished from Budd's face, reappeared. He leaned back in his chair, his mind apparently relieved, and said: 'Oh now, now, now! That's an exaggeration. Oh yes, that's just a little exaggeration, I assure you! What I told the Sergeant was that there had been a misunderstanding between Mr Fletcher and me.'

'What was the misunderstanding?' asked Hannasyde.

Mr Budd looked reproachful. 'Now, Superintendent, have a heart! You don't expect a man in my position to disclose the nature of strictly confidential transactions. It wouldn't be right. It wouldn't be honourable.'

'You are mistaken: I do expect just that. We shall probably save time if I tell you at once that Mr Fletcher's private papers are at this moment in the possession of the police. Moreover, what you refuse to tell me your ledgers will no doubt show.'

The look of reproach deepened. More in sorrow than in anger, Budd said gently: 'Come, Superintendent, you know you can't act in that high-handed fashion. *You're* not a fool, *I'm* not a fool. Where's the sense in trying to get tough with me? Now, I ask you!'

'You will find that I have it in my power to get remarkably tough with you,' replied Hannasyde brutally. 'On your own showing, you visited Mr Fletcher on the night of his murder; you admit that a quarrel took place –'

'Not a quarrel, Superintendent! Not a quarrel!'

'– between you; you can bring no evidence to prove that you left the house at the time you stated. Added to these facts, there is enough documentary evidence amongst Mr Fletcher's papers to justify my applying for a warrant to search these premises.'

Budd flung up a hand. 'Don't let's have any unpleasantness! You're not treating me as you should, Superintendent. You've got nothing against me. Didn't I go round to Scotland Yard the moment I read the shocking news? Didn't I tell your Sergeant the whole truth? This isn't what I expected. No, it certainly is not what I expected. I've never been on the wrong side of the Law, never in my life. But what reward do I get for that?'

Hannasyde listened to this plaint with an unmoved countenance. Without troubling to reply to it, he said, consulting a paper he had in his hand: 'On 10 June Mr Fletcher wrote to you, instructing you to buy ten thousand shares in Huxton Industries.'

'That's correct,' said Budd, eyeing him with a little perturbation. 'I don't deny it. Why should I?'

'It was what is known, I believe, as a dead market, was it not?'

Budd nodded.

'Did you buy those shares, Mr Budd?'

The directness of the question startled Budd. He stared at Hannasyde for a moment, then said feebly: 'That's a funny question to ask. I had my instructions, hadn't I? Perhaps I didn't approve of them; perhaps it didn't seem to me wise to invest in Huxton Industries; but was it my business to advise Mr Fletcher?'

'Did you buy those shares?'

Budd did not answer immediately, but kept his troubled gaze on Hannasyde's face. It was plain that he was at a loss, perhaps uncertain of what Fletcher's papers might have revealed. He said uneasily: 'Suppose I didn't? You know that a block like that isn't bought in the twinkling of an eye. It would look funny, wouldn't it? I know my business better than that.'

'At the time when you received Mr Fletcher's instructions to buy, Huxton Industries were not quoted?'

'Moribund company,' said Budd tersely.

'The stock was, in your opinion, worthless?'

Budd shrugged.

'You were no doubt surprised at receiving instructions to buy such a large block of shares?'

'Maybe I was. It wasn't my business to be surprised. Mr Fletcher may have had a tip.'

'But your own opinion was that Mr Fletcher had made a mistake?'

'If it was, that's neither here nor there. If Mr Fletcher wanted the shares it wasn't anything to do with me. I bought them. Why, if you know so much you'll know that there's been considerable activity in Huxton Industries. That's me.'

'Buying?'

'What else would I be doing, I should like to know?' said Budd, almost indulgently. 'Now, I'm going to be frank with you, Mr Hannasyde. There's no reason why I should be, not a ha'p'orth of reason, but I've nothing to hide, and I'm anxious to help the police in every way I can. Not that my dealings with Mr Fletcher can help you, but I'm a reasonable man, and I realise that you want to know about this little deal. The fact is, the misunderstanding that took place between Mr Fletcher and me occurred over these instructions. Now, it struck you as remarkable – I think we can say it was remarkable – that Mr Fletcher should have wanted to buy ten thousand shares in a company which was dying. It struck me that way too. It would anyone, wouldn't it? I put it to you! Well, what do I do? I ask myself if there's been a mistake in the typing. Very easy to add an extra nought, isn't it? So I ring up my client, to verify. I ask him, am I to buy a thousand shares? He says yes. He's impatient: wants to know why I need to question my instructions. I don't get a chance to tell him. While I'm explaining, he rings off. Now where's the sense in trying to pull the wool over your eyes? There's none. I know that. I slipped up. Yes, Mr Hannasyde, I slipped up. The first time in twenty years I've got to accuse myself of carelessness. I don't like admitting it. You wouldn't yourself. I ought to have got written confirmation from my client that a thousand shares was what he wanted. That's what I neglected to do. I bought a thousand shares on his behalf, in small packets. The shares rise as a result. Then I get a telephone call from my client. He's seen the record of the transactions on the ticker: he knows that's me. He rings up to know whether I've fulfilled instructions. I tell him yes. He's in a high good humour. Him and me have done business for years; I've obeyed orders, so he lets me in on the secret. That was his way: there wasn't anything mean about him. Not a thing! He tells me IPS Consolidated are taking over Huxton Industries, and if I want to buy, to buy quick, but discreetly. Get the idea? He tells me they'll go to fifteen shillings. That's the truest thing you know. Maybe they'll go higher. Then what happens? He says in his joking way, now did I think he was mad to buy ten thousand shares? Plain as I'm speaking now he said it. Ten thousand. You get it? Ten thousand, and I've got one thousand, and the shares have risen from half-a-crown to seven-and-six. They aren't going to sink again, either. No sir, Huxton Industries is on the up and up. So where am I? What am I going to do? There's only one thing to *be* done. I do it. I go down to see Mr Fletcher. He knows me; he trusts me; he'll believe what I say. Because it's the truth. Was he pleased? No, Mr Hannasyde. Would you be? But he was a gentleman. A perfect gentleman, he was. He sees it was the result of a misunderstanding. He's sore, but he's fair. We part on good terms. Forgive and forget. That's the truth in a nutshell.'

Hannasyde, on whom this frank recital did not seem to have made quite the desired impression, said dampingly:

'Not quite, surely? How was it that Mr Fletcher, who, you say, watched the records as they appeared on the ticker, failed to notice that the shares weren't rising as much as they must have done had you bought ten thousand?'

There was an uncomfortable silence. Mr Budd pulled himself together, and said glibly: 'Why, you don't suppose Mr Fletcher had nothing better to do than to watch the ticker, do you, Superintendent? No, no, the little deal I was putting through for him was nothing more than a side-line for him.'

'I should like to see your books,' said Hannasyde.

For the first time a sharp note came into Budd's rather unctuous voice: 'I don't show my books to anyone!'

Hannasyde looked at him under frowning brows. 'Is that so?' he said.

Mr Budd lost some of his colour. A rather sickly smile was brought into action. 'Now, don't get me wrong! Be fair, Mr Hannasyde! That's all I ask of you. Be fair! If it was to get about I'd shown my books to a soul outside this office I should lose half my clients.'

'It won't,' said Hannasyde.

'Ah, if I could be sure of *that*!'

'You can be.'

'Well, look here, Mr Hannasyde, I'm a reasonable man, and if you show me a warrant, I've nothing to say. But if you haven't got one, I'm not showing my books to you. Why should I? There's no reason. But the instant you walk in here with a warrant you won't find me making trouble.'

'If you're wise you won't make trouble under any circumstances,' said Hannasyde. 'I'll see your books now.'

'You can't do it,' said Budd, doggedly staring into his eyes. 'You can't come that high-handed stuff in my office. I won't put up with it.'

'Do you realise,' said Hannasyde sternly, 'the position you are in? I am giving you a chance to clear yourself of suspicion of –'

'I had nothing to do with the murder! Why, you know that, Mr Hannasyde! Didn't I come right away to Scot –'

'The fact of your having come to Scotland Yard has no bearing on the case whatsoever. You have just told me a story a child wouldn't believe, and, for reasons best known to yourself, you refuse to substantiate it by the evidence of your books. You leave me no alternative –'

'No, no!' Budd said quickly. 'Don't let's get hasty! No use getting hasty! I didn't see it like that, that's all. You'll be wasting your time if you arrest me. You don't want to do that, now do you? I'm not a violent man. You couldn't think I'd break anyone's head open! Why, I couldn't do it! Just couldn't do it! As for what I told you, well, perhaps it wasn't exactly the truth, but I swear to you –'

'Never mind about swearing to me. What was the truth?'

Mr Budd licked his lips, shifting restlessly in his chair. 'It was a miscalculation on my part. It might have happened to anyone. I never dreamed of IPS taking over Huxton Industries. It looked to me like a little flutter. A man's got to do the best he can for himself, hasn't he? You would yourself. There's nothing criminal in it.'

'Get on!' said Hannasyde. 'You thought the shares would sink back again, didn't you?'

'That's the way it was!' answered Budd eagerly. 'If Mr

Fletcher had let me into the secret earlier, it needn't have happened. Wouldn't have happened.'

'Instead of buying the ten thousand shares you were told to buy, you played a little game of your own, didn't you?'

'A man's got to take a chance sometimes,' Budd pleaded. 'You know how it is! I didn't mean to do anything wrong.'

Hannasyde ignored this extremely unconvincing statement. 'Buying and then selling, and again buying and selling, with the profits finding their way into your pocket. That's what you did? The ticker recorded the transactions, but Fletcher was not to know what you were up to. Then he let you in on the secret – I believe that part of your story – and you found yourself with one thousand shares only of the ten thousand you were instructed to buy, and the market steadily rising. Is that the true story?'

'You – you ought to have been in business yourself, Mr Hannasyde,' said Budd unhappily. 'It's wonderful the way you spotted it!'

'And on the night he was murdered you had gone down to spin some kind of a yarn to Mr Fletcher to account for your being unable to deliver the correct number of shares?'

Budd nodded. 'That's the way it was. A bit of bad luck, Mr Hannasyde. I don't deny I acted foolishly, but –'

'I take it Mr Fletcher was very angry?'

'He was angry. I didn't blame him. I saw his point. But he couldn't do anything, not without coming out into the open. He wouldn't do that. See? He couldn't afford to have it known he had been buying Huxton Industries under cover. You haven't got anything on me, Mr Hannasyde. You'll only regret it if you do anything impulsive. Take my word for it!'

He looked anxiously at Hannasyde as he spoke, beads of sweat standing on his brow. When he found that he was not, apparently, to be arrested, he heaved a gusty sigh of relief, and wiped his face with a large silk handkerchief.

Hannasyde went away to promote inquiries into the state of Neville Fletcher's finances.

Meanwhile, Sergeant Hemingway, arriving betimes in Marley, found PC Glass awaiting him with his customary air of gloomy disapproval. The Sergeant was in a cheerful frame of mind, and took instant exception to his subordinate's joyless mood. 'What's the matter with you?' he demanded. 'Colic, or something?'

'Nothing is the matter with me, Sergeant,' replied Glass. 'I enjoy perfect health.'

'Well, if that's the way you look when you're enjoying yourself I hope I never see you when you're feeling a bit blue,' said the Sergeant. 'Do you ever smile? I won't say laugh, mind you! Just smile!'

'Sorrow is better than laughter,' said Glass stiffly. 'For by the sadness of the countenance the heart is made better.'

'If it's my heart you're talking about, you're wrong!' responded the Sergeant instantly.

'I see no reason for mirth,' Glass said. 'I am troubled; I am bowed down greatly; I go mourning all day long.'

'Look here, let's get this straight!' begged the Sergeant. 'Have you really got anything to mourn about, or is this just your idea of having a good time?'

'I see sin upon sin discovered by reason of one man's death. I see how abominable and filthy is man, which drinketh iniquity like water.'

'You know, when I came down here this morning,' said the Sergeant, restraining himself with a strong effort, 'I was feeling all right. Nice sunny day, birds singing, the case beginning to get interesting. But if I have to listen to much more of that kind of talk I shall have the horrors, which isn't going to help either of us. You forget about iniquity and think about this case you're supposed to be working on.'

'It is that which is in my mind,' said Glass. 'An evil man is slain, but by his death hidden sins are laid bare. There is not one implicated in the case who can say: "I am blameless; there is no spot on me."'

'Today's great thought!' said the Sergeant. 'Of course no one can say there's no spot on them! What did you expect! You know, your trouble is you take things too hard. What have other people's spots got to do with you, anyway? I may not know as much as you do about the Bible, but what about the mote in your neighbour's eye, eh?'

'It is true,' said Glass. 'You do right to reprove me. I am full of sin.'

'Well, don't take on about it,' recommended the Sergeant. 'Let's get down to business. Nothing fresh come to light, I suppose?'

'I know of nothing.'

'You'd better come along up to Greystones with me. I'm going to have a look for that blunt weapon myself.'

'It's not there.'

'That's what you think. What's all this I was hearing

from the Superintendent about young Neville producing a hopeful-looking paper-weight?'

Glass's brow darkened. 'They that are of froward heart are an abomination to the Lord,' he said coldly. 'Neville Fletcher walks in vanity. He is of no account.'

'What do you know about him?' inquired the Sergeant. 'Anything, or nothing?'

'I think him an irreligious man, who despises the Word. But I know no other ill of him.'

'What about the Norths?'

'He is said to be an upright man, and such I believe him to be. She speaks with a lying tongue, but she did not strike the blow that killed Ernest Fletcher.'

'No, not unless she did it with a sledge-hammer,' agreed the Sergeant. 'It's my belief that when we find him Charlie Carpenter is going to tell us who killed Fletcher. You heard about him, didn't you?'

'I heard, but I did not understand. What is known of this Carpenter?'

'He's a small-time criminal. Done time and came out of gaol about a year ago. We found his finger-prints on the late Ernest's desk.'

Glass frowned. 'How is such an one concerned in the case? Truly, the way is dark.'

'Not as dark as you think,' replied the Sergeant. 'Carpenter was mixed up with one of the late Ernest's little bits of fluff. That crack of yours about the girl in the photograph having an end as bitter as wormwood was one of your luckier shots. That was Angela Angel, the same that committed suicide sixteen months ago. It looks as though she didn't want to go on living when the late Ernest shook her off – supposing he was the boy-friend, which it's pretty certain he was. Silly little fool, of course, but you can't help feeling sorry for the kid.'

'The soul that sinneth, it shall die,' Glass said harshly. 'Is it thought that Carpenter slew Ernest Fletcher?'

'That's what we can't make out. We shan't till we lay our hands on him. It looks a cinch, on the face of it, but somehow it doesn't fit with what we know of him. My own idea is that Charlie thought he saw his way to putting the black on the late Ernest, over Angela's death.'

'It is possible. But he would not then kill Fletcher.'

'You wouldn't think so, but when you've seen as much crime as I have, my lad, you'll know that the more improbable a thing seems to be the more likely it is it'll turn out to be a fact. But I won't deny you've made a point. What the Chief thinks is that Carpenter may have seen the real murderer.'

Glass turned his arctic gaze upon the Sergeant. 'How should that be? Why should he remain silent if it were so?'

'That's easy. He's not the sort to go running to the police. He'd have to explain why he was at Greystones, for one thing.'

'True. Is his habitation known to you?'

'If you'd talk plain English, we'd get on better,' remarked the Sergeant. 'No, it isn't known to me, but I'm hoping it soon will be. Meanwhile, we've got to see what we can find out about friend North.' He saw the question in Glass's eyes, and added: 'Oh, you don't know about that little problem play, do you? According to the Chief, Mrs North thinks North was the man she saw in the garden. So what must she do but alter her evidence to suit this new development? Lying lips about hits her off.'

'Why should she think it?'

'Because it turns out that he was sculling around without an alibi at the time. The Chief's working on him now. Then there's Budd. He's been up to no good, or I'm a Dutchman.'

They had by this time reached Greystones. As they turned in at the front gate, Glass suddenly said: 'The day cometh that shall burn them as an oven; and all the proud, yea, and all that do wickedly shall be stubble!'

'You may be right, but it won't be in your time, my lad, so don't you think it!' replied the Sergeant tartly. 'Now you can go and make yourself useful. The butler's a friend of yours, isn't he?'

'I know him. I do not call him a friend, for I have few friends.'

'You surprise me!' said the Sergeant. 'Still, if you're acquainted with him, that ought to be good enough. You go and have a chat with him – just a nice, casual chat.'

'An idle soul shall suffer hunger,' said Glass austerely.

'Not when it's idling with a butler. Or thirst either, if it comes to that,' retorted the Sergeant.

'Thy tongue deviseth mischiefs, like a sharp razor working deceitfully,' Glass told him. 'Simmons is an honest man, in the way of Light.'

'Yes, that's why I'm handing him over to you,' said the Sergeant. 'And I don't want any more backchat! You'll get that butler talking, and see what you can pick up.'

Half-an-hour later the Sergeant, standing before the wall at the end of the garden, and gazing thoughtfully at one of the espaliers growing against it, was interrupted in his cogitations by the arrival on the scene of Neville Fletcher and Miss Drew.

'Oh, here's the Sergeant!' said Neville. 'He's a nice man, Sally: you'll like him.'

The Sergeant turned, foreboding in his breast. The monocle in Miss Drew's eye confirmed his fears. He regarded her with misgiving, but, being a polite man, bade her good-morning.

'You're looking for the weapon,' said Miss Drew. 'I've given a good deal of thought to that myself.'

'So have I. I was even constructive,' said Neville. 'But Malachi told me to stand in awe, and sin not.'

The Sergeant's lips twitched, but he said dryly: 'Well, from all I hear, sir, that was about what you were asking for.'

'Yes, but he also advised me to commune with my own heart upon my bed, and be still, which I maintain was unreasonable at three in the afternoon.'

'I rather think of making a study of Malachi,' announced Miss Drew. 'He's probably a very interesting case – psychologically speaking. He ought to be psycho-analysed, I think.'

'You're right, miss; he ought,' agreed the Sergeant, regarding her with a kindlier light in his eye. 'Ten to one, it would come out that he had something happen to him when he was an infant that would account for the kink he's got now.'

'Dropped on his head?' inquired Neville.

'Oh no, it was probably some seemingly trivial episode which affected his subconscious,' said Sally.

'My precious!' said Neville, with spurious fondness. 'He hasn't got one.'

The Sergeant could not allow this assertion to pass. 'That's where you're wrong, sir. Everyone's got a subconscious.'

Neville's interest was at once aroused: 'Let us sit down, and talk this over. I can see you're going to support Miss Drew, but though I know little, if anything, about the subject I have a very agile brain, and I'm practically certain to refute all your statements. We will have a lovely argument, shall we?'

'Very nice, I'm sure, sir,' said the Sergeant, 'but I'm not here to argue with you. It would be a waste of my time.'

'It wouldn't be half such a waste of time as staring at that broken branch,' said Neville. 'Argument with me is very stimulating to the brain, and as a matter of fact that branch, which looks like a clue, is a snare for the unwary.'

The Sergeant looked at him rather narrowly. 'Is it, sir? Perhaps you can tell me how it comes to be broken?'

'I can, of course, but it isn't awfully interesting. Are you sure you wouldn't rather –'

'It might be very interesting to me,' interposed the Sergeant.

'You're wrong,' Neville said. 'It looks to you as though someone climbed over the wall, using the espalier as a foothold, doesn't it?'

'Yes,' replied the Sergeant. 'It looks remarkably like that to me.'

'You're jolly clever,' said Neville, 'because that's exactly what did happen.'

'It did, did it?' The Sergeant eyed him with acute suspicion. 'Are you trying to get funny with me, sir?'

'No, I wouldn't dare. You mightn't think it, but I'm

frightened of you. Don't be misled by my carefree manner: it's a mask assumed to hide my inward perturbation.'

'That I might believe,' said the Sergeant grimly. 'But I'd like to hear a little more about this branch. Who climbed over the wall?'

'Oh, I did!' replied Neville, with his seraphic smile.

'When?'

'The night my uncle was murdered.' He observed the Sergeant's expression, and said: 'I can see you think there's a catch coming, and, of course, if your mind is running on the murder, there is. I climbed over the wall when everyone, including the policeman parked in the hall, thought I'd gone to bed. Oh, and I climbed out of my bedroom window as well. I'll show you.'

'Why?' demanded the Sergeant.

Neville blinked at him. 'Policeman in the hall. I didn't want him to know I was going out. It would have put unsuitable ideas into his head – same sort of ideas that you're toying with now, which all goes to show that policemen have very dirty minds. Because I'm innocent. In fact, I had to go and confer with an accomplice.'

'You . . . Now, look here, sir!'

Sally interrupted to say: 'I hand it to you; you're as clever as stink, Neville.'

'Don't be coarse, precious: the Sergeant isn't mealy-mouthed, but he doesn't like to hear young women being vulgar.'

'What I'd like to hear,' said the Sergeant, 'is the truth of this story you're trying to gammon me with!'

'Of course you would,' said Neville sympathetically. 'And just because I like you, I'll tell you. I went round by stealth to tell Mrs North that my uncle had been murdered.'

The Sergeant's jaw dropped. 'You went round to tell – And why, may I ask?'

'Well, obviously it was important to her to know, on account of her sordid financial transactions with Uncle Ernie,' explained Neville.

'So you knew about that, did you, sir?'

'Yes, didn't I make that clear? I was her accomplice.'

'And a damned bad one!' struck in Sally.

'She shouldn't have bullied me into it. I don't wonder you look surprised, Sergeant. You're perfectly right, it wasn't in my line at all. However, I did try to make my uncle disgorge the IOUs. That's what Simmons meant when he told you that he heard my uncle telling me to go to hell, before dinner.' He paused, watching the Sergeant through his long lashes. 'You know, you're awfully quick,' he told him. 'I can see that you've hardly finished thinking that that gives me a motive for having committed the murder, before your mind has grasped the flaw in that theory. Not, mind you, that I could have got hold of those IOUs, even if I had murdered my uncle. I haven't actually tried, but I'm pretty sure I couldn't open a safe. Miss Drew could – at least, she says she could, but I noticed that when it came to the point she went to pieces a bit. That's the worst of women: they can never carry anything in their heads. If she had had her criminal notes with her she would have made some very violent stuff which she calls soup, and blown the safe up. You mustn't think I encouraged her, because though I may look effeminate I'm not really, and the sort of primeval crudity which characterises the female mind nauseates me.'

The Sergeant, who had listened to this remarkable speech with an air of alert interest, said: 'And why, sir, did you think it was so important that Mrs North should know that your uncle was dead?'

'Well, naturally it was important,' said Neville patiently. 'You people were bound to discover the IOUs, and if you don't think that their presence in my uncle's safe was extremely incriminating, why on earth did your Superintendent go and grill the poor girl?'

The Sergeant stared at him, unable immediately to think of a suitable rejoinder. He was relieved of the necessity of answering.

'Why boasteth thou thyself in mischief, O mighty man?' demanded the condemnatory voice of PC Glass.

Eight

The Sergeant, who had not heard his subordinate's approach across the lawn, jumped, but Neville proved himself to be Glass's equal by retorting without an instant's hesitation: 'Am I a sea or a whale that thou settest a watch over me?'

This question, delivered as it was in a tone of pained surprise, took Glass aback, and had also the effect of warming the Sergeant's heart towards Neville.

Miss Drew said dispassionately: 'The devil can quote Scripture for his own use. All the same, that's a jolly good bit. Where did you find it?'

'Job,' responded Neville. 'I found some other good bits, too, but unfortunately they aren't quite drawing-room.'

'Whoso despiseth the Word,' announced Glass, recovering from the shock of having been answered in kind, 'shall be destroyed!'

'That'll do!' intervened the Sergeant. 'You go and wait for me in the drive, Glass!' He waited until the constable had withdrawn, and then said: 'Well, sir, you've told me a very straightforward story, but what I'm asking myself is, why didn't you tell it before?'

'You didn't notice the espalier before,' said Neville.

'It might be better for you, sir, if you told the truth about your doings on the night of the murder without waiting to be questioned,' suggested the Sergeant, with a touch of severity.

'Oh no! You'd have thought it very fishy if I'd been as expansive as all that,' said Neville.

Upon reflection, the Sergeant privately agreed with him. However, all he said was that Neville would be wise not to try to be too clever with the police.

'You may be right,' answered Neville, 'but your Superintendent said that no good would come of my taking the Press to my bosom, and lots of good came of it. I've got my picture in the papers.'

'You have?' said the Sergeant, diverted in spite of himself. 'What, you're not going to tell me they went and printed all that International spy stuff?'

'No,' replied Neville regretfully. 'Not that, but one of the eager brotherhood really thought I was the Boots.'

Sally gave a crow of mirth. 'Neville, is that what you told them? Oh, do let me see your interview!'

'I will, if the Sergeant doesn't mind putting off my arrest for ten minutes.'

The Sergeant said: 'You know very well I've got nothing to arrest you on, sir.'

'But wouldn't you love to do it?' murmured Neville.

'You get along with you, sir,' recommended the Sergeant.

To his relief, Neville obeyed his command, linking his arm in Sally's, and strolling away with her towards the house. Out of earshot, she said: 'You spilled more than I bargained for.'

'Diverting his mind.'

'I hope to God you didn't say too much.'

'Yes, so do I,' agreed Neville. 'One comfort is that we shall soon know. How's the heroine of this piece doing?'

'If you mean Helen –'

'I do, darling, and if one of your sisterly fits is coming on, go home and do not bore me with it.'

'Gosh, how I do dislike you!' exclaimed Sally.

'Well, you're not singular,' said Neville comfortingly. 'In fact, I'm getting amazingly unpopular. Aunt Lucy gets gooseflesh whenever she sets eyes on me.'

'I'm not surprised. I must say, I think –'

'What compels you?' inquired Neville.

'Oh shut up! I *will* say that I think it's fairly low of you to get yourself photographed as the Boots. Miss Fletcher's got enough to bear without your antics being added to the rest.'

'Not at all,' he replied. 'My poor aunt was becoming lachrymose, and no pleasure to herself or me. The paper that printed my story, carefully imported into the house by me, has been another of my diversions. Indignation not profitable, but better than aimless woe. How's Helen?'

'She's all right,' said Sally, a note of reserve in her voice.

A sleepy but intelligent eye was cocked at her. 'Ah, the atmosphere a trifle strained? I wondered why you came round here.'

'It wasn't that at all. I wanted to take another look at the lay-out. And I thought it might be a good thing to evaporate for a bit. John's not going up to town till after lunch.'

'Don't tell me it's a necking-party!' said Neville incredulously.

She gave a short laugh. 'No. But I'm giving it a chance to become one. If only John weren't so – so idiotically unapproachable!'

'These strong men! Oh, do tell me! If it turns out to be John who killed Ernie, do we seek to cover up the evidence of his guilt, or not?'

She did not answer, but, as they reached the drawing-room window, pulled her arm away from his, and said abruptly: 'Are you capable of speaking the truth, Neville?'

'Didn't you hear me just now, speaking the truth to the Sergeant?'

'That was different. What I want to know is this, are you in love with Helen?'

'Oh, God give me strength!' moaned Neville. 'A chair – brandy – a basin! Romance, as pictured by Sally Drew! Tell me, does anyone *really* read your works?'

'All very well,' said Sally, critically surveying him. 'But you're quite a good actor, and I can't get it out of my head that you agreed to try and wrest those IOUs from Ernie. I haven't before seen you falling over yourself to render assistance to people.'

'No, darling, and believe me, you won't see it again. Not that I did. If I fell it was because I was pushed. Don't tell me you've inserted this repulsive notion into John's head!'

'I haven't, of course, but I shouldn't be altogether surprised if it were there. I may be wrong, but one thing I do know, and that is that he's being extremely guarded – not to say frozen.'

'You'd be guarded if you looked like being pinched for murder.'

She let her monocle drop. 'Neville, do you think there's a danger of that?'

'I do, of course. What is more, I don't think that the further instalment of Helen's adventures on the fatal night are going to be as helpful to John as she no doubt felt they would be.'

'No,' said Sally bluntly. 'Nor do I. If she'd only keep her mouth shut . . . By the way, John doesn't know anything about her second interview with the Superintendent, so don't go and let it out!'

'How simple life would be without friends! Why, in the name of all that's feeble-minded —'

'Because he'd be bound to ask why she went back to the study, of course, and that would tear the whole thing wide open. She'd have to tell him about the IOUs.'

'Let's go and write an anonymous letter to John, divulging the whole story, shall we?' suggested Neville. 'It would be a kindness to them both, and I don't in the least mind doing people kindnesses if it doesn't cost me anything.'

Sally sighed. 'I darned nearly told him myself, when he first arrived. Only Helen was so terrified of his knowing that I didn't. And since then . . . Oh, I don't know! She may be right. I can't make John out. Neville, *what brought him home*?'

'Dear heart, will you purge your mind of the belief that I'm good at riddles?'

'He doesn't suspect her of having had an affair with Ernie. Apparently he told her he didn't.'

'Well, it's nice to know that he hasn't joined the great majority.'

She looked sharply at him. 'Is that what people have been thinking? Go on, tell me!'

'People are so lewd,' murmured Neville.

'Has there been talk? Much of it?'

'Oh no! Just a little light-hearted gossip to pass the time.'

She was silent for a moment, frowning. At last she said: 'That's bad. Easily discovered, and saddles John with a motive. If he got wind of that . . . Hang it, he wouldn't burst home just to bash Ernie on the head! It's archaic.'

Neville handed her a cigarette, and lit one himself. 'You could work that up into a plausible story if you put your mind to it,' he said. 'While in Berlin, John heard repercussions of the gossip –'

'Why in Berlin?' she interrupted.

'That I can't tell you. You'll probably be able to think out several attractive answers for yourself. He returned to remonstrate with Ernie –'

'I don't see John remonstrating.'

'No, darling; if you'd seen John remonstrating you'd be a suspect yourself.'

'What I mean is –'

'We know, we know! Have it your own way! He came home to issue an ultimatum. Ernie got under his skin, and without taking much thought he knocked him on the head.'

'Several flaws,' said Sally. 'Why did he enter by the side gate, if not with malice aforethought?'

'State entry heralded by butler leading to undesirable publicity. Gossip amongst servants, possibility of encountering Aunt Lucy. Lots of answers.'

'All right. What did he do with the weapon?'

'Not a fair question. Doesn't apply exclusively to John. Whoever killed Ernie disposed of the weapon with such skill as to provide this case with its most baffling feature.'

'Very nice,' said Sally. 'You've been reading my books. But let me tell you that I'm not a believer in these sudden flashes of brilliance on the part of murderers. When I think out a bit of dazzling ingenuity for my criminal to indulge in, it usually costs me several hours of brain-racking thought.'

'The human mind sharpened by fear –'

'Bosh!' said Sally, flicking the ash from the end of her cigarette. 'In my experience, the human mind, when under the influence of fear, rushes round in frantic circles. No, thanks: that theory doesn't go big with me at all. As I see it, there was one person who had time, motive and opportunity to kill Ernie, and lashings of time in which to dispose of the weapon.'

He met her look with a flickering smile, and lifted his hand. 'Oh, no! *This hand of mine Is yet a maiden and an innocent hand, Not painted with the crimson spots of blood.*'

'Round of applause from the gallery. But quotations prove nothing. You could have done it, Neville.'

'Oh, but why stop at me? Perhaps Aunty Lucy did it, with one of her Indian clubs. I believe she wields them with considerable vigour.'

'Don't be silly. Why should she?'

'Heaven knows. If you don't fancy her, what about Simmons?'

'Again why?'

'And again, Heaven knows. Why leave all the brain-work to me? You think.'

'Yes, well, I see very little point in thinking out fantastic motives for Miss Fletcher and Simmons while you're right under my nose, complete with a motive I don't have to hunt for.'

He looked bored. 'Well, if you're going to make me the favourite, I shall lose all interest. The crime becomes at once pedestrian and commonplace. Oh, here's my poor aunt! Come and help us to solve the mystery, Aunt Lucy. My theory is that you did it.'

Miss Fletcher, who had entered the drawing-room, came over to the window, but said in a voice of shocked indignation: 'I'm sure I don't know where you get your dreadful tongue from, Neville. It certainly wasn't from your dear father. I know it is only thoughtlessness, but the things you say are in the very worst of bad taste. And you haven't even bought an armband!'

'I know. I thought it would look like the fall from the sublime to the ridiculous if I did,' he explained, indicating with a wave of his hand her funereal attire.

'One likes to show respect for the dead,' she said. 'Oh, Miss Drew, so kind of your sister to send such beautiful flowers!' She pressed Sally's hand, and added: 'I expect you must find this all *most* interesting. I always think it so clever of you to write books. So complicated, too. Not that I've read them, of course. I find I'm too stupid to understand detective stories, but I always put them down on my library list.'

'You wouldn't be so encouraging if you knew what she's up to,' said Neville. 'She's trying to prove that I murdered Ernie.'

'Oh no, dear!' said Miss Fletcher distressfully. 'I'm afraid Neville's often very thoughtless, but he wouldn't do a thing like that.'

'Why on earth you can't keep a still tongue in your head baffles conjecture!' Sally told Neville wrathfully.

'His poor father was very talkative,' explained Miss Fletcher. 'Dear Ernie, too, was always good company. But unfortunately Neville has got into a bad habit of mumbling, which makes it very difficult to hear what he says. Neville, I have just discovered that there will have to be an inquest. Can nothing be done to stop it?'

'No. Do you mind?' he inquired.

'Well, dear, it's not very *nice*, is it? We've never had such a thing in the family. So common! I wonder if Mr Lawrence could do anything about it? I think I will go and ring him up.'

'But Miss Fletcher – !' began Sally, only to be silenced by having her foot trodden on by Neville.

Miss Fletcher, recommending Neville to take care of his guest, drifted away. Neville said softly: 'You know, you're a menace. Leave my aunt to me, will you?'

'But what's the use of letting her think there needn't be an inquest? It isn't very considerate of you to –'

'Of course it's not considerate! It wasn't considerate of me to discover that I hadn't a shirt fit to wear this morning, or a pair of socks without holes in them; and it won't be considerate of me when I think up a new annoyance, which I shall do as soon as this inquest-business begins to wear thin. You've got a disgustingly sentimental idea that bereaved persons ought to be humoured, cosseted, and given plenty of time in which to indulge their grief. I shouldn't be at all surprised to find that you're one of those paralysing monsters of unselfishness, with a bias towards self-sacrifice, and a strong yen for shouldering other people's burdens.'

Sally gave a gasp. 'Go on! It's the rankest kind of boloney, but I should be interested to know how you defend it.'

'Shouldn't place people under obligations,' said Neville briefly. 'Nearly always intolerable. Effect on your own character probably disastrous.'

'Why?'

'Spiritual conceit.'

She polished her monocle. 'There's something in what you say,' she admitted. 'Not much, but a grain of truth. Sorry I tried to butt in on your plans for Miss Fletcher's consolation. I very nearly took a hand in Helen's differences with John, too. A small, inner voice bade me hold my peace.'

'A woman's instinct!' said Neville, deeply moved. 'Not but what I sympathise with your purely rational desire to disperse the fog they grope in. But one should never forget that some people fair revel in fog.'

'Helen isn't revelling in any of this,' Sally replied. 'Married couples who can't get on rather bore me in the ordinary way, but though I think she's been cavorting around like a prize ass my withers are a trifle wrung by Helen's troubles. They really do seem to have gathered thick and fast upon her. The worst of it is, I can't be sure which way John will jump if he discovers the truth.'

'Baffling man – John,' agreed Neville.

'Well, he is. Just consider it! He arrives in England, unexpectedly, the day Ernie is murdered, and turns up here the next morning, suspecting that the footprints discovered in the garden might be Helen's.'

'Oh no, did he really? That leads us to suppose that he knew something.'

'Yes, but what? Helen says he doesn't suspect her of having had any kind of liaison with Ernie. But when he walked in on us yesterday the general impression I got was that an iceberg had drifted in. In fact, he was coldly angry, and not loving any of us very noticeably.'

'Forgive the interruption, but if he thought Helen was mixed up in a murder case, there was a certain amount of excuse for peevishness. I don't want to be old-world, but wife's admitted presence in home of noted lady-killer is enough to make most men feel a trifle out of humour.'

'I know, and if he'd raged at her I could have understood it. He was just deadly polite.'

'Obviously the moment for Helen to put over a big act as repentant wife.'

'That what I hope she is doing, but she's so burned up over the whole thing that she seems to have lost grip. Of course, if John were to say: "Darling, tell me all," I expect she would. But he isn't that sort. They must have let themselves drift an awful way apart.'

The same thought was in Helen's mind at that moment. She had just entered the library, where her husband sat writing at his desk, and almost before she closed the door behind her she wished that she were on the other side of it.

North looked up, regarding her in a way which did not tend to put her any more at her ease. 'Do you want me, Helen?' he asked impersonally.

'I – No, not exactly. Are you busy?'

He laid down his pen. 'Not if you wish to talk to me.'

This reply, though possibly intended to be encouraging, had the effect of making Helen feel a very long way away from him. She moved across the room to a chair by the window, and sat down in it. 'It's such a long time since we talked together – really talked – that I seem to have forgotten how,' she said, trying to speak lightly.

His face hardened. 'Yes.'

She realised that hers had been an unfortunate remark. She said, not looking at him: 'We – we ought to talk this thing over, don't you think? It concerns us both, doesn't it?'

'Certainly. What do you want to say?'

She tried to formulate sentences in her brain; he neither moved nor spoke, but sat watching her. Suddenly she raised her eyes, and said abruptly: 'Why did you come home like that? So unexpectedly, and without a word to me?'

'I thought, Helen, that you already knew the answer to that question.'

'I? How could I know?'

'You informed me that you did. You said that I had come home to spy on you.'

She flushed. 'I didn't mean it. I was upset.'

'That you were upset by my arrival is not, my dear Helen, a very reassuring thought.'

'Not that! Ernie's death – that policeman asking me such ghastly questions!'

'We should get on better,' he remarked, 'if you did not lie to me. I know you rather well. You were horrified to see me.'

She looked rather hopelessly across at him. 'Oh,

what's the use of talking like this? It only leads to misunderstandings, and bitterness.'

After a moment's silence, he answered levelly: 'Very well. What did you want to talk to me about? Fletcher's murder?'

She nodded. 'Yes.'

'It seems to be very much on your nerves.'

'Wouldn't it be on yours?'

'That would depend on whether I felt either grief, or fear.'

'Grief! Oh no! But I was there that evening. I don't want to be dragged into it. You must see how awful my position is!'

'Had you not better tell me exactly what happened?' he suggested.

'I did tell you. I think I've made the Superintendent realise that it would be no use asking me to identify the man I saw, but –'

'Just a moment, Helen. It is time we understood one another. Did you, in fact, recognise that man?'

'No!' she said quickly. 'I never saw his face.'

'But you have some idea, haven't you, who he was?'

She said in a low voice: 'If I had I shouldn't tell a soul. You can be sure of that.'

'In that case, there does not seem to be much point in pursuing the matter further,' he said. 'The only advice I can possibly give you, as things are, is to keep calm, and to say as little as you can.' He picked up his pen again, but after writing a couple of lines, said, without looking up: 'By the way, have you any objection to telling me why Neville Fletcher came to see you on the night of the murder?'

She gave an uncontrollable start, and faltered: 'How do you know? Who told you?'

'Baker saw him leave the premises, and mentioned it to me this morning.'

'Do you encourage the servants to report to you who visits me?'

'No,' he replied imperturbably.

'Neville came to tell me Ernie had been killed.'

He looked up at that. 'Indeed! Why?'

'He knew I was a friend of Ernie's. I suppose he thought I'd want to know. He's always doing mad things. You simply can't account for anything he says or does.'

'What does he know about this business?'

'Nothing. Only what we all know.'

'Then why did he think it necessary to visit you at midnight to tell you what you would certainly know a few hours later?'

'He'd seen my footprints,' she said desperately. 'He thought they might be mine. He came to find out.'

'If Neville leapt to the conclusion that the footprints were yours he must enjoy a greater share of your confidence than I suspected. What is there between you?'

She pressed her hands to her throbbing temples. 'Oh, my God, what do you take me for? Neville! It's – it's almost laughable!'

'You misunderstand me. I wasn't suggesting that there was any love between you. But your explanation of his visit is altogether too lame to be believed. Did he by any chance *know* that you were at Greystones that evening?'

'No, of course not! How could he? It was a guess, that's all.'

'Not even Neville Fletcher would make such a guess

without having very good reason for doing so. Am I to understand that you were so much in the habit of visiting Fletcher in that – you will have to forgive me if I call it clandestine – manner, that it was a natural conclusion for Neville to arrive at?'

'Oh no! Neville knew all the time that I didn't feel about Ernie except as a friend.'

He raised his brows. 'Was your possible relationship with Fletcher of interest to Neville?'

'No. No, of course not. But I've known Neville for years.' Her voice tailed off uncertainly.

'I am quite aware of that. I too have known Neville – or shall we say, have been acquainted with him? – for years. Are you asking me to believe that that extremely detached young man asked you to explain your dealings with his uncle?'

She could not help smiling, but there was fright in her eyes. 'No. Actually, I told him.'

'You told Neville Fletcher . . . I see. Why?'

She muttered: 'No reason. It – sort of came out. I can't explain.'

'That at least is evident,' he said harshly.

'You don't believe anything I say.'

'Do you find that surprising?'

She was silent, staring down at her clasped hands.

'Is Neville in love with you?'

She said, with genuine surprise: 'Neville? Oh no, I'm sure he's not!'

'You must forgive me for being so ignorant,' he said. 'So little have I spied on you that I'm not at all up to date. Who, at the moment, is an enamoured swain? Is Jerry Maitland still in the running?'

'If I told you no one had ever been in the running you'd believe that as little as you believe the rest of my story.'

'As I have yet to hear the rest of your story, I can't answer that. Oh, don't insult my intelligence by telling me that I have heard it!'

Her lips were trembling. 'If you think that, is this the way to get me to tell you the whole truth? You treat me as though I were – as though I were a criminal, and not your wife!'

'My wife!' He gave a short laugh. 'Is not that a trifle farcical?'

'If it is, it's your fault!' she said in a choking voice.

'Oh, undoubtedly! I failed to satisfy you, didn't I? You wanted more excitement than was to be found in marriage with me, and one man's love was not enough for you. Tell me this, Helen; would you have married me if I had not been a rich man?'

She made a gesture, as though thrusting his words away from her, and rose jerkily to her feet, and stood with her back to him, staring out of the window. After a moment she said in a constricted tone: 'If they don't arrest me for Ernie's murder, you had better divorce me.'

'They won't arrest you. You needn't let that bugbear ride you.'

'Things look very black against me,' she said wearily. 'I don't know that I care much.'

'If things look black, you've kept something from me which must be of vital importance. Are you going to tell me what it is?'

She shook her head. 'No. When the case is over – if we

come out of it intact – I'll make it possible for you to divorce me.'

'I'm not going to divorce you. Unless –' He stopped.

'Well? Unless?'

'Unless there's someone else whom you've fallen in love with enough to – But I don't believe there is. You don't fall in love, Helen. All you want is a series of flirtations. But if I am to help you now –'

'Why should you?' she interrupted.

'Because you're my wife.'

'The whole duty of a husband, in fact. Thank you, but I would prefer you to keep out of it.'

'I can't do that.'

'You were a fool to come down here!' she said.

'Possibly, but if you were to be dragged into the case there was nothing to be done.'

She turned. 'To save your own good name? Do you hate me, John?'

'No.'

'You're indifferent, in fact. We're both indifferent.' She came away from the window. 'I don't want to be divorced. I realise that all this mess – Ernie's death, the scandal, everything! – has been my fault, and I'm sorry. In future, I'll be more careful. There really isn't anything more to be said, is there?'

'If you don't trust me enough to tell me the whole truth, nothing.'

'I trust you as much as you trust me!' she said fiercely. 'You know how much that is! Now, if you please, let's banish the whole subject. Do you mean to come home to dinner tonight?'

He was looking rather narrowly at her, and did not

answer. She repeated the question; he replied in his usual cold way: 'No, I shall dine in town. I may be late back. Expect me when you see me.'

Nine

Sergeant Hemingway left Greystones in a thoughtful mood. An exhaustive search had failed to discover the hiding-place of any weapon, but one fact had emerged with which he seemed to be rather pleased.

'Though why I should be I can't tell you,' he said to Glass. 'It makes the whole business look more screwy than ever. But in my experience that's very often the way. You start on a case which looks as though it's going to be child's play, and you don't seem to get any further with it. By the time you've been at work on it a couple of days you've collected enough evidence to prove that there couldn't have been a murder at all. Then something breaks, and there you are.'

'Do you say that the more difficult a case becomes the easier it is to solve?' asked Glass painstakingly.

'That's about the size of it,' admitted the Sergeant. 'When it's got so gummed up that each new fact you pick up contradicts the last I begin to feel cheerful.'

'I do not understand. I see around me only folly and sin and vanity. Shall these things make a righteous man glad?'

'Not being a righteous man, I can't say. Speaking as a humble flatfoot, if it weren't for folly and sin and vanity I wouldn't be where I am now, and nor would you, my lad. And if you'd stop wasting your time learning bits of the Bible to fire off at me – which in itself is highly insubordinate conduct, let me tell you – and take a bit of wholesome interest in this problem, you'd probably do yourself a lot of good. You might even get promoted.'

'I set no store by worldly honours,' said Glass gloomily. 'Man being in honour abideth not: he is like the beasts that perish.'

'What you do want,' declared the Sergeant with asperity, 'is a course of Bile Beans! I've met some killjoys in my time, but you fairly take the cake. What did you get out of your friend the butler?'

'He knows nothing.'

'Don't you believe it! Butlers always know something.'

'It is not so. He knows only that harsh words passed between the dead man and his nephew on the evening of the murder.'

'Young Neville explained that,' said the Sergeant musingly. 'Not that I set much store by what he says. Pack of lies, I daresay.'

'A lying tongue is but for the moment,' observed Glass, with melancholy satisfaction.

'You can't have been about the world much if that's what you think. Do you still hold to it that the man you saw on the night of the murder wasn't carrying anything?'

'You would have me change my evidence,' said Glass, fixing him with an accusing glare, 'but I tell you that a man that beareth false witness is a maul, and a sword, and a sharp arrow!'

'No one wants you to bear false witness,' said the Sergeant irritably. 'And as far as I'm concerned, you're a sharp arrow already, and probably a maul as well, if a maul means what I think it does. I've had to tell you off once already for giving me lip, and I've had about enough of it. Wait a bit!' He stopped short in the middle of the pavement and pulled out his notebook, and hastily thumbed over the leaves. 'You wait!' he said darkly. 'I've got something here that I copied out specially. I knew it would come in useful. Yes, here we are! *He that being often reproved hardeneth his neck, shall suddenly be destroyed.*' He looked up to see how this counter-blast was being received, and added with profound satisfaction: '*And that without remedy!*'

Glass compressed his lips, but said after a moment's inward struggle: 'Pride goeth before destruction, and an haughty spirit before a fall. I will declare my iniquity, I will be sorry for my sin.'

'All right,' said the Sergeant, returning his notebook to his pocket. 'We'll carry on from there.'

A heavy sigh broke from Glass. 'Mine iniquities have gone over my head; as an heavy burden they are too heavy for me,' he said in a brooding tone.

'There's no need to take on about it,' said the Sergeant, mollified. 'It's just got to be a bad habit with you, which you ought to break yourself of. I'm sorry if I told you off a bit roughly. Forget it!'

'Open rebuke,' said Glass with unabated gloom, 'is better than secret love.'

The Sergeant fought for words. As he could think of none that were not profane, and felt morally certain that Glass would, without hesitation, condemn those with

Biblical aphorisms, he controlled himself, and strode on in fulminating silence.

Glass walked beside him, apparently unaware of having said anything to enrage him. As they turned into the road where the police station was situated, he said: 'You found no weapon. I told you you would not.'

'You're right,' said the Sergeant. 'I found no weapon, but I found out something you'd have found out two days ago if you'd had the brains of a louse.'

'He that refraineth his lips is wise,' remarked Glass. 'What did I overlook?'

'Well, I don't know that it was any business of yours, strictly speaking,' said the Sergeant, always fair-minded. 'But the grandfather clock in the hall is a minute slow by the one in the late Ernest's study, which synchronised with your watch. What's more, I found out from Miss Fletcher that it's been like that for some time.'

'Is it important to the case?' asked Glass.

'Of course it's important. I don't say it makes it any easier, because it doesn't, but that's what I told you: in cases like this you're always coming up against new bits of evidence which go and upset any theory you may have been working on. On the face of it, it looks as though the man you saw – we'll assume it was Carpenter – did the murder, doesn't it?'

'That is so,' agreed Glass.

'Well, the fact of that hall clock's being a minute slow throws a spanner in the works,' said the Sergeant. 'In the second act of her highly talented performance, Mrs North stated that that clock struck the hour, which was 10 p.m., while she was in the hall, on her way to the front door. You saw Carpenter making his getaway at 10.02.

That gave him a couple of minutes in which to have killed the late Ernie, disposed of the weapon, and reached the gate. It's my opinion it couldn't have been done, but at least there was an outside chance. Now I discover that when Mrs North left the study it wasn't 10.00, but 10.01, and that's properly upset things. It begins to look as though Carpenter wasn't in on the murder at all, but simply went down to try his luck at putting the black on the late Ernie, and was shown off the premises as described by Mrs North. In fact, it wouldn't surprise me if Carpenter turns out to be one of those highly irrelevant things that seem to crop up just to make life harder. The real murderer must have been hiding in the garden, waiting for his opportunity, and while you were taking notice of Carpenter, and deciding to go and investigate, he was doing the job.'

Glass considered this for a moment. 'It is possible, but how did he make his escape? I saw no one in the garden.'

'I daresay you didn't see anyone, but you didn't go looking behind every bush, did you? You flashed your torch round, and *thought* there was no one in the garden. There might have been, and what was to stop him making his getaway while you were in the study?'

They had reached the police station by this time. Glass paused on the steps, and said slowly: 'It does not seem to me that it can have happened like that. I do not say it was impossible, but you would have me believe that between 10.01, when Mrs North left the house, and 10.05, when I discovered the body, a man had time to come forth from his hiding-place, enter the study, slay Ernest Fletcher, and return to his hiding-place. It is true that I myself did not enter the study until 10.05, but as I came up the path must I not have seen a man escaping thence?'

'You know, when you keep your mind on the job you're not so dumb,' said the Sergeant encouragingly. 'All the same, I've got an answer to that one. Who says the murderer escaped by way of the side gate? What was to stop him letting himself out the same way Mrs North did – by the front door?'

Glass looked incredulous. 'He must be a madman who would do so! Would he run the risk of being seen by a member of the household, perhaps by Mrs North, who had only a minute or two before passed through the study door into the hall, as he must have known, had he been lying in wait as you suggest?'

'Heard you coming up the path, and had to take a chance,' said the Sergeant.

'Folly is joy to him that is destitute of wisdom!' said Glass scornfully.

'Well, for all you know he was destitute of wisdom,' replied the Sergeant. 'You go and get your dinner, and report here when you've had it.'

He went up the steps, and into the building. It was not until he had passed out of Glass's sight that it occurred to him that the constable's last remark might not have been directed at the unknown murderer. A wrathful exclamation rose to his lips; he half turned, as though to go after Glass; but thought better of it. Encountering the Station Sergeant's eye, he said: 'Somebody here must have had a grudge against me when they saddled me with that pain in the neck.'

'Glass?' inquired Sergeant Cross sympathetically. 'Chronic, isn't he? Mind you, he isn't usually as bad as he's been over this case. Well, it stands to reason, doesn't it? His sort has to have a bit of sin in front of them to get properly wound up, as you might say. Do you want him taken off?'

'Oh no!' said the Sergeant, with bitter irony. 'I like being told-off by constables. Makes a nice change.'

'We'll take him off the job,' offered Cross. 'He's not used to murder-cases, that's what it is. It's gone to his head.'

The Sergeant relented. 'No, I'll put up with him. At least he's a conscientious chap, and apart from this nasty habit he's got of reciting Scripture I haven't anything against him. I daresay he's got a fixation, poor fellow.'

An hour later, mellowed by food, he was propounding this theory to Superintendent Hannasyde, who arrived at the police station just as his subordinate came back from a leisurely dinner.

'You never know,' he said. 'We shall quite likely find that he had some shocking experience when he was a child, which would account for it.'

'As I have no intention of wasting my time – or letting you waste yours – in probing into Glass's past, I should think there is nothing more unlikely,' replied Hannasyde somewhat shortly.

The Sergeant cast him a shrewd glance, and said: 'I told you this wasn't going to be such a whale of a case, Chief. Said so at the start. Bad morning?'

'No, merely inconclusive. Budd had been double-crossing Fletcher; Neville Fletcher seems to be up to his eyes in debt; and North did not spend the evening of the 17th at his flat.'

'Well, isn't that nice?' said the Sergeant. 'Stage all

littered up with suspects, just like I said it would be! Tell me more about friend Budd.'

Hannasyde gave him a brief account of the broker's exploits. The Sergeant scratched his chin, remarking at the end of the tale: 'I don't like it. Not a bit. You can say, of course, that if he had to hand over nine thousand shares which he hadn't got, and couldn't get without pretty well ruining himself, he had a motive for murdering the late Ernest. On the other hand, what he said to you about Ernest's not being able to come out into the open to prosecute him rings very true. Very true indeed. He's not my fancy at all. What about North?'

'North, unless I'm much mistaken, is playing a deep game. He told me that after dinner at his club he returned to his flat, and went early to bed. What actually happened was that he returned to his flat shortly after 8.30 p.m., and went out again just before 9.00. He came back finally at 11.45.'

'Well, well, well!' said the Sergeant. 'No deception? All quite open and above-board?'

'Apparently. He paused to exchange a word with the hall porter on his way in at 8.30; when he went out the porter offered to call a taxi, and he refused, saying he would walk.'

'Who saw him come in later, Chief?'

'The night porter. He says that he caught sight of North stepping into the lift.'

'Well, for a man who impressed you as having a head on his shoulders he doesn't seem to me to be doing so very well,' said the Sergeant. 'What was the use of his telling you he'd spent the evening at his flat when he must have known you could bust the story wide open at the first blow?'

'I don't know,' Hannasyde replied. 'Had it been Budd, I should have thought that he had got into a panic, and lost his head. But North wasn't in a panic, and I'm quite sure he didn't lose his head. What I do suspect is that for some reason, best known to himself, he was stalling me.'

The Sergeant thought it over. 'Stalling you till he could have a word with his wife. I get it. I'd call it a risky game to play, myself.'

'I don't know that I think that would worry him much.'

'Oh, that sort, is he?' said the Sergeant. 'A little course of Ichabod wouldn't do him any harm, by the sound of it.'

Hannasyde smiled, but rather absently. 'He wasn't at his office this morning, and as his secretary didn't seem to think he was going there today, I came down to see him here. But he's going to be difficult, just because he doesn't say a word more than he need.'

'So is young Neville going to be difficult,' said the Sergeant. 'But not, believe me, for the same reason. That bird talks so much you have a job to keep up with him. What do you make of him having the nerve to tell me he climbed out of his bedroom window, and over the garden wall, the night the late Ernest was murdered, just to go and tell Mrs North all about it? Said he was her accomplice over the business of those IOUs of hers.'

Hannasyde frowned. 'Cool hand. It might be true.'

'Cool! I believe you! Brass isn't the word for what he's got. However, I'm bound to admit I've got a soft corner for him. He laid old Ichabod out with the neatest right counter you ever saw.'

'What?'

'Figure of speech,' explained the Sergeant. 'He landed a Biblical text which Ichabod wasn't expecting, and which pretty well crumpled him up. But that's nothing to go on. I wouldn't put it above him to bump his uncle off, if it happened to suit his book. Though, now I come to think of it,' he added reflectively, 'it would be more in his line to have stuck a knife in his ribs. No; if it weren't for the fact that there's no trace of the weapon, and not one hiding-place that I could spot, I wouldn't fancy him at all for the role of murderer. Which brings me to the only bit of useful evidence I picked up. The hall clock is a minute slow, Chief.'

Hannasyde looked at him. 'If that is so,' he said slowly, 'it makes Mrs North's evidence practically valueless.'

'The second batch, you mean? It does look like it, doesn't it? Not that I ever set much store by it myself, from what you told me of her. Mind you, I don't say the murder couldn't still have happened but what I do say is that the man Glass saw – call him Charlie Carpenter – couldn't have done it. It must have been Budd, which I *don't* think, young Neville, North, or the dizzy blonde herself.'

Hannasyde shook his head. 'I can't swallow that, Hemingway. If we are to assume that Mrs North's evidence was true, it means that Fletcher did not re-enter the study until 10.01. You yourself put the time it would take him to sit down at his desk again and start to write his letters at two minutes at the least. That leaves two minutes for the murderer to walk in, kill him, and get away again. Less, for though Glass didn't actually enter the study until 10.05, he must have had the window in view for quite a minute, on his way up the path.'

'Yes, that's what he said,' replied the Sergeant. 'I admit it would be cutting it a bit fine. What's your idea, Chief? Think Mrs North's first story was the true one?'

'No,' said Hannasyde, after a pause. 'I think she did go back into the study. If she didn't let herself out of it as she described, I don't see how her finger-prints came to be on the panel. But the fact of the hall clock's being slow points to a discrepancy somewhere in her story. She stated that the man X left the study with Ernest at 9.58, that she went back into it, and left it as the hall clock struck 10.00. Now, the only times we *know* to be correct are 10.02, when Glass saw X making off; and 10.05, when he discovered Fletcher's body. That left us with a difference of four minutes, between the time Mrs North said X left and the time Glass actually saw him leave. We could just, and only just, account for that by assuming that X doubled back to the study, murdered Fletcher, and again made off. But if Fletcher returned to the study not at 10.00, but at 10.01, then there is no possibility of X's having returned, committed the murder, and reached the gate again. So either X left by the side gate at 9.58, to be followed in four minutes by a second man – Y, if you like; or the first man, X, was a pure fabrication of Mrs North's.'

'Hold on, Super! I'll have to see it on paper,' said the Sergeant. He wrote for a moment or two, and regarded the result with disgust. 'Yes, that is a hopeful-looking mess,' he remarked. 'All right – X is out. So what? We know the North dame hid in the garden, because we found her footprints. Yes, I get it. Y, who is obviously North, was with the late Ernest; she recognised his voice – or maybe she didn't: I haven't worked that bit out. Anyway, Y killed Ernest while Mrs North was in the garden, and bunked. Mrs North then entered the study to have a look-see, and – for reasons which I won't attempt to fathom – made off by way of the front door. You can make the times fit if you juggle with them. Someone may have passed down Maple Grove when Y reached the gate, which would mean that he'd have to wait till whoever it was had cleared off before making his getaway. Or, if you prefer it, Mrs North didn't leave at 10.01, but later. Though why she should make that bit up, I don't quite see. That eliminates X, and fits the only facts we know to be certain.'

'You can eliminate X if you like,' interposed Hannasyde, 'but you can't eliminate Charlie Carpenter. Where does he fit into this otherwise plausible story?'

The Sergeant sighed. 'That's true. If we've got to have him in, then he's Y, and North is X – eliminated. Yes, that's all right. Mrs North didn't recognise his voice, but she caught a glimpse of him, and thought he might be her husband. Hence her erroneous evidence. How's that?'

'Not bad,' conceded Hannasyde. 'But if North is eliminated, will you tell me why he stated that he spent the evening in his flat, when in actual fact he did nothing of the kind?'

'I give it up,' said the Sergeant despairingly. 'There isn't an answer.'

Hannasyde smiled. 'There might be. It's just possible that North had nothing to do with the murder, but suspects that his wife had.'

The Sergeant stared at him. 'What, and deliberately chucked his own alibi – if any – overboard, so as to be all set to leap in and take the rap for his wife? Go on, Super! You don't believe that!'

'I don't know. He might. Rather that type of man.'

'Regular film star, he sounds to me,' said the Sergeant, revolted. 'Red blood, and hair on his chest, too, I should think.' He turned his head, as the door opened, and encountered the solemn stare of PC Glass. 'Oh, so you're back, are you? Well, if you're working on this case, I suppose you'd better come in. I daresay I'll be able to think up a job for you.'

Hannasyde nodded. 'Yes, come in, Glass. I want you to cast your mind back to the night of the murder. When you were walking along Vale Avenue, on your beat, do you remember seeing anyone, beyond the man who came out of the side gate of Greystones? Anyone who might, at about 10.00 p.m., have been passing the front entrance to Greystones?'

Glass thought deeply for a moment, and then pronounced: 'No, I remember no one. Why am I asked this question?'

'Because I have reason to doubt the truth of Mrs North's statement, that she left Greystones by the front door, at a minute after 10.00. What I want is a possible passer-by, who may or may not have seen her.'

'If that is so, the matter is simple,' said Glass. 'There is a pillar-box at the corner of Vale Avenue and Glynne Road, where she dwells, which is cleared at 10.00 p.m. each night. I do not doubt that the postman saw her, if she was indeed upon her way home at that hour.'

'Nice work, Ichabod!' exclaimed the Sergeant. 'You'll end up in the CID yet.'

A cold eye was turned upon him. 'A man that flattereth his neighbour spreadeth a net for his feet,' said Glass, adding, since the Sergeant seemed unimpressed: 'Even the eyes of his child shall fail.'

'Well, don't sound so cocky about it,' said the Sergeant. 'And as it happens I haven't got any children, so now where are you?'

'We won't discuss the matter,' interposed Hannasyde in a chilling tone. 'You will please remember, Glass, that you are talking to your superior officer.'

'To have respect of persons is not good,' said Glass seriously. 'For, for a piece of bread that man will transgress.'

'Oh, will he?' said the indignant Sergeant. 'Well, he won't – not for fifty pieces of bread! What next!'

'That'll do,' said Hannasyde, a tremor in his voice. 'Get hold of that postman, Glass, and discover at what time he cleared the box, whether he saw Mrs North, and if so, whether she was carrying anything. Got that?'

'Yes, sir.'

'All right, that's all. Report here to me.'

Glass withdrew. As the door closed behind him, Hannasyde said: 'Why do you encourage him, Skipper?'

'Me? Me encourage him?'

'Yes, you.'

The Sergeant said: 'Well, if you call it encouraging him to tell him where he gets off –'

'I believe you enjoy him,' said Hannasyde accusingly.

The Sergeant grinned. 'Well, I've got to admit it adds

a bit of interest to the case, waiting for him to run dry. You'd think he must have got pretty well all he's learnt off his chest by now, wouldn't you? He hasn't, though. I certainly have to hand it to him: he hasn't repeated himself once so far. Where do we go from here?'

'To North's house,' replied Hannasyde. 'I must see if I can get out of him what he was doing on the night of the murder. You, I think, might put in a little good work in the servants' hall.'

But when he arrived at the Chestnuts Hannasyde was met by the intelligence that North had left the house immediately after lunch. The butler was unable to state his master's destination, but did not think, since he was driving himself in his touring car, that he was bound for his City office.

After a moment's consideration, Hannasyde asked to have his card taken to Mrs North. The butler accepted it, remarking repressively that he would see whether it were convenient for his mistress to receive him, and ushered him into the library.

Here he was presently joined by Miss Drew, who came in with her monocle screwed firmly into her eye, and a cigarette stuck into a long amber holder. 'My sister's resting, but she'll be down in a moment,' she informed him. 'What do you want to see her about?'

'I'll tell her, when she comes,' he replied politely.

She grinned. 'All right: I can take a snub. But if it's about that epic story Neville Fletcher burbled into your Sergeant's ears, I can tell you now you're wasting your time. It leads nowhere.'

'Epic story? Oh, you mean his adventures on the night of his uncle's death! No, I haven't come about that.'

'I quite thought you might have. I shouldn't have been altogether surprised had you asked to see me.'

'No? Are you concerned in those adventures?'

'Actually, I'm not, but Neville, who, you may have noticed, is rather reptilian, told the Sergeant, in his artless way, that I had plans for opening Ernie Fletcher's safe.'

'And had you?'

'Well, yes and no,' said Sally guardedly. 'If I'd had my criminal notebook with me, and time to think it out, I believe I could have had a stab at it. But one very valuable thing this case has taught me is that in real life one just doesn't have time. Of course, if I'd been writing this story, I should have thought up a perfectly plausible reason for the fictitious me to have had the means at hand of concocting the stuff you call soup. I should have turned myself into a scientist's assistant, with the run of his laboratory, or something like that. However, I'm nothing of the sort, so that wasn't much good.'

Hannasyde looked at her with a good deal of interest. 'Mr Fletcher's story was true, then, and not an attempt to keep the police amused?'

'You seem to have weighed him up pretty accurately,' commented Sally. 'But, as it happens, he really did come here to tell Helen (*a*) that his uncle had been murdered, and (*b*) that he hadn't managed to get hold of her IOUs. That, naturally, looked very bad to me. Of course, it was idiotic of my sister to co-opt Neville in the first place: she'd have done better to have put me on to it. You won't misunderstand me when I tell you that I was all for abstracting those IOUs from the safe before you could get your hands on them. Unfortunately, there was a policeman mounting guard over the study, which completely cramped my style.'

'I quite see your point,' said Hannasyde. 'But if you've made a study of crime you must know that it would have been quite culpable of you to have abstracted anything at all from the murdered man's safe.'

'Theoretically, yes; in practice, no,' responded Sally coolly. 'I knew that the IOUs had nothing whatsoever to do with the case. Naturally you can't be expected to know that, and just look at the trouble they're causing you! Not to mention the waste of time.'

'I appreciate your point of view, Miss Drew, but, as you have already realised, I don't share it. It seems to me that the IOUs may have a very direct bearing on the case.'

She gave a chuckle. 'Yes, wouldn't you love me to pour my girlish confidences into your ears? It's all right: I'm going to. If you're toying with the notion that my sister may have been the murderess, I can put you right straight away. Setting aside the fairly evident fact that she simply hasn't got it in her to smash anyone's head in, there wasn't a trace of blood on her frock or her cloak when she came home that night. If you want me to believe that she could have done the deed, and not got one drop of blood on her, you'll have to hypnotise me. Of course, I don't expect you to pay much heed to what I say, because I'm bound to stand by my sister, but you can interrogate her personal maid, can't you? She'll tell you that none of my sister's clothes have disappeared, or have been sent to the cleaners' during the past week.' She paused, extracted the end of her cigarette from the holder, and stubbed it out. 'But, as I see it, you don't really think she did it. The man you suspect is my brother-in-law, and I'm sure I don't blame you. Only there again I may be able to help you. You can take it from me that he doesn't know of the existence of those IOUs. I've no doubt that sounds a trifle fatuous to you, but it happens to be true. And – just in case you haven't grasped this one – he doesn't suspect my sister of having had any what-you-might-call improper dealings with Ernest Fletcher.' She stopped, and looked critically at him. 'I'm not making a hit with you at all. Why not? Don't you believe me?'

'Yes, I believe you're telling me what *you* believe to be the truth,' he answered. 'But it is just possible that you don't know the whole truth. If – for the sake of argument – your brother-in-law is the man I'm looking for, it must be obvious to you that he wouldn't give anything away, even to you.'

'That's perfectly true,' conceded Sally fair-mindedly. 'But there's one other point: my brother-in-law's no fool. If he'd done it, he'd have taken darned good care to have covered up his tracks.' She frowned suddenly, and began to fit another cigarette into her holder. 'Yes, I see there's a snag there. You think that he meant to, but that Helen's getting mixed up in it gummed up the works. You may be right, but if I were you I wouldn't bank on it.'

'At my job,' said Hannasyde, 'one learns not to bank on anything.'

He turned, for the door had opened, and Helen had come into the room. She looked tired, and rather strained, but greeted him quite calmly. 'Good-afternoon. I'm sorry to have kept you waiting. I was lying down.'

'I'm sorry to be obliged to disturb you, Mrs North,' he replied, 'but there are one or two points in your evidence which I want to go over with you again.'

She moved to a chair by the fireplace. 'Please sit down. I can't tell you anything more than I have, but, of course, I'll answer any questions you want to ask me.'

He took a seat beside a table near her, and laid on it his notebook. 'I am going to be perfectly frank with you, Mrs North, for I think it will save a great deal of time and misunderstanding if you know what facts are in my possession. Now, the first thing I am going to tell you is that I have proof that a certain man, who need not concern you much, since it is in the highest degree unlikely that you have ever heard of him, visited Ernest Fletcher at some time during the evening on which he was murdered.'

Her eyes were fixed upon his face with an expression in them of painful anxiety, but she merely said in a low voice: 'No doubt he was the man I saw. Go on, please.'

He opened his notebook. 'I am going to read to you, Mrs North, the sequence of events, between the hours of 9.35 and 10.05, according to your own evidence, and to that of the Constable who discovered Fletcher's body. If I have got any of the times wrong, you must stop me. To begin with, at 9.35 you arrived at the side entrance of Greystones. You noticed a short, stout man come out of the gate, just before you reached it, and walk away towards Vale Avenue.'

She was clasping the arms of her chair rather tensely, but when he paused, and looked inquiringly at her, she replied with composure. 'Yes, that is correct.'

'You entered the garden of Greystones, walked up the path, and found Ernest Fletcher alone in his study.'

'Yes.'

'At 9.45, after a short dispute with Fletcher, you left the study, by the way you had entered, unattended, and were about to go home, when you heard footsteps approaching up the path. You then concealed yourself behind a bush a few feet from the path.'

'Yes. I've already told you all this.'

'Just a moment, please. You were able to see that this new visitor was a man of medium height and build, wearing a light Homburg hat, and carrying no stick in his hand; but you were not able to recognise him.'

She said nervously: 'I thought he seemed to be quite an ordinary-looking person, but I only caught a glimpse of him, and the light had practically gone. I couldn't *swear* to anything about him.'

'We won't go into that at present. This man entered the study through the window, closing it behind him, and remained there until approximately 9.58. At 9.58, he came out of the study, followed by Fletcher, who escorted him in a leisurely fashion to the gate. As soon as both men were out of sight round the bend in the path, you went back into the study to search in the desk for your IOUs. You heard Fletcher returning to the house, and you escaped from the study before he reached it, passing through the door into the hall. While you were in the hall, the tall-case clock there struck the hour of 10.00. But I must tell you, Mrs North, that the clock was a minute slower than the one in the study, so that the time was actually one minute past ten.'

'I don't see –'

'I think you will, for I am coming now to the evidence of the Constable. At 10.02 he observed, from the point where Maple Grove runs into Vale Avenue, a man coming out of the side gate of Greystones, and making off towards the Arden Road. Thinking the circumstance suspicious, he made his way down Maple Grove, entered the garden of Greystones by the side gate, and walked up the path to the study window. There he discovered the body of Ernest Fletcher, lying across the desk, with his head smashed. The time then, Mrs North, was 10.05 p.m.'

She faltered: 'I don't think I understand.'

'If you think it over, I feel sure you will,' he suggested. 'If your evidence is true, Fletcher was alive at one minute past ten.'

'Yes,' she said hesitantly. 'Yes, of course he must have been.'

'Yet at 10.02 the Constable saw an unknown man coming out of the garden-gate; and by 10.05 Fletcher was dead, and there was no trace to be found of his murderer.'

'You mean it couldn't have happened?'

'Consider it for yourself, Mrs North. If you say that the man you saw left at 9.58, who was the man the Constable saw?'

'How can I possibly tell?'

'Can you suggest any reason to account for his presence in the garden?'

'No, of course I can't. Unless he murdered Ernie.'

'In considerably less than a minute?'

She stared at him uncomprehendingly. 'I suppose not. I don't know. Are you – are you accusing *me* of having murdered Ernie Fletcher?'

'No, Mrs North. But I am suggesting that you have falsified your evidence.'

'It's not true! I did see Ernie taking that man to the gate! If there was another man in the garden, I knew nothing of it. You've no right to say I falsified my evidence! Why should I?'

'If, Mrs North, you did, in point of fact, recognise the man who entered the garden, that in itself might constitute a very good reason for falsifying your evidence.'

Sally's hand descended on her sister's shoulder, and gripped it. 'Quiet. You're not obliged to answer.'

'But I didn't! What I told you was true! I know nothing about the second man, and since I heard Ernie whistling just before I went into the hall I presume he was alive at a minute past ten. You want me to say he didn't see that man out, but you won't succeed! He *did*!'

'That's enough,' said Sally. She looked across at Hannasyde. 'My sister is entitled to see her solicitor before she answers any questions, I think. Well, she isn't going to say any more now. You've heard her evidence: if you can't make it fit with your constable's evidence, that's your look out, not hers.'

She spoke with considerable pugnacity, but Hannasyde replied without any apparent loss of temper: 'Certainly she may consult her solicitor before answering me. I think she would be wise to. But perhaps she will be good enough to tell me where I may find Mr John North?'

'I don't know!' Helen said sharply. 'He didn't tell me where he was going. All I can tell you is that he isn't coming back to dinner, and may be late home.'

'Thank you,' said Hannasyde, rising to his feet. 'Then I won't detain you any longer, Mrs North.'

Helen stretched her hand towards the bell, but Sally said curtly: 'I'll see him out,' and strode to the door and opened it.

When she returned to the library she found her sister pacing up and down, a twisted handkerchief being jerked between her hands. She looked at her under frowning brows, and inquired: 'So now what?'

'What am I going to do?'

'Search me. Do you feel inclined to tell me the truth?'

'What I have already said is the truth, and nothing will make me go back on it!' Helen said, holding Sally's eyes with her own.

There was a slight pause. 'All right,' Sally said. 'I don't know that I blame you.'

Ten

Joining his superior outside the gate, Sergeant Hemingway said: 'Nothing much to be made of it my end. Did you shake the fair Helen?'

'No. She's sticking to it that her story's true. She's bound to, of course. I didn't expect her to go back on it. What I did want to do – and what I rather fancy I succeeded in doing – was to frighten her. Did you get anything out of the servants?'

'Precious little. The butler saw young Neville walking off down the drive at about 12.30 that night, which makes it look as though what he told me was true. Otherwise, I wasted my time. Old-fashioned sort of servants: been employed there several years, seem to be fond of both master and mistress, and aren't talking. Come to think of it, it's a pity there aren't more like them – though not from our point of view. Did you get the impression Mrs North was working in cahoots with her husband, or what?'

'I don't know. Her sister warned her not to answer me until she'd seen her solicitor, so I didn't press the matter.'

'Just about what that dame with the eyeglass would do!' remarked the Sergeant disapprovingly. 'In my young days women didn't know anything about such things. I don't believe in all this emancipation. It isn't natural. What are we going to do now? Get after young Neville?'

'No. I'm going back to the police station. It's no use my tackling Neville. I haven't anything against him, except the state of his bank overdraft, and he knows it. I'm hoping Glass may have managed to make contact with that postman. As far as I can see, the two people we've got to get hold of are North and Carpenter. I'll put a call through to North's office, and find out if he's there, or has been there. With any luck Jevons has been able to ferret out some more information about Angela Angel. I put him on to that first thing this morning. Which reminds me that there's one thing I want to pick up, and that's a photograph of Fletcher. We'll call in at Greystones on our way, and borrow one from his sister. I take it no photograph was found amongst Angela Angel's possessions?'

'Only a few of stage pals, and one of Charlie Carpenter. I asked Jimmy Gale particularly, but he was positive there wasn't one of the man who'd been keeping her. Few flies on the late Ernest. Think Angela's an important factor, Chief?'

Hannasyde did not answer for a moment. As they turned in at the front gate of Greystones, he said: 'I hardly know. If North's our man, I should say not. But in some way or other she seems to be linked up with the case. It won't do any harm to see what we can find out about her.'

He rang the front-door bell, and in a few minutes the door was opened by Simmons, who, however, told them that his mistress had gone out. Hannasyde was about to ask him if he could produce a photograph of his master when Neville strayed into the hall from a room overlooking the drive, and said with his shy, slow smile: 'How lovely for me! I was getting so tired of my own company, and I daren't go out in case you're having me watched. My aunt wouldn't like it if I became conspicuous. But where's the Comic Strip? You don't mean to tell me you haven't brought him?'

The Sergeant put up a hand to his mouth. Neville's large eyes reproached him. 'You can't like me as much as I thought you did,' he said, softly slurring his words. 'I've learnt two new bits to say to him, and I'm sure I shan't be able to carry them in my head much longer.'

The Sergeant had to fight against a desire to ask what the new bits might be. He said: 'Ah, I daresay, sir!' in a non-committal tone.

Young Mr Fletcher, who seemed to have an uncanny knack of reading people's thoughts, said confidentially: 'I know you want me to tell you what they are. I would – though you oughtn't to try and pick my brains, you know – if it weren't for the Superintendent's being with you. You understand what I mean: they're awfully broad – not to say vulgar.'

The Sergeant cast an imploring glance at his superior, who said with an unmoved countenance: 'You can tell the Sergeant some other time, Mr Fletcher. I called in the hope of seeing your aunt, but perhaps you can help me in her stead. Have you a photograph of your uncle which you could let me borrow for a few days?'

'Oh no!' said Neville. 'I mean, I haven't. But if I had I wouldn't lend it to you: I'd give it to you.'

'Extremely kind of you, but –'

'Well, it isn't really,' Neville explained, 'because I hate photographs. I'll tell you what I'll do: I'll give you the one that stands on a table all to itself in the drawing-room. As a matter of fact, I was wondering what next I could do to annoy my aunt.'

'I have no wish to annoy Miss Fletcher. Isn't there some other –'

'No, but I have,' said Neville in his gentle way. 'I shan't tell her I gave it to you, and then she'll organise a search for it. That will be uncomfortable, of course, but since I started to do good turns I've found that they invariably entail a certain amount of self-immolation, which has a very degrading effect on the character.' Talking all the time, he had led the way into the drawing-room, where, as he had described, a large studio portrait of his uncle stood in solitary state upon an incidental table. He stopped in front of it, and murmured: 'Isn't it a treat?'

'I don't want to borrow a photograph which Miss Fletcher obviously values,' said Hannasyde somewhat testily. 'Surely there must be another somewhere.'

'Oh, there is, beside my aunt's bed! But I shan't let you have that, because it wouldn't suit my book. There's an almost indistinguishable but certainly existent line drawn between the counter and the added irritant.'

'I'm bothered if I know what you're talking about, sir!' said the Sergeant, unable to contain himself. 'Nice way to treat your poor aunt!'

The flickering gaze rested on his face for an instant. 'Yes, isn't it? Will you have it with or without frame, Superintendent?'

'Without, please,' Hannasyde replied, looking at him a little curiously. 'I think I understand. Your methods are slightly original, aren't they?'

'I'm so glad you didn't say eccentric,' said Neville, extracting the portrait from its frame. 'I hate being called eccentric. Term employed by mediocre minds to describe pure rationalism. Now I will hide the frame, and bribe Simmons to keep his mouth shut. Practically the only advantage I have yet discovered in inheriting a fortune is the ability it confers on one to exercise the unholy power of bribery.'

'And then I suppose you'll join in the search for it?' said the Sergeant, torn between disapproval and amusement.

'No, that would savour strongly of hypocrisy,' answered Neville serenely. 'There you are, Super-intendent. I shan't invite you to stay and have tea, because my aunt might come back.'

Once outside the house, the Sergeant said: 'Came over me in a flash! Do you know what that silly smile of his makes me think of, Super?'

'No, what?'

'That picture people make such a fuss about, though why I've never been able to make out. Pie-faced creature, with a nasty, sly smile.'

'The Mona Lisa!' Hannasyde laughed suddenly. 'Yes, I see what you mean. Odd young man. I can't make up my mind about him at all.'

'There are times,' said the Sergeant, 'when I'd ask nothing better than to be able to pin this murder on to him. However, I'm bound to say it isn't, to my way of thinking, arty enough for him. My lord would go all out for something pretty subtle, if you ask me.'

'I shouldn't be at all surprised if you're right,' said Hannasyde.

In another few minutes they boarded an omnibus which set them down within a stone's throw of the police station. PC Glass had not returned from his quest, and Hannasyde, having ascertained over the telephone that North was not at his office, put through a call to Scotland Yard, and asked whether Inspector Jevons had come in. He was soon connected with the Inspector, who had, however, little to report. He had discovered the block of flats in which her unknown protector had installed Angela Angel, but her apartment had been rented by a man calling himself Smith. The hall porter was sure he would recognise the gentleman if he saw him again, and described him as being slim, dark, and very well dressed.

Hannasyde glanced at his watch, and decided to return to London, leaving the Sergeant to pick up any information that Glass might bring in. He appointed a meeting-time at Headquarters, and went off, bearing the portrait of Fletcher with him.

It was some little while before Glass presented himself, and when he did arrive he appeared to be suffering from strong indignation. He no sooner set eyes on the Sergeant than he said sternly: 'Whoso causeth the righteous to go astray in an evil way, he shall fall himself into his own pit!'

'What on earth's the matter with you?' said the Sergeant. 'You can't have been on the jag, because the pubs aren't open yet.'

'Let them be ashamed and confounded together that seek after my soul to destroy it! I will turn away mine eyes from beholding vanity; I am like a green olive tree in the house of the Lord.'

'Look here, what the devil have you been up to?' demanded the Sergeant.

Glass fixed him with a sombre glare. 'Mine eyes have beheld lewdness, and a Babylonish woman!' he announced.

'Where?' asked the Sergeant, suddenly interested.

'In a glittering house of corruption I have seen these things. I have escaped from an horrible pit.'

'If you mean what I think you do, all I can say is that I'm ashamed of you,' said the Sergeant severely. 'What were you doing in that kind of a house, I'd like to know? The Chief told you to find the postman; instead of obeying orders you go and –'

'I have done as I was bidden. I have found him though my feet were led in the path of destruction.'

'Now, look here, my lad, that's quite enough. There's no need to go nuts over the postman's morals. It doesn't matter to you where you found him, as long as you did find him – though I must say I'd no idea postmen got up to those kinds of larks in the suburbs. Did you get his evidence?'

'I summoned him forth from that place of sin, yes, and his wife also –'

'What?' exclaimed the Sergeant. 'Here, where *was* the poor fellow?'

'In a playhouse, which is an habitation of the devil.'

'Do you mean to tell me all this song and dance is because the postman took his wife to the pictures in his off-time?' gasped the Sergeant. 'It's my belief you're crazy! Now, cut it out, and let's get down to brass tacks!

Did he see Mrs North on the night of the murder, or did he not?'

'I have roared by reason of the disquietness of my heart,' apologised Glass, with a groan. 'But I will make my report.' He produced a notebook, and with a bewilderingly sudden change from zeal to officialdom, read in a toneless voice: 'On the night of 17 June, having cleared the box at the corner of Glynne Road at 10.00 p.m. precisely, the postman, by name Horace Smart, of 14 Astley Villas, Marley, mounted his bicycle, and proceeded in an easterly direction, passing the gates of Greystones. Smart states he saw a woman walking down the drive.'

'Did he notice whether she was carrying anything?'

'He states that she carried nothing, that when he saw her she had one hand raised to hold her hair against the breeze. With the other she held up the skirts of her dress.'

'Did he recognise –' The Sergeant broke off to answer the telephone, which at that moment interrupted him. 'Scotland Yard? Right! Put 'em through . . . Hullo? Hemingway speaking.'

'We've got Carpenter for you,' announced a voice at the other end of the line.

'You have?' said the Sergeant incredulously. 'Nice work! Where is he?'

'We don't know that, but we can tell you where he will be this evening. Got it through Light-Fingered Alec, who says Carpenter's hanging out in a basement room at 43 Barnsley Street, W. That's –'

'Half a shake!' said the Sergeant, reaching for a pencil. '43 Barnsley Street, W. – basement room. Where is Barnsley Street?'

'I'm telling you. You know the Glassmere Road? Well, Barnsley Street leads out of it into Letchley Gardens.'

'Letchley Gardens? Classy address for friend Carpenter.'

'It would be if he lived there, but he doesn't. Barnsley Street's not so hot. No. 43 looks like a lodging-house. Do you want Carpenter pulled in?'

'I thought you said you didn't know where he was?'

'We don't, but his landlady might.'

The Sergeant thought for a moment, and then said: 'No. You never know, and we don't want to give him warning we're on to him. He'll keep till he gets home. I'm meeting the Superintendent at the Yard when I get through here. We'll go along to this Barnsley Street then, and catch his lordship unawares.'

'Well, from what Light-Fingered Alec told Fenton, you won't find him till latish. He's got a job in some restaurant. Anything else we can do for you?'

'Not that I know of. If he's working in a restaurant, the Chief may decide to pick him up in the morning. Anyway, I'll be seeing you. So long!' He replaced the receiver, and said with satisfaction: 'Well, now we are getting on, and no mistake!' He found that Glass was still waiting, open notebook in hand, and his eyes fixed on his face, and said: 'Oh yes, you! What was I saying?'

'You were about to ask me whether the man Smart recognised the woman he saw. And I answer you, No. He rode upon the other side of the road, and saw but the figure of a female, her robe caught up in one hand, the other smoothing her hair, which the breeze ruffled.'

'Oh well, there doesn't seem to be much doubt it was Mrs North, anyway!' said the Sergeant. He collected his papers together and got up. The Constable was apparently still brooding over the experience through which he had passed, for he said with a shudder: 'The lamp of the wicked shall be put out: but the tabernacle of the righteous shall flourish.'

'I daresay,' agreed the Sergeant, bestowing his papers in his case. 'But if the picture you saw was wicked enough to set you off like this, all I can say is I wish I'd seen it. I've never struck a really hot one in my life – not what I call hot, that is.'

'How long shall thy vain thoughts lodge within thee?' demanded Glass. 'I tell you, when the wicked perish there is shouting!'

'You go off home, and treat yourself to a nice aspirin,' recommended the Sergeant. 'I've had enough of you for one day.'

'I will go,' Glass replied, restoring his notebook to his pocket. 'I am tossed up and down as the locust.'

The Sergeant deigned no reply, but walked out of the office. Later, when he met Superintendent Hannasyde in his room at Scotland Yard, he said: 'You've properly put your foot into it now, Chief. Turned poor old Glass into a locust, that's what you've done. You never heard such a commotion in your life!'

'What on earth – ?'

'Led his feet into a horrible pit,' said the Sergeant with unction. 'I've sent him off duty to get over it.'

'What are you talking about?' said Hannasyde impatiently. 'If you'd forget Glass and attend to this case –'

'Forget him! I wish I could! Thanks to you, he's been to the pictures, and what he's got to say about it would make your hair stand on end. However, he found the postman, and Mrs North *was* seen about ten o'clock – though not recognised – and she was not carrying anything. So at any rate she was speaking the truth about the time she left Greystones. You heard about Carpenter?'

'Yes, I've been talking to Fenton about that. From what he could pick up from this Light-Fingered Alec of his, it looks as though we ought to find Carpenter at home any time after 9.30 p.m. We'll drop round to see him, Skipper.'

The Sergeant nodded. 'Right you are. What time?'

'Oh! Give him half-an-hour's law, just to be sure of catching him. I'll meet you at the corner of Glassmere Road and Barnsley Street at 10.00 p.m. Meanwhile, you'll like to hear that the hall porter at Chumley Mansions recognised Fletcher's photograph as soon as I showed it to him. He was "Smith" all right.'

'Well, we never had much doubt, did we?' said the Sergeant. 'Was he able to tell you anything more?'

'Nothing of much use to us. Like everyone else who came into contact with Fletcher, he seems to have found him invariably pleasant. He knows nothing more about the girl than he told Gale at the time of her death.'

'I must say it looks as though Angela Angel's suicide and the late Ernest's murder do hang together,' pondered the Sergeant. 'But I'm damned if I see where North fits into it, if they do.'

'We shall probably know more when we've heard what Carpenter has to say,' replied Hannasyde.

'What you might call the key to the whole mystery,' agreed the Sergeant.

He arrived a little before ten o'clock at the appointed rendezvous that evening, and found Barnsley Street to be a drab road connecting the main thoroughfare of Glassmere Road with the prim respectability of Letchley Gardens. Glassmere Road, which the Sergeant knew well, was a busy street, and at the corner of Barosley Street, close to an omnibus stopping-place, was a coffee-stall. The Sergeant bought himself a cup of coffee, and entered into idle chat with the proprietor. He was soon joined by Hannasyde, who came walking along the Glassmere Road from an Underground Railway Station a few hundred yards distant.

'Evening,' Hannasyde said, nodding to the coffee-stall proprietor. 'Not much of a pitch, this, is it?'

'Not bad,' replied the man. He jerked his thumb over his shoulder. 'I get folks coming out of the Regal Cinema later on. Of course, it's quiet now, but then, it's early. Can't complain.'

The Sergeant pushed his empty cup and saucer across the counter, bade the man a cheerful good-night, and strolled away with his superior.

The sky was overcast, and although the daylight had not yet failed entirely, it was growing dark. Barnsley Street, curling round in a half-circle towards Letchley Gardens, was ill lit, a depressing street lined with thin, drab houses. No. 43 was discovered midway down it. A card in the window on the ground-floor advertised Apartments, and a shallow flight of six steps led up to the front door. A light was burning at the top of the house, but the basement was in darkness. 'Looks as though we're too early,' remarked the Sergeant, pulling the bell-knob. 'Of course, if he's got a job at a really swell restaurant, it isn't likely he'd be back yet.'

'We can but try,' Hannasyde replied.

After an interval, the Sergeant pulled the bell again. He was about to pull it a third time when a light appeared in the fanlight over the door, and slip-shod feet were heard approaching inside the house.

The door was opened by a stout lady of disagreeable aspect, who held it slightly ajar, and said pugnaciously: 'Well? What do you want? If you've come about lodgings, I'm full up.'

'If I had, that would break my heart,' said the Sergeant instantly. 'I don't know when I've taken such a fancy to anyone as I have to you. Came over me the instant I laid eyes on you.'

'I don't want none of your sauce,' responded the lady, eyeing him with acute dislike.

'Well, tell me this: is Mr Carpenter in?'

'If it's him you want, why don't you go down the area steps? Pealing the bell, and having me down from the top of the house, as though I'd nothing better to do than run up and down stairs the whole evening!'

'Run?' said the Sergeant. 'Go on! You couldn't! Now, put a sock in it, and let's have a real heart to heart. Is Charlie Carpenter in?'

She said grudgingly: 'Yes, he's in. If you want him, you can go down and knock on his door.'

'Thank you for nothing,' said the Sergeant. 'You let me see this running act of yours. You and me will trip downstairs, and you'll do the knocking, after which you'll tell Mr Charlie Carpenter to shut his eyes and open the door, and see what the fairies have brought him.'

'Oh, I will, will I?' said the lady, bristling. 'And who says so?'

The Sergeant produced his card, and showed it to her.

'That's the name, Clara, but if you like you can call me Willy, seeing that you're so stuck on me. Come on, now, get a move on!'

She read the card painstakingly, and seemed to feel an increased aversion from him. 'I'm a respectable woman, and I don't want any busies nosing round my house, nor there's no reason why I should have them what's more. If that young fellow's been up to any tricks, it's no business of mine, and so I'll have you know!'

'Well, now that I know it, let's get going,' said the Sergeant.

She led the way, grumbling under her breath, to the top of the basement stairs. Hannasyde nodded to the Sergeant, and himself remained on the doorstep, keeping a strategic eye on the area.

No reply was made to the landlady's imperative knock on the door of the basement room, nor was any sound audible.

'Funny. He don't generally go to bed early,' remarked the landlady, renewing her assault upon the door. 'I daresay he's gone out again. Well, I hope you're satisfied, that's all.'

'Just a moment, sister!' said the Sergeant, pushing her aside. 'No objection to my having a look round, have you?'

He turned the handle as he spoke. The door opened, and he groped for the light-switch. 'Looks as though you're right,' he remarked, stepping into the room.

But the landlady was not right. Charlie Carpenter had not gone out. He was lying fully dressed across the bed that was pushed against the wall opposite the door, and he was, as the Sergeant saw at a glance, dead.

The landlady, peeping over the Sergeant's shoulder, gave a piercing shriek, and cowered away from the door into the gloom of the passage.

'Shut up!' said the Sergeant curtly. He walked across the room, and bent over the tumbled body, feeling its hands. They were quite warm.

Hannasyde's voice sounded on the stairs. 'Anything wrong, Hemingway?' he called.

The Sergeant went to the door. 'We're just a bit too late, Chief, that's what's wrong,' he said. 'You come and see.'

Hannasyde descended the stairs, cast one shrewd glance at the landlady's pallid countenance, and strode into the front room.

The Sergeant was standing beside the bed, his bright eyes dispassionately surveying the dead man. At Hannasyde's involuntary exclamation, he looked up. 'Something we *weren't* expecting,' he remarked.

Hannasyde bent over the body, his face very grim. Carpenter had been killed as Ernest Fletcher had been killed, but whereas Fletcher had apparently been taken unawares, some struggle had taken place in this dingy basement room. A chair had been overturned, a mat rucked up, and above the dead man's crumpled collar a bruise on his throat showed dark on the white skin.

'Same method – probably the same weapon. But this man knew what to expect,' Hannasyde muttered. He glanced over his shoulder. 'Get on to the Department, Hemingway. And get rid of that woman. Tell her she'll have to answer questions. Not that she's likely to know anything.'

The Sergeant nodded, and went out. Left alone in the

room, Hannasyde turned his attention from the body to his surroundings. These told him little enough. The room was sparsely furnished, but had been embellished by a number of photographs and coloured pictures, some framed, some pinned on the wall, or stuck into the frame of the spotted mirror over the fireplace. A curtain, drawn across one corner of the room, concealed from view several cheap suits, and a few pairs of shoes. On the dressing-table before the window were ranged bottles of hair oil, shaving lotion, nail varnish, and scent. Hannasyde grimaced at them, and taking out his handkerchief, covered his hand with it, and pulled open the two top drawers of the table. A motley-coloured collection of socks and handkerchiefs was all that one contained, but in the other, under a pile of ties, were scattered a number of letters, old programmes, playbills, and Press cuttings.

Hannasyde had gathered all these together into a heap by the time the Sergeant returned, and was standing looking at a photograph, cut from a picture paper, which he held in his hand. He looked round as the Sergeant entered the room, and held the cutting out to him without comment.

The Sergeant took it, and read out: '*Snapped at the Races, the Hon. Mrs Donne, Miss Claudine Swithin, and Mr Ernest Fletcher.* You don't say! Well, X has been eliminated all right, hasn't he, Chief? Find anything else?'

'Not yet. I'll wait till the room's been gone over for possible finger-prints.' Still with his hand wrapped up, he extracted the key from the door, fitted it in again on the outside, and went out.

The Sergeant followed him, watched him lock the

door and pocket the key, and said: 'The old girl's in the kitchen. What do you want me to do?'

'Find out if the man at the coffee-stall saw anyone passing down this road about half-an-hour ago. Wait, I'll try and get out of the landlady exactly when Carpenter came home.'

He walked down the passage to the kitchen at the back of the house, where he found the landlady fortifying herself with gin. She whisked the bottle out of sight when he appeared, and broke at once into a torrent of words. She knew nothing; and her poor husband, whom the shock would kill, was upstairs in bed with the influenza, and she had been with him for the past hour. All she could take her oath to was that Carpenter was alive at 9.30, because he had shouted up the stairs to her, wanting to know if a parcel of shoes hadn't come for him from the cobbler, as though she wouldn't have put it in his room if it had, as she told him, pretty straight.

'Steady! Could anyone have entered the house without your knowing it?' Hannasyde asked.

'They did, that's all I know,' she said sullenly. 'If someone got in, it must have been by the area door, and it isn't my blame. Carpenter, he ought to have bolted it when he come in. 'Tisn't the first time he's been too lazy to put the chain up. The key's lost. I've been meaning to get a new one made.'

'Did he use that door?'

'Yes, he did. Saved trouble, see?'

'Who else is in the house?'

'Me and my 'usband, and my gal, Gladys, and the first-floor front.'

'Who is that?'

'A very nice lady. Stage, but she's resting.'

'Who is on the ground-floor?'

'No one. He's away. His name's Barnes. He travels in soap.'

'How long has Carpenter lodged here?'

'Six months. He was a nice young fellow. Smart, too.'

'Were you friendly with him? Did he tell you anything about himself?'

'No. Ask no questions and you'll be told no lies, is what I say. As long as he paid his rent, nothing else didn't matter to me. I guessed he'd had his bit of trouble, but I'm not one for poking my nose into what don't concern me. Live and let live's my motto.'

'All right, that's all for the present.' Hannasyde left her, and went along the passage to the door that gave on to the area. The bolts were drawn back, and the chain hung loose beside the wall.

A few minutes later the police ambulance drew up outside the house. The divisional surgeon, the photographer, and the finger-print expert were soon busy in the basement room, and a fresh-faced young sergeant was dispatched to assist Hemingway in his search for possible witnesses.

Sergeant Hemingway returned just after Carpenter's body had been removed, and joined Hannasyde in the basement room, where he was engaged, with the help of an inspector, in searching through the dead man's possessions.

'Well?' Hannasyde said.

'Yes, I got something,' the Sergeant answered. 'The coffee-merchant only arrived at his pitch at 9.30, since when, Chief, the only person he's seen come down the road, setting aside you, me and the Constable on his beat, was a medium-sized man in evening dress, who walked quickly down the other side of the street, making for the taxi-rank in Glassmere Road. And what do you make of that?'

'Any description?'

'No. He didn't notice him particularly. Says it was too dark to see his face. But what he does say, Super, is that he wasn't wearing an overcoat, and he wasn't carrying anything in his hands. Talk about history repeating itself! I don't need to ask if you've found the weapon here. I wouldn't believe you if you said you had.'

'I haven't. Did you find anyone to corroborate the coffee-stall owner's evidence?'

'If you can call it corroboration,' said the Sergeant with a sniff. 'There's a couple propping the wall up at the other end of the street. You know the style: kissing and canoodling for the past hour. I wouldn't set much store by what they say, but for what it's worth the girl seems to think she saw a gentleman in evening dress and an opera hat pass by about half-an-hour ago. Not what you'd call a lot of traffic on this road. I've put Lyne on to the houses opposite, on the chance someone may have been looking out of a window.'

'Did the couple at the other end of the street notice whether the man in evening dress was carrying a stick?'

'Not they. First thing they said was they hadn't noticed anyone at all. I had to press them a bit before they came out of the ether, so to speak. Then the girl remembered seeing a man with a white shirt-front on the other side of the road, and the boy-friend says after thinking hard, yes, he believes he did see someone, only he didn't look at him particularly, and whether it was before or after the

Constable passed them, he wouldn't like to say. Actually, it was just before, if the coffee-merchant is to be believed, which I think he is. What's more, they were going opposite ways, and there's an outside chance they may have passed each other. Shall I get hold of the chap who has this beat?'

'Yes, as soon as possible. Obviously he saw nothing suspicious, but if he did meet the man in evening dress he may be able to describe him.'

'Not much doubt who he was, if you ask me,' said the Sergeant. 'It's North all right. But what he does with his weapon has me fairly beat. Sleight-of-hand isn't in it with that chap. You got any ideas, Chief?'

'No. Nor have I any idea why, if it was he, he had to kill Carpenter.'

The Sergeant stared at him. 'Well, but it's plain enough, isn't it, Chief? Carpenter must have seen the murder of the late Ernest. My own hunch is that he was trying his hand at blackmailing North for a change.'

'Look here, Hemingway, if Carpenter was shown off the premises at 9.58 by Fletcher, how can he have seen the murder?'

'Perhaps he wasn't shown off the premises,' said the Sergeant slowly. 'Perhaps Mrs North made that up.' He paused, and scratched his chin. 'Yes, I see what you mean. Getting what you might call involved, isn't it? It looks to me as though Charlie Carpenter knew a sight more about this business than we gave him credit for.'

Eleven

The amorous couple, interrogated at the police station by Hannasyde, were eager to be of assistance, but as their evidence was vague, and often contradictory, it was not felt that either could be considered a valuable witness. The girl, who was an under-housemaid enjoying her evening out, no sooner discovered that the fact of her having seen a man in evening dress was considered important by the police than she at once began to imagine that she had noticed more than she had at first admitted.

'I thought he looked queer,' she informed Hannasyde. 'Oo, I thought, you do look queer! You know: funny.'

'In what way funny?' asked Hannasyde.

'Oh, I don't know! I mean, I can't say exactly, but there was something about him, the way he was walking – awfully fast, you know. He looked like a gangster to me.'

At this point her swain intervened. 'Go on!' he said. 'You never!'

'Oh, I did, Syd, honest, I did!'

'You never said nothing to me about it.'

'No, but I got a *feeling*,' said Miss Jenkins mysteriously.

'You and your feelings!'

'Tell me this,' interposed Hannasyde. 'Was the man dark or fair?'

But Miss Jenkins refused to commit herself on this point. Pressed, she said that it was too dark to see. Mr Sydney Potter said indulgently: 'You never sor a thing. It was this way, sir: me and my young lady were having what you might call a chat. We didn't notice no one particularly. What I mean is, not to be sure of them.'

'Did you see the man in evening dress?'

Mr Potter said cautiously: 'Not to remember, I didn't. There was two or three people passed, but I didn't take no notice. It's like this: I do seem to think there was a toff walking down the other side of the road, but I wouldn't like to swear to it.'

'Yes, and he must have met the policeman, what's more,' put in Miss Jenkins. 'It was just a minute after he went by that I saw the policeman. Fancy if he done it under the policeman's nose, as you might say. Oo, some people haven't half got a nerve! I sort of *know* it was a gangster.'

'You're barmy! The policeman came by ages before,' said Mr Potter fondly. 'Go on, put a sock in it! You don't remember nothing.'

This opinion was shared by Sergeant Hemingway, who said disgustedly as soon as the couple had departed: 'Nice pair of witnesses, I *don't* think! If they were carrying on the whole evening like they were when I found them, it's a wonder to me they saw anyone. Proper necking-party. I'm bothered if I know how people keep it up for the hours they do. The girl wants to see her picture in the papers, I've met her sort before.

Potter's not much better, either. In fact, they're neither of them any good.'

'Except that the girl did see a man in evening dress, which corroborates the coffee-stall proprietor's story. We'll see what the policeman has to say. If the girl was speaking the truth about his having passed just after she saw the man in evening dress, we may get somewhere.'

But when Constable Mather, a freckle-faced and serious young man, came in, he said regretfully that when he passed up Barnsley Street he had seen nothing of any man in evening dress.

'There you are!' said Hemingway, exasperated. 'What did I tell you? Just making up a good tale, that's all the silly little fool was doing.'

Hannasyde addressed the young policeman. 'When you passed, did you happen to notice whether the light was on in the basement of No. 43?'

'That's Mrs Prim's,' said Mather. 'If you'll excuse me, I'll have to think a minute, sir.'

The Sergeant regarded him with bird-like curiosity, and said: 'Either you know or you don't.'

The grave grey eyes came to rest on his face. 'Not till I've walked up the road, sir. I'm doing that now – if you wouldn't mind waiting a minute. I find I can think back if I do that.'

'Carry on,' said Hannasyde, quelling the sceptical Sergeant with a frown.

There was a pause, during with PC Mather apparently projected his spirit back to Barnsley Street. At last he said with decision: 'Yes, sir, it was. No. 39 – that's Mrs Dugdale's – had a window open, but she's got bars up, so it didn't matter. Then the next house, which is

No. 41, was all dark, and after that there was one with the basement light on. That was No. 43.'

'I see,' Hannasyde said. 'You feel sure of that?'

'Yes, sir.'

'You didn't hear any sounds coming from that basement room, or notice anything wrong?'

'No, sir. The blind was drawn down, and I didn't hear anything.'

'If the light was on, the murderer may have been there,' said the Sergeant. 'In fact, it looks to me as though he was there, having done in Carpenter, waiting till you'd passed to make his escape.'

The Constable looked distressed. 'Yes, sir. I'm sure I'm very sorry.'

'Not your fault,' said Hannasyde, and dismissed him.

'Nice case, isn't it?' said the Sergeant. 'Now we only want to find that the taxi-driver didn't happen to notice what his face looked like, and we'll be sitting pretty.'

He was not destined to be disappointed. Some time later, when he and Hannasyde were back at Scotland Yard, a message was received to the effect that one Henry Smith, taxi-driver, while waiting in the rank in Glassmere Road, had been engaged by a gentleman in evening dress, and directed to drive to the Piccadilly Hotel. Whether his fare had actually entered the hotel, he was unable to say. He had not inspected the gentleman closely, but retained an impression of a man of medium height and build. He did not recall the man's face particularly; he was just an ordinary, nice-looking chap.

'Well, at any rate it can't have been Budd,' remarked the Sergeant. 'No one in their senses would call him nice-looking. We've drawn a blank on the finger-prints, Chief. Whoever did this job wore gloves.'

'And no trace of the weapon,' Hannasyde said, frowning. 'A heavy, blunt instrument, wielded with considerable strength. In fact, exactly the same instrument that was used to kill Fletcher.'

'It's nice to think we didn't overlook it at Greystones, at all events,' said the Sergeant cheerfully. 'The murderer must have walked off with it under his hat. Have you got anything out of Carpenter's papers?'

'Nothing that looks like being of much assistance. There's this.'

The Sergeant took a limp, folded letter from him, and spread it open. A glance at the signature made him exclaim: 'Angela! Well, well, well!'

The letter, which was undated, was not a long one. Written in a round, unformed hand, it began abruptly: *Charlie – By the time you get this I won't be at our old address any more. I don't think you really care, but I wouldn't want to do it without telling you, because in spite of everything, and the wrong you have fallen into, dear Charlie, and the evil companions, and everything, I don't ever forget the old times. But I know now it wasn't the real thing, because I have found the real thing, and I see everything differently. I shan't tell you his name, because I know you, Charlie, you are without truth and would make trouble if you could. Don't think it is because of the disgrace you have got into that I am leaving you, because I know now that love is as strong as death, and if it had been the real thing I would have stuck to you, because many waters cannot quench love, neither can the floods drown it. They used to teach us that that bit and all the rest was about the Church, but I know better now.*

The Sergeant read this missive, remarking as he gave

it back to Hannasyde: 'She *had* got it bad, hadn't she? Fancy anyone feeling that way about the late Ernest! Looks as though she must have written it when Charlie was in jug. What you might call corroborative evidence only. She probably did do herself in for love of the late Ernest, and Charlie *was* the sort of dirty little squirt who'd put the black on anyone if he saw his way to it. And where are we now? Do you take it that Carpenter saw the late Ernest murdered?'

'If he did, it raises one or two questions,' replied Hannasyde. 'Did the murderer not only see Carpenter, but also recognise him? Or did Carpenter recognise the murderer, and attempt to blackmail him?'

'Look here, Chief, are we casting North for the part, or are we assuming the murderer is an entirely new and unsuspected character, whom we haven't even laid eyes on?'

'How do I know? I admit, nearly everything points to North. Not quite, though. In favour of that theory, we have North's unexpected return to England, his unexplained movements on the night of the murder, Mrs North's peculiar behaviour, and the presence of a man in Barnsley Street tonight who corresponds vaguely with his description. Against it, I think we ought to set North's character first. I have his sister-in-law's word for it that he's no fool, and I believe it. But what could be more blundering and foolish than to murder a second man in precisely the same way as he murdered the first?'

'I don't know so much,' interrupted the Sergeant. 'Come to think of it, it's worrying us a bit, isn't it? If he's the smart Alec you say he is, it might strike him as a pretty fruity idea to do in his victims as clumsily as he could. Moreover, it's not as dumb as it looks. He doesn't leave his finger-prints behind him, and he's got some trick of concealing his weapon which a conjurer couldn't better.'

'Yes, I've thought of that,' admitted Hannasyde. 'But there are other points. Where and when did a man in his position come into contact with Carpenter?'

'At Greystones, on the night of the late Ernest's murder,' replied the Sergeant promptly. 'Look, Super! Supposing you forget Mrs North's second instalment for the moment. Take it that Carpenter was hiding in the garden all the time she was with the late Ernest –'

'What the devil would he be hiding for, if he had come to blackmail Fletcher?'

The Sergeant thought for a moment. 'How about his having hidden for exactly the same reason Mrs North did? He may have been walking up the path when he heard her open the gate behind him –'

'Impossible. If that were so, he must have met Budd, and he didn't.'

'All right,' said the Sergeant, in long-suffering accents. 'We'll take it he was there all the time. Came in while Budd was with the late Ernest. Instead of hopping out of his hiding-place the instant Budd left, he waited a moment to be sure the coast was clear. Then Mrs North came into the garden, and he continued to lie low. When she left the late Ernest, North had just arrived. She hid, just as she told us, recognised her husband, and bunked – No, she didn't, though! The postman saw her leaving by the front entrance just after 10.00! Wait a bit! Yes, I've got it. North killed the late Ernest somewhere between 9.45 and 10.00, and left by way of the garden-gate, watched by Mrs North, and our friend Charlie. Not knowing of Charlie's presence, Mrs North slipped into the study, just to see what kind of fun and games had been going on, found the late Ernest, got into a panic, and bunked through the house. Carpenter, meanwhile, made his exit by way of the garden-gate – time 10.02 – was seen by Ichabod, and bolted in the same direction that North had taken. He came in sight of North, followed him –'

'Followed him where?'

'Back to town, I suppose. He must have tracked him to his flat to have found out who he was. After that he tried his blackmailing game on North, and North naturally had to eliminate him. How do you like that?'

'Not much,' said Hannasyde.

'Well, if it comes to that I don't fancy it a lot myself,' confessed the Sergeant. 'The trouble is that whichever way you look at it that North dame's story gums up the works. We've got to believe she hid behind the bush at some time or other, because we found her footprints. Similarly we've got to believe she went back into the house, because of the postman's evidence.'

'Exactly,' said Hannasyde. 'And, according to your latest theory, she went back into the study when Fletcher was dead. Now, you've seen the photographs. Do you seriously think that a rather highly strung woman, seeing what she must have seen from the window, deliberately went into the study?'

'You never know what women will do when they want something badly, Chief. She wanted her IOUs.'

'That won't do, Hemingway. She could not have opened the desk drawer without moving Fletcher's body.

She must have known that before she set foot in the room. We can take it she didn't go in to try and render first aid, because if she had she'd have called for help, not stolen out of the house without saying a word to anyone.'

'She might have done that if she knew the murderer was her husband.'

'If she knew that I can't think she'd have gone into the study at all. Unless she and he are working together, which hypothesis is against all the evidence we have, I don't believe she saw the murder done.'

'Wait, Super! I've got it!' the Sergeant said. 'She couldn't see into the study from behind the bush, could she?'

'No.'

'Right! North leaves at 10.02. He's the man Ichabod saw. Mrs North, not knowing what's been happening, creeps up to the study window to see. That's reasonable, isn't it?'

'So far,' agreed Hannasyde. 'Where's Carpenter? Still in ambush?'

'That's right. Now, you say Mrs North wouldn't have gone through the study. She had to!'

'Why?'

'Ichabod!' said the Sergeant triumphantly. 'By the time she was all set to do a disappearing act down the path, he must have reached the gate. She wouldn't risk hiding in the garden with the late Ernest lying dead in the study. She had to get clear somehow, and her best chance was through the house.'

Hannasyde looked up with an arrested expression in his eyes, 'Good Lord, Skipper, you may be right! But what happened to Carpenter?'

'If he was hidden behind one of the bushes by the path he could have sneaked back to the gate as soon as Ichabod passed him on his way to the study. Must have done.'

'Yes, possibly, but bearing in mind the fact that the other man left the garden at 10.02, and made off as fast as he could walk towards the Arden Road, and was seen by Glass to turn the corner into it, how did Carpenter manage (a) to guess in which direction he'd gone, and (b) to catch up with him?'

'There you have me,' owned the Sergeant. 'Either he had a lot of luck, or it didn't happen.'

'Then how do you account for his having known who North was? The Norths have been kept out of the papers so far.' He paused, tapping his pencil lightly on the desk. 'We've missed something, Hemingway,' he said at last.

'If we have, I'd like to know what it is!' replied the Sergeant.

'We've got to know what it is. I may find it out from North, of course, but somehow I don't think I shall. He's more likely to stand pat, and say nothing.'

'He'll have to account for his movements last night, and the night of the late Ernest's murder.'

'Yes. But if he gives me an alibi he can't substantiate and I can't check up on, I shall be no better off than I am now. Unless I can trace the connection between him and Carpenter, or prove he was in Barnsley Street last night, I haven't any sort of case against him. Unless I can rattle his wife into talking – or him, through her,' he added.

'I suppose it's just possible North may have had a meal at that restaurant friend Charlie was working at,' suggested the Sergeant doubtfully.

'I should think it in the highest degree unlikely,' replied Hannasyde. 'North's a man of considerable means, and if you can tell me what should take him to a fly-blown restaurant off the Fulham Road I shall be grateful to you. You were with me when I visited the place: can you picture North there?'

'No, but no more I can at any of those joints in Soho,' said the Sergeant. 'But it's a safe bet he's dined at most of those.'

'Soho's different.' Hannasyde collected the scattered documents before him, and put them away in his desk. 'Time we both went home, Skipper. There's nothing more to be done till we've seen North. I propose to pay him a visit first thing in the morning – before he's had time to leave the house, in fact. I'll leave you to look after this end of the business. No need for you to attend the inquest. See what you can dig out of Carpenter's past history. I'll take Glass along with me to the Norths', just in case I need a man.'

'He'll brighten things up for you, anyway,' remarked the Sergeant. 'I'm sorry I shan't be there to hear him give his evidence at the inquest. I bet it's a good turn.'

Superintendent Hannasyde reached Marley at half-past eight on the following morning, but he was not the first visitor to the Chestnuts. At twenty minutes to nine, as Miss Drew sat down to a solitary breakfast, a slender figure in disreputable grey flannel trousers, a leather-patched tweed coat, and a flowing tie, was ushered into the room by the slightly affronted butler.

'Hullo!' said Sally. 'What do you want?'

'Breakfast. At least, I've come to see if you've got anything better than we have. If you have, I shall stay. If not, not. Kedgeree at home. On this morning of all mornings!'

'Are you going to the inquest?' asked Sally, watching Neville inspect the contents of the dishes on the hotplate.

'No, darling, but I'm sure you are. Herrings, and kidneys and bacon, and a ham as well! You do do yourselves proud. I shall start at the beginning and go on to the end. Do you mind? Something rather nauseating in the sight of persons eating hearty breakfasts, don't you think?'

'I am what is known as a good trencher-woman,' replied Sally. 'Roll, or toast? And do you want tea or coffee, or would you like a nice cup of chocolate to go with all that food?'

'How idly rich!' sighed Neville, drifting back to the table. 'Just coffee, darling.'

'You're one of the idle rich yourself now,' Sally reminded him. 'Rich enough to buy yourself a decent suit, and to have your hair cut as well.'

'I think I shall get married,' said Neville meditatively.

'Get married?' exclaimed Sally. 'Why?'

'Aunt says I need someone to look after me.'

'You need someone to furbish you up,' replied Sally, 'but as for looking after you, I've a shrewd notion that in your backboneless way, Mr Neville Fletcher, you have the whole art of managing your own life weighed up.'

He looked up from his plate with his shy, slow smile. 'Art of living. No management. Is Helen a witness?'

She was momentarily at a loss. 'Oh, the inquest! No, she hasn't been subpœnaed so far. Which means, of course, that the police are going to ask for an adjournment.'

'I expect she's glad,' said Neville. 'But it's a great disappointment to me. One of life's mysteries still unsolved. Which story would she have told?'

'I don't know, but I wish to God she'd tell the true story to John, and be done with it. You've no idea of the atmosphere of cabal and mystery we live in. I have to think before I speak every time I wish to make an observation.'

'That must come hard on you,' said Neville. 'Where are they, by the way?'

'In bed, I should think. John didn't get in till very late last night, and Helen hardly ever appears till after breakfast. I suppose Miss Fletcher's going to the inquest?'

'Then you suppose wrong, sweetheart.'

'Really? Very sensible of her, but I made sure she'd insist on going.'

'I expect she would if she happened to know it was being held today,' he agreed.

She regarded him curiously. 'Do you mean you've managed to keep it from her?'

'No difficulty,' he answered. 'Entrancingly womanly woman, my aunt. Believes what the male tells her.'

'But the papers! Doesn't she read them?'

'Oh yes! Front and middle page of *The Times*. All cheaper rags confiscated by adroit nephew, and put to ignoble uses.'

'I hand it to you, Neville,' said Sally bluntly. 'You've been a brick to Miss Fletcher.'

He gave an anguished sound. 'I haven't! I wouldn't know how! You shan't tack any of your revolting labels on to me!'

At that moment Helen came into the room. Her eyes looked a little heavy, as though from lack of sleep, and the start she gave on seeing Neville betrayed the frayed state of her nerves. 'Oh! You!' she gasped.

'I never know the answer to that one,' remarked Neville. 'I expect it's similarly dramatic, but I can't be dramatic at breakfast. Do sit down!'

'What are you doing here?' Helen asked.

'Eating,' replied Neville. 'I wish you hadn't come down. I can see you're going to disturb the holy calm which should accompany the first meal of the day.'

'Well, it's my house, isn't it?' said Helen indignantly.

Sally, who had risen, and walked over to the side-table, came back with a cup and saucer, which she handed to her sister. 'You look pretty rotten,' she said. 'Why did you get up?'

'I can't rest!' Helen said with suppressed vehemence.

'Night starvation,' sighed Neville.

Helen cast an exasperated glance at him, but before she could retort, the butler came into the room, and said austerely: 'I beg your pardon, madam, but Superintendent Hannasyde has called, and wishes to see the master. I have informed him that Mr North is not yet down. Would you have me wake the master, or shall I request the Superintendent to wait?'

'The Superintendent?' she said numbly. 'Yes. Yes, you must tell the master, of course. Show the Superintendent into the library. I'll come.'

'What for?' asked Sally, when the butler had withdrawn. 'He didn't ask for you.'

'It doesn't matter. I must see him. I must find out what he wants. Oh dear, if only I could *think*!'

'Can't you?' asked Neville solicitously. 'Not at all?'

'For the Lord's sake, drink your tea, and don't agitate!' said Sally. 'If I were you I'd let John play his own hand.'

Helen set her cup and saucer down with a jar. 'John is not your husband!' she said fiercely, and walked out of the room.

'Now we can resume the even tenor of our way,' said Neville, with a sigh of relief.

'I can't,' replied Sally, finishing her coffee in a hurry. 'I must go with her, and try to stop her doing anything silly.'

'I love people who go all out for lost causes,' said Neville. 'Are you a member of the White Rose League too?'

Sally did not trouble to reply to this, but went purposefully out of the room. Her arrival in the library coincided with that of the butler, who informed Hannasyde that Mr North was shaving, but would be down in a few minutes.

Helen looked at her sister, with a frown in her eyes. 'It's all right, Sally. I don't need you.'

'That's what you think,' said Sally. ' 'Morning, Superintendent. Why, if it isn't Malachi! Well, that is nice! Now we only want a harmonium.'

'A froward heart,' said Glass forbiddingly, 'shall depart from me. I will not know a wicked person.'

Helen, who had not previously encountered the Constable, was a little startled, but Sally responded cheerfully: 'Quite right. Evil associations corrupt good manners.'

'Be quiet, Glass!' said Hannasyde authoritatively. 'You have asked me, Mrs North, why I wish to see your husband, and I will tell you quite frankly that I wish to ask him to explain his movements on the night of Ernest Fletcher's death.'

'And what could be fairer than that?' said Sally.

'But my husband told you! You must remember. Surely you remember! He spent the evening at the flat.'

'That's what he told me, Mrs North, but it was unfortunately not true.'

Sally had been engaged in the task of polishing her monocle, but this remark, dropped like a stone into a mill pond, made her look up quickly. 'Good bluff,' she remarked. 'Try again.'

'I'm not bluffing, Miss Drew. I have proof that between the hours of 9.00 p.m. and 11.45 p.m. Mr North was not at his flat.'

Helen moistened her lips. 'That's absurd. Of course he was. He can have had no possible reason for having said so if it weren't true.'

Hannasyde said quietly: 'You don't expect me to believe that, do you, Mrs North?'

Sally stretched out her hand for the cigarette-box. 'Obviously not. According to your idea, my brother-in-law may have been at Greystones.'

'Precisely,' nodded Hannasyde.

A flash of anger made Helen's eyes sparkle. 'Be quiet, Sally! How dare you suggest such a thing?'

'Keep cool. I haven't suggested anything that wasn't already in the Superintendent's mind. Let's look at things sanely, shall we?'

'I wish you'd go away! I told you I didn't need you!'

'I know you wish I'd go away,' replied Sally imperturbably. 'The Superintendent wishes it too. It stands out a mile that his game is to frighten you into talking. If you've a grain of sense you'll keep your mouth shut, and let John do his own talking.'

'Very perspicacious, Miss Drew,' struck in Hannasyde. 'But your words imply that there would be danger in your sister's being frank with me.'

Sally lit her cigarette, inhaled deeply, and expelled the smoke down her nostrils. 'Quite a good point. But I'm nearly as much in the dark as you are. Not entirely, because I have the advantage of knowing my sister and her husband pretty well. Do let's be honest! It must be evident to a child that things look rather black against my brother-in-law. He apparently had a motive for killing Ernest Fletcher; his sudden return from Berlin was unexpected and suspicious, and now you seem to have collected proof that the alibi he gave you for 17 June was false. My advice to my sister is to keep her mouth shut. If her solicitor were here I fancy he would echo me. Because, Mr Superintendent Hannasyde, you are trying to put over one big bluff. If you'd any real evidence against my brother-in-law you wouldn't be wasting your time talking to my sister now.'

'Very acute of you, Miss Drew; but aren't you leaving one thing out of account?'

'I don't think so. What is it?'

'You are preoccupied with the idea of Mr North's possible guilt. It is quite natural that you should not consider the extremely equivocal position of your sister.'

She gave a scornful laugh. 'You don't think she had anything to do with it!'

'Perhaps I don't. But I may think that she knows much more than she has told me. You wish me to be frank, so

I will tell you that Mrs North's evidence does not tally with those facts which I know to be true.'

Helen came forward, throwing up a hand to silence her sister. 'Yes, you told me that the last time you were here. I agree with what Miss Drew says; it is time to be frank, Superintendent. You believe that the man I saw was my husband, and that I recognised him. Is not that so?'

'Let us say, Mrs North, that I consider it a possibility.'

'And I tell you that it is not so!'

'That is what I propose to find out,' said Hannasyde. 'You yourself have given me two separate accounts of your movements on the night of the 17th. The first was before your husband arrived here on the morning after the murder; the second, which was apparently designed to convince me, first, that the mysterious man seen by you was shown off the premises by Fletcher himself; and, second, that Fletcher was alive at 10.00 p.m., you told me after the arrival of your husband. You will admit that this gives me food for very serious thought. Added to this, I have discovered that Mr North left his flat at 9.00 p.m. on the evening of the 17th, and only returned to it at 11.45.'

Helen was white under her delicate make-up, but she said perfectly calmly: 'I appreciate your position, Super-intendent. But you are wrong in assuming that my husband was implicated in the murder. If you have proof that he was not in the flat on the evening of the 17th, no doubt you are right. I know nothing of that. What I do know is that he had no hand in the murder of Ernie Fletcher.'

'Yes, Mrs North? Shall we wait to hear what he himself may have to say about that?'

'It would be useless. As far as I know, he was nowhere near Greystones on the night of the 17th. It is quite possible that he may try to convince you that he was, for – for he is the sort of man, Superintendent, who would protect his wife, no matter how – how bad a wife she had been to him.'

Her voice quivered a little, but her face was rigid. Sally caught her breath on a lungful of smoke, and broke into helpless coughing. Hannasyde said quite gently: 'Yes, Mrs North?'

'Yes.' Helen's eyes stared into his. 'You see, I did it.'

Hannasyde said nothing. Glass, who had been watching Helen, said deeply: 'It is written, speak ye every man the truth to his neighbour. Surely the net is spread in vain in the sight of any bird!'

'Not this bird!' choked Sally. 'Helen, don't be a fool! Don't lose your head!'

A faint smile just curved Helen's lips. She said, still with her gaze fixed on Hannasyde's face: 'My evidence was true as far as it went. Ernie Fletcher did show the stranger off the premises, and I did return to the study to search for my IOUs. What was untrue was my story that I got out of the room before he returned to it. I didn't. He found me there. He sat down at his desk. He laughed at me. Taunted me. I saw it was no use trying to plead with him. I – I suppose I must have been mad. I killed him.'

Sally, who had by this time recovered from her coughing fit, said witheringly: 'With your little hatchet. Don't you realise that this isn't a gun-pulling affair, you cuckoo? Whoever killed Ernie did it by violence. If you'd tried to bat him on the head I don't say you wouldn't have hurt him, but you haven't the necessary strength to smash his skull.'

'I caught him unawares. I think I must have stunned him. At that moment, I was so – so angry I wanted to kill him. I hit him again and again . . .' Her voice failed; a shudder shook her, and she raised her handkerchief to her lips.

'A highly unconvincing narrative,' said Sally. 'You know, if you make up much more of this gruesome story you'll be sick. I can just see you beating someone's head in!'

'Oh don't, don't!' whispered Helen. 'I tell you I wasn't myself!'

'Mrs North,' interposed Hannasyde, 'I think I ought to inform you that it is not enough merely to say that you murdered a man. You must prove that you did so, if you wish me to believe you.'

'Isn't that for you to do?' she said. 'Why should I convict myself?'

'Don't be silly!' said Sally. 'You've confessed to a murder, so presumably you want to be convicted. All right, let's hear some more! How did you do it? Why weren't there any bloodstains on your frock? I should have thought you must have been splashed with blood.'

Helen turned a ghastly colour and groped her way to a chair. 'For God's sake, be quiet! I can't stand this!'

Glass, standing by the wall like a statue of disapproval, suddenly exclaimed: 'Woman, thou shalt not raise a false report!'

'Be quiet!' snapped Hannasyde.

The Constable's glacial blue eyes seemed to scorn him, and turned towards Helen, who had raised her head, and was staring at him in fright and doubt. He said to her in a milder tone: 'Deceit is in the heart of them that imagine evil. The fear of man bringeth a snare: but whoso putteth his trust in the Lord shall be safe.'

Hannasyde said angrily: 'Another word from you, and –'

'Hold on!' interrupted Sally. 'He has my vote. What he says is absolutely right.'

'That is as may be,' responded Hannasyde. 'But he will nevertheless hold his tongue! Mrs North, if you killed Ernest Fletcher, perhaps you will tell me what was the implement you used, and what you did with it?'

There was a brief silence. Helen's eyes travelled from one sceptical face to another. An interruption occurred, in the shape of Mr Neville Fletcher who at that moment appeared at the open window, a cup and saucer in one hand, and a slice of toast in the other. 'Don't mind me,' he said, with his sweet smile. 'I heard your last pregnant words, Superintendent, and I'm all agog to hear the answer. Why, there's Malachi!' He waved the piece of toast to the unresponsive Constable, and seated himself on the low window-sill. 'Do go on!' he said invitingly to Helen.

Hannasyde looked consideringly at him for an instant, and then turned back to Helen. 'Yes, go on, Mrs North. What was the implement, and what did you do with it?'

'I'll tell you,' Helen said breathlessly. 'You've seen the – the implement. A heavy bronze paper-weight sur- mounted by a statuette. It was on Mr Fletcher's desk. I caught it up, and struck him with it, several times. Then I escaped by way of the front door, as I told you. I hid the paper-weight under my cloak. When I reached home I –

washed it, and later, when – when Mr Neville Fletcher visited me, I – I gave it to him, and he restored it, as you know!'

Her eyes were fixed imploringly on Neville, who was staring at her with his mouth open. He blinked, shut his mouth, swallowed, and said faintly: 'Oh, give Malachi permission to speak! He'll say it all so much better than I can. Something about one's sins finding one out. Now I don't fancy this piece of toast any more. God give me strength!'

Sally found her tongue, 'Helen! You can't do that! Good Lord, you're trying to make Neville an accessary after the fact! It's too thick!'

'Thank you, darling!' said Neville brokenly. 'Take this cup and saucer away from me. My hand shakes like a reed. Women!'

'Well, Mr Fletcher?' said Hannasyde. 'What have you to say to Mrs North's accusation?'

'Don't worry!' said Neville. 'Chivalry has practically no appeal for me whatsoever. It's a wicked lie. I produced the paper-weight to create a little diversion. I suppose Miss Drew told her sister about it. That's all.'

'Yes, I did,' admitted Sally. 'And I'm very sorry, Neville. I never dreamed Helen would use the story like this!'

'The ruthlessness of the so-called gentle sex!' he said. 'But I can disprove it. The paper-weight was never on Ernie's desk. It came from the billiard-room. Ask any of the servants. You might even ask my aunt.'

'It's true!' Helen said, in a strained, unnatural voice. 'Neville had nothing to do with the murder, but he replaced the paper-weight for me. Neville, it isn't as though anyone suspects you of killing Ernie! Just – just to have put a paper-weight back isn't such an awful thing to admit to!'

'Nothing doing!' said Neville firmly. 'I've no doubt you think I should look noble as a sacrifice, but I've never wanted to look noble, and I won't be made to.'

'Neville –'

'Now, don't waste your breath in arguing with me!' he begged. 'I know I ought to be falling over myself with desire to save your husband from arrest, but, strange as it may seem to you, I'm not. In fact, if it's to be his arrest for murder, or mine for being an accessary, I'd a lot rather it was his.'

'You are hardly to be blamed,' said a cool voice from the doorway. 'But may I know upon what grounds I am to be arrested for murder?'

Twelve

At the sound of her husband's voice, Helen had started to her feet, turning an anguished face of warning towards him. He looked at her, slightly frowning, then with deliberation shut the door and came forward into the room.

'You've timed your entry excellently, John,' said Sally.

'So it seems,' he replied. His glance took in Glass, and Hannasyde, and Neville. 'Perhaps you will tell me why my house has been invaded at this singularly inappropriate hour of the day?'

'John!' The faint cry came from Helen. 'I'll tell you. Don't ask them! Oh, won't you let me speak to him alone? Superintendent, I beg of you – you must realise – give me five minutes, only five minutes!'

'No, Mrs North.'

'You're inhuman! You can't expect me to break such news to him in public – like this! I can't do it! I won't do it!'

'If your sister and Mr Fletcher choose to withdraw they may do so,' said Hannasyde.

'You too! Oh, please! I won't run away! You can guard the door and the window!'

'No, Mrs North.'

'Gently, Helen.' North walked across the room to where she was standing, and held out his hand. 'You needn't be afraid to tell me,' he said. 'Come, what is it?'

She clasped his hand with both of hers, looking up into his face with dilated eyes full of entreaty. 'No. I'm not afraid. Only of what you'll think! Don't say anything! Please don't say anything! You see, I've just confessed to the Superintendent that it was I – that it was I who killed Ernie Fletcher!'

A silence succeeded her words. North's hold on her hand tightened a little; he was looking down at her, his own face rather pale, and set in grim lines. 'No,' he said suddenly. 'It's not true!'

Her fingers dug into his hand. 'It is true. You don't know. You weren't there. You *couldn't* know! I struck him with a heavy paper-weight that stood on his desk. There was a reason –'

His free hand came up quickly to cover her mouth. 'Be quiet!' he said harshly. 'You're demented! Helen, I order you to *be quiet*!' He turned his head towards Hannasyde. 'My wife doesn't know what she's saying! There's not a word of truth in her story!'

'I need more than your assurance to convince me of that, Mr North,' replied Hannasyde, watching him.

'If you think she did it you must be insane!' North said. 'What evidence have you? What possible grounds for suspecting her?'

'Your wife, Mr North, was the last person to see Ernest Fletcher alive.'

'Nonsense! My wife left the garden of Greystones while an unknown man was in Fletcher's study with him.'

'I'm afraid you are labouring under a misapprehension,' said Hannasyde. 'Mrs North, on her own confession, did not leave the garden while that man was with Ernest Fletcher.'

North's eyelids flickered. 'On her own confession!' he repeated. He glanced down at Helen, but her head was bowed. He led her to a chair, and pressed her gently down into it, himself taking up a position behind her, with one hand on her shoulder. 'Just keep quiet, Helen. I should like the facts, please, Superintendent.'

'Yes, Mr North. But I, too, should like some facts. At my previous interview with you, you informed me that you spent the evening of the 17th at your flat. I have discovered this to have been untrue. Where were you between the hours of 9.00 p.m. and 11.45 p.m.?'

'I must decline to answer that question, Superintendent.'

Hannasyde nodded, as though he had been expecting this response. 'And yesterday evening, Mr North? Where were you between the hours of 9.15 and 10.00?'

North was regarding him watchfully. 'What is the purpose of that question?'

'Never mind the purpose,' said Hannasyde. 'Do you choose to answer me?'

'Certainly, if you insist. I was in Oxford.'

'Can you prove that, Mr North?'

'Are my whereabouts last night of such paramount importance? Haven't we wandered a little from the point? I've asked you for the facts of the case against my wife. You seem curiously disinclined to state them.'

Sally, who had retreated to the big bay window, and

was listening intently, became aware of Neville's soft voice at her elbow. 'What a lovely situation! Shall you use it?'

Hannasyde took a minute to reply to North. When he at last spoke it was in his most expressionless voice. 'I think perhaps it would be as well if you were put in possession of the facts, Mr North. Your wife has stated that at 9.58, on the night of the murder, Ernest Fletcher escorted this unknown visitor to the garden-gate. While he was doing this Mrs North re-entered the study, with the object of obtaining possession of certain IOUs of hers which were in Fletcher's possession. According to her story, Fletcher returned to find her there. A quarrel took place, which terminated in Mrs North's striking Fletcher with the paper-weight which, she informs me, stood upon the desk. She then escaped from the study by the door that leads into the hall, leaving her finger-prints on one of the panels. The time was then one minute past ten. At five minutes past ten Constable Glass here discovered the body of Ernest Fletcher.'

From the window, Sally spoke swiftly. 'Leaving out something, aren't you? What about the man whom Glass saw leaving the garden at 10.02?'

'I have not forgotten him, Miss Drew. But if either of your sister's stories is to be believed he can hardly have had anything to do with Fletcher's murder.'

'Either?' protested Neville. 'You've lost count. She's told three to date.'

'I think we need not consider Mrs North's first story. If her second story, that she left the study at 10.01, just before Fletcher returned to it, was correct, the man seen by the Constable cannot have had time to commit the murder. If, on the other hand, it is true that she herself killed Fletcher –'

Helen raised her head. 'It's true. Must you go on? Why don't you arrest me?'

'I warn you, I shall strenuously deny my alleged part in your unprincipled story,' said Neville.

'I never suggested that you were my – my accomplice!' Helen said. 'You didn't know why I wanted you to take the paper-weight back!'

'Oh no, and I wouldn't guess, would I?' said Neville. 'And to think that in a misguided moment I told the Sergeant I *was* your accomplice! I can almost feel the cruel prison bars closing round me. Sally, I appeal to you! Did your unspeakable sister give me a paper-weight on that memorable night?'

'Not in my presence,' replied Sally.

'She would hardly have done so in your presence, Miss Drew,' said Hannasyde.

'Good God, you don't believe that story?' Sally exclaimed. 'Are you suggesting that Mr Fletcher was in it too? Next you'll think I had a hand in it! Is no one immune from these idiotic suspicions of yours?'

'No one who was in any way concerned in the case,' he replied calmly. 'You must know that.'

'How true! how very true!' said Neville. 'There isn't one of us who doesn't suspect another of us. Isn't that delightfully succinct?'

'It is so!' Glass, who had been silently listening and watching, spoke in a voice of righteous wrath. 'I have held my peace, reading the thoughts you harbour! How long will ye imagine mischief against a man? Ye shall be slain, all of you: as a bowing wall shall ye be, as a tottering fence!'

'I'm like a tottering fence already,' said Neville. 'But as for you, you're like an overflowing scourge. Isaiah, 28,15. Why isn't the Sergeant here?'

'Oh, for God's sake – !' Helen cried out. 'I've told you what happened, Superintendent! Can't you put an end to this?'

'Yes, I think so,' he said.

'Just a moment!' North interposed. 'Before you take a step which you will regret, Superintendent, had you not better inquire a little more fully into one thing which seems to have been left out of your calculations?'

'And what is that, Mr North?'

'*My* movements on the night of Fletcher's murder,' said North.

Helen twisted round in her chair. 'No, John! No! You shan't, you shan't! I *beg* of you, don't say it! John, you don't want to break my heart!' Her voice broke piteously; she caught at his hands, and gripped them hard in hers, tears pouring down her face.

'Now look what you've done!' said Neville. 'You know, this will have to go down in the annals of my life as a truly memorable morning.'

'Helen!' North said, in a curious voice. 'Helen, my dear!'

'What *were* your movements on the night of the 17th, Mr North?'

'Does it matter? I killed Fletcher. That's all you want to know, isn't it?'

'No!' panted Helen. 'He's only saying it to save me! You can see for yourself he is! Don't listen to him!'

Hannasyde said: 'It is by no means all I want to know, Mr North. At what hour did you arrive at Greystones?'

'I can't tell you. I didn't consult my watch.'

'Will you tell me just what you did?'

'I walked up the path to the study, entered it, told Fletcher why I had come –'

'Why had you come, Mr North?'

'That I do not propose to tell you. I then killed Fletcher.'

'With what?'

'With the poker,' said North.

'Indeed? Yet no finger-prints or bloodstains were discovered upon the poker.'

'I wiped it, of course.'

'And then?'

'Then I left the premises.'

'How?'

'By the way I came.'

'Did you see anyone in the garden, or the road?'

'No.'

'What took you to Oxford yesterday?'

'A business conference.'

'A business conference of which your secretary knew nothing?'

'Certainly. A very confidential conference.'

'Did anyone besides yourself know that you were going to Oxford?'

'Both my partners.'

'What proof can you give me that you actually were in Oxford last night?'

'What the devil has my visit to Oxford got to do with Fletcher's murder?' North demanded. 'Of course I can bring proof! I dined at my college, if you must know, and spent the evening with my old tutor.'

'When did you leave your tutor?'

'Just before midnight. Anything else you'd like to know?'

'Nothing else, thank you. I shall ask you presently to give me the name and address of your tutor, so that I can just check up on your story.'

Helen got up jerkily. 'You don't believe all he's told you! It isn't true! I swear it isn't!'

'No, I only believe that your husband was in Oxford yesterday evening, Mrs North. But I think you had better not swear to anything more. You have already done your best to obstruct the course of justice, which is quite a serious offence, you know. As for you, Mr North, I'm afraid your account of the murder of Fletcher doesn't fit the facts. If I am to believe that you killed him, I must also believe the story your wife told me at the police station on the day I first interviewed you both. Your wife did leave Greystones by way of the front drive just after ten o'clock, for she was seen. That means that you murdered Fletcher, cleaned the poker with such scrupulous care as to defy even the microscope, and reached the side gate all within the space of one minute. I sympathise with the motive that prompted you to concoct your fairy story, but I must request you to stop trying to hinder me.'

'What, didn't he do it after all?' said Neville. 'You don't mean to tell me we're right back at the beginning again? How inartistic! How tedious! I can't go on being interested; it's time we reached a thrilling climax.'

'There's a catch in it somewhere, and I can't spot it,'

said Sally, frowning at Hannasyde. 'What makes you so sure my brother-in-law's innocent?'

'The fact that he was not in London last night, Miss Drew.'

Helen put out a wavering hand and grasped a chairback. 'He didn't do it?' she said, as though she hardly understood. 'Are you trying to trick me into saying something – something –'

'No,' Hannasyde replied. 'When Mr North has told me just where he really was on the evening of the 17th I shall be satisfied that neither of you murdered Ernest Fletcher. You, at least, could never have done so.'

She gave a queer little sigh, and crumpled up in a dead faint.

'Oh, damn you, Superintendent!' exclaimed Sally, and went quickly forward.

She was thrust somewhat unceremoniously out of the way. North went down on his knee, gathered Helen into his arms, and rose with her. 'Open the door!' he ordered curtly. Over his shoulder he said: 'I went to see a friend of mine on the evening of the 17th. You can verify that. Peter Mallard, 17 Crombie Street. Thanks, Sally: I shan't need your assistance.'

The next instant he was gone, leaving his sister-in-law meekly to shut the door behind him.

Neville covered his eyes with his hand. 'Drama in the home! Oh, my God, can you beat it? He thought she did it, and she thought he did it, in the best Lyceum tradition. And they performed their excruciating antics on empty stomachs!'

'Trouble and anguish have taken hold on me!' suddenly announced Glass. 'They will deceive every one his neighbour, and will not speak the truth: they have taught their tongue to speak lies!'

'You know, I won't say that I don't appreciate Malachi,' remarked Neville critically, 'but you must admit that he has a paralysing effect on conversation.'

Hannasyde said briefly: 'You can wait in the hall, Glass.'

'Rebellion,' said Glass, 'is as the sin of witchcraft, and stubbornness is an iniquity and idolatry. Therefore I will depart as I am bidden.'

Hannasyde refused to be drawn into any sort of retort, merely waiting in cold silence until Glass had left the room. Neville said: 'I wish you'd brought the Sergeant. You don't understand how to play up to Malachi a bit.'

'I have no wish to play up to him,' replied Hannasyde. 'Miss Drew, when your sister feels well enough to see me, I want to have a short talk with her.'

'All right,' said Sally, lighting another cigarette.

He looked at her. 'I wonder if you would perhaps go and find out when I may see her?'

'Don't leave me, Sally, don't leave me!' begged Neville. 'My hand must be held. Suspicion has veered in my direction. Oh, I do wish John had done it!'

'I'm not going,' replied Sally. 'For one thing, I wouldn't be so tactless; for another, this problem is just beginning to get interesting. You needn't mind me, Superintendent: carry on!'

'I know what's coming,' said Neville. 'Who were you with last night?'

'Precisely, Mr Fletcher.'

'But it's very awkward: you've no idea how awkward!' said Neville earnestly. 'I can see that you're asking a very pregnant question, of course. But it would make things much easier for me if you'd tell me what the secret of last night is.'

'Why?' said Hannasyde. 'All I wish you to do is to tell me where you were yesterday evening. Either you know why I'm asking this, or you don't – in which case you can have no possible objection to answering the question.'

'You know, that sounds very specious to me,' said Neville. 'I can see myself falling headlong into a trap. How terribly right Malachi always is! He warned me against deceit repeatedly.'

'Am I to understand that you have been practising deceit?'

'Oh yes! I lied to my aunt,' said Neville. 'That's what makes it all so awkward. I told her I was coming here last night, to see Miss Drew. I can't but see that that is going to cast an extremely bilious hue over my whole story.'

'You didn't come here, in fact?'

'No,' said Neville unhappily.

'Where did you go?'

'I'd better tell the truth, hadn't I?' Neville asked Sally. 'One is at such a disadvantage with the police: they always know more than they say. On the other hand, if I tell the truth now I may find it awfully hard to lie afterwards.'

'Mr Fletcher, this sort of thing no doubt amuses you, but it fails entirely to amuse me!' said Hannasyde.

'You must think I've got a perverted sense of humour!' said Neville. 'I haven't; I'm not in the least abnormal: it's only other people's troubles that amuse me. I'm wriggling in the toils.'

'I am still waiting for an answer to my question, Mr Fletcher.'

'If I had my way you'd wait for ever,' said Neville frankly. 'Oh God, why didn't I go to Oxford, and call on *my* tutor? He'd have been very glad to see me, too. You mightn't think it, but they all hoped for great things of me at Oxford. You know: Fellowships, and what-nots. I was thought to have an intellect.'

'That doesn't surprise me at all,' said Hannasyde dryly.

'Yes, but doesn't it all go to show that a classical education is so much dross? Double firsts – yes, I did really! – are of no practical use whatsoever. Oh, let us end this ghastly suspense! I was in London last night.'

'Intrigue!' said Sally, her eyes dancing. 'He lied to his aunt, and went to the great, wicked city! Spill it, Neville! What haunt of vice did you visit?'

'I didn't. I wish I had. All I sought was rational companionship.'

'Beast! You could have found that here!'

'Oh no, darling! No, really! Not with Helen in the offing!'

'Where did you find this rational companionship?' interrupted Hannasyde.

'I didn't. I went to call upon one Philip Agnew, who lives in Queen's Gate, and pursues a delightfully scholarly and ineffective career at the South Kensington Museum. But he was out.'

'Indeed? So what did you do?'

'I wandered lonely as a cloud, trying to think of anyone besides Philip whom I could bear to consort with. But I couldn't, so I came home, and went to bed.'

'Thank you. At what hour did you leave Greystones?'

'Oh, but I don't know! After dinner. I expect it was somewhere between half-past eight and nine.'

'How were you dressed?'

'God, I can see the pit yawning at my feet! You could get the answer to that one out of my aunt, or Simmons, couldn't you? Black tie, Superintendent. Rather a nice one, too. Even my aunt was pleased.'

'Did you wear an overcoat?'

'What, in the middle of June? No, of course not.'

'Hat?'

'Yes.'

'What sort of a hat?'

'A black felt hat.'

'What, that thing?' exclaimed Sally.

'It's a very good hat. Besides, I haven't got another.'

'Forgive the interruption,' said Sally to Hannasyde, 'but if you are trying, as I gather you are, to convict Mr Fletcher of having murdered his uncle, do you mind telling me how you account for the man Malachi saw leaving Greystones at 10.02?'

'I have an idea, Miss Drew,' replied Hannasyde deliberately, 'that that man is dead.'

Neville blinked at him. 'Did – did I kill him?' he asked in an anxious voice.

'Someone killed him,' said Hannasyde, looking searchingly at him.

'Who was he?' Sally demanded.

'His name was Charles Carpenter. He was present at Greystones on the night of the murder, and was murdered yesterday evening between the hours of 9.30 and 10.00.'

'How do you know he was present at Greystones?'

'His finger-prints were discovered, Miss Drew.'

'Oh! Known to the police, was he?'

'How acute!' said Neville admiringly. 'I should never have thought of that.'

'Yes, he was known to the police,' said Hannasyde. 'But before the police could interrogate him he was killed – as Ernest Fletcher was killed.'

'Can't we pretend he murdered my uncle?' begged Neville.

'No, Mr Fletcher, we can not.'

'Killed because he knew too much,' said Sally, getting up, and beginning to walk up and down the room. 'Yes, I see. Not Neville, though. Any weapon discovered?'

'No,' said Hannasyde. 'In both cases, the murderer contrived to conceal his weapon with – let us say – extraordinary ingenuity.'

'Oh!' Sally threw him a somewhat scornful smile. 'You think that points to Mr Fletcher, do you? There's a difference, Superintendent, between ingenuity of mind and practical cleverness. Neville – practically speaking – is half-witted.'

'I suppose I ought to be grateful,' murmured Neville. 'What was my weapon, by the way? You know, I don't want to upset the only theory left to you, but I doubt very much if I could nerve myself to commit an act of such repulsive violence – let alone two of them.'

'Just a moment!' Sally intervened. 'My sister's evidence now becomes of vital importance. I'd better go and see if she's fit enough to see you, Superintendent.'

'I should be very grateful to you if you would,' said Hannasyde.

'I will, but I don't suppose I shall be frightfully popular,' said Sally, going to the door.

'Tell her a man's life is at stake,' recommended Neville, swinging his legs over the window-sill, and stepping into the room. 'That'll appeal to her morbid mind.'

Sally went upstairs to her sister's bedroom. She entered to find that Helen, having recovered consciousness, was indulging in a comfortable fit of weeping on her husband's shoulder, gasping at intervals: 'You didn't do it! You didn't do it!'

'No, darling, of course I didn't do it. If you'd only told me!'

Sally paused for a moment in the doorway, and then came in and shut it behind her. 'Delicately nurtured female suffering from a fit of strong hysterics?' she inquired. 'Come on, Helen. Snap out of it! You're wanted downstairs.' She walked into the adjoining bathroom, discovered a bottle of sal volatile in the medicine-chest, mixed a ruthless dose of it, and returned to the bedroom, and put the glass into North's hand. 'Push that down her throat,' she said.

'Come, Helen! Drink this!' North commanded.

Helen gulped some of the mixture and choked. 'Oh! *Filthy* stuff! I'm all right; really I am! Oh, John, tell me it's true, and I'm not dreaming? It wasn't you I saw that awful night?'

'Of course it wasn't. Is that what you have been thinking all this time?'

'I've been so much afraid! Then that ghastly Superintendent told me you weren't in your flat that evening, and it seemed to make it quite certain. I hoped you'd get away while I talked to the police. That's why I sent Baker up to tell you. I hoped you'd understand it was a warning.'

'Was that why you told the Superintendent you had committed the murder?' he asked.

'Yes, of course. I couldn't think of anything else to do. I was too unhappy to mind what happened to me. It didn't matter.'

He took her hands, and held them. 'You cared as much as that, Helen?'

'John, John, I've always cared! You thought I didn't, and I know I behaved like a beast, but I never meant to let this awful gulf grow between us!'

'It was my fault. I didn't try to understand. I even made you afraid to turn to me when you were in a mess. But, Helen, believe me, I never meant to lose your trust like that! I would have got you out of it, no matter what it cost me!'

'Oh, no, no, it was all my utter folly! Oh, John, forgive me!'

Sally polished her monocle. 'Don't mind me!' she said.

North raised his head. 'Oh, Sally, do go away!'

'I would if I could. Don't think it's any pleasure to me to watch a couple of born idiots dripping all over one another,' said Miss Drew with brutal frankness. 'I'm here on a mission. The Superintendent wants to see Helen. Do you think you could pull yourself together, sister?'

Helen sighed, still clinging to North's hand. 'I never want to set eyes on the Superintendent again.'

'I daresay, but you happen to be an important witness. Now that you aren't labouring under the delusion that John's a murderer, the police would like to hear your evidence all over again. Take another swig of sal volatile! Tell me, John: why *did* you come back from Berlin in such a hurry?'

'It doesn't matter any longer,' he said.

Sally opened her eyes at that. 'What a lurid thrill! Did you get an anonymous letter about Helen's goings-on?'

'No. Not anonymous.'

Helen swallowed some more sal volatile. 'Who?' she asked, flushing.

'Never mind. It wasn't what your somewhat vulgar sister thinks. In fact, it was a metaphorical kick in the pants for me. So I came home.'

'And very helpful you were,' said Sally. 'You spread such a blight all over everywhere that even I began to think Helen might be wise not to tell you all.'

'It was – a little difficult,' he replied. 'Helen was so obviously dismayed at seeing me, and so obviously afraid of my finding out the nature of her dealings with Fletcher –'

'That,' said Sally, 'was your cue, and you missed it. If you'd gone the right way to work, she would have told you the whole story.'

'Yes,' said North. 'But I wasn't sure that I wanted to hear it.'

'An ostrich act? You? Well, I wouldn't have thought it of you,' said Sally.

Helen pulled his hand to her cheek. 'And thinking that, you – you tried to get yourself arrested to save me! Oh, John!'

'I'm sorry, Helen. We seemed to have lost one another.'

Sally took the empty glass away from her sister. 'Look

here, do you mind postponing all this? You've got to come down and tell the Superintendent exactly what did happen on the fatal evening. At the moment he looks like pinching Neville for the murder, which I'm not at all in favour of. I don't know whether your evidence will be any good to him, but it might be. Shove some powder on your nose, and come downstairs.'

Helen got up and went rather wearily to her dressing-table. 'All right, if I must. Though why you should care, I don't know. I thought you had no use for Neville.'

'I have never,' said Miss Drew, inaccurately, but with dignity, 'allowed vulgar prejudice to influence my judgment. Moreover, I don't share your conviction that as long as John isn't pinched for the murder it doesn't matter who is. Are you ready?'

Helen passed a comb through her hair, patted the waves into place, critically surveyed her profile with the aid of a hand-mirror, and admitted that she was ready.

Hannasyde was awaiting them in the library still with Neville. North said to him, with a slight, rueful smile: 'We owe you an apology, Superintendent. I rather think we've rendered ourselves liable to criminal prosecution.'

'Yes, you've been thoroughly obstructive,' replied Hannasyde, but with a twinkle. 'Now, Mrs North, will you please tell me exactly what did happen while you were at Greystones on the 17th?'

'I did tell you,' she said, raising her eyes to his face. 'It was quite true, my story. Really, it was!'

'Which one?' inquired Neville.

'The one I told the Superintendent at the police station that day. I did hide behind the bush, and I did go back into the study to look for my IOUs.'

'And the man you saw enter the study? You're quite sure that Fletcher saw him off the premises before 10.00 p.m.?'

'Yes, absolutely.'

'And you heard Fletcher returning towards the house just before you left the study?'

She nodded. 'Yes, and he was whistling. I heard his step on the gravel path. He was strolling, I think, not hurrying at all.'

'I see. Thank you.'

Sally saw that he was frowning a little, and said shrewdly: 'You don't like my sister's evidence, Superintendent?'

'I wouldn't say that,' he answered evasively.

'Just a moment,' said Neville, who had been jotting some notes down on the back of an envelope. 'Do you think I could have done this? 10.01, my uncle alive and kicking; 10.02, man seen making off down Maple Grove; 10.05, my uncle discovered dead. Who was the mysterious second man? Did he do it? Was I he? And if so, why? Actions strange and apparently senseless. I shall resist arrest.'

'No question of arrest,' announced Sally. 'There's no case against you. If you did it, what was your weapon?'

Neville pointed a long finger at Hannasyde. 'The answer is in the Superintendent's face, loved one. The paper-weight! The paper-weight which I myself introduced into the plot.'

Hannasyde remained silent. Sally replied: 'Yes, I see that. But if you had murdered Ernie, it would have taken some nerve to make the police a present of your weapon.'

'Yes, wouldn't it?' he agreed. 'I should have stuttered with fright. Besides, I don't see the point. What would I do it for?'

'Oh, the overweening conceit of the murderer!' said Sally. 'That's a well-known feature of the homicidal mind, isn't it, Superintendent?'

'You have made a study of the subject, Miss Drew,' he answered non-committally.

'Of course I have. But my own opinion is that Neville doesn't suffer from that kind of conceit. You can say it was a piece of diabolical cunning, if you like, but there again there's an objection. There was no reason why you should suspect the paper-weight more than any other of the weapons there must be at Greystones. So why should he have brought it to your notice?'

'Perverted sense of humour,' supplied Neville. 'The murderer's freakish turn of mind. I shall soon begin to believe I'm guilty. Oh, but just think of me murdering a man for his millions! No, I won't subscribe to it: it's a repulsive solution to an otherwise recherché crime.'

'Yet it is, I believe, a fact that your financial condition, at the time of your uncle's death, was extremely precarious?' said Hannasyde.

North, who had been standing behind his wife's chair in silence, intervened at this, saying in his even way: 'That question, Superintendent, should surely not be put to Mr Fletcher in public?'

Neville blinked. 'Oh, isn't that sweet of John? And I quite thought he didn't like me!'

Hannasyde said, with something of a snap: 'Quite right, Mr North. But as, at the outset of this interview, I made it plain that I wished to interrogate him in private, and he refused to allow Miss Drew to leave the room, you will agree that discretion on my part would be quite superfluous. I am, however, still prepared to see Mr Fletcher alone, if he wishes it.'

'But I don't, I don't!' said Neville. 'I should dither with fright if closeted with you alone. Besides, Miss Drew is acting as my solicitor. I shouldn't dare to open my mouth if she weren't here to check my irresponsible utterances.'

'Then perhaps you will tell me whether I am correct in saying that you were very awkwardly placed, as regards finance, at the time of your uncle's death?'

'Well, no,' answered Neville diffidently. 'I didn't find anything awkward about it.'

'Indeed! Are you prepared to state that you had a credit balance at your bank?'

'Oh, I shouldn't think so!' said Neville. 'I never have at the end of the quarter.'

'Were you not, in fact, very much overdrawn?'

'I don't know. Was I?'

'Isn't this a little unworthy of you, Mr Fletcher? Did you not receive a communication from your bank, on the 14th of the month, informing you of the state of your overdraft?'

'Ah, I thought that was what it was about!' said Neville. 'It generally is. Though not always, mind you. The bank once wrote to me about some securities, or something, of mine, and it led to quite a lot of trouble, on account of their stamping the name of the bank on the envelope. Because, of course, when I saw that I put the letter into the waste-paper basket. I mean, wouldn't you?'

'Are you asking me to believe that you did not open the bank's letter?'

'Well, it'll make things much easier for you if you do believe it,' said Neville engagingly.

Hannasyde looked a little non-plussed, but said: 'You did not, then, apply to your uncle for funds to meet your liabilities?'

'Oh no!'

'Did you perhaps know that it would be useless?'

'But it wouldn't have been,' objected Neville.

'Your uncle had not warned you that he would not be responsible for your debts?'

Neville reflected. 'I don't think so. But I do remember that he was most annoyed about an episode in my career that happened in Budapest. It was all about a Russian woman, and I didn't really want Ernie to interfere. But he had a lot of hidebound ideas about the honour of the name, and prison being the final disgrace, and he would insist on buying me out. He didn't like me being County Courted either. I've always thought it would probably save a lot of bother to be declared bankrupt, but Ernie couldn't see it in that light at all. However, I don't want to speak ill of the dead, and I expect he meant well.'

'Unpaid bills do not worry you, Mr Fletcher?'

'Oh, no! One can always fly the country,' said Neville, with one of his sleepy smiles.

Hannasyde looked rather searchingly at him. 'I see. A novel point of view.'

'Is it? I wouldn't know,' said Neville innocently.

Helen, who had been leaning back in her chair, as though exhausted, suddenly said: 'But I don't see how it could have been Neville. It isn't a bit like him, and anyway, how could he have done it in the time? He wasn't anywhere in sight when I left the house.'

'Peeping at you over the banisters, darling,' explained Neville. 'When you think that Helen was in the study at 10.00 p.m., and my dear friend Malachi at 10.05, I had a lot of luck, hadn't I? What do you think, Superintendent?'

'I think,' said Hannasyde, 'that you had better consider your position very carefully, Mr Fletcher.'

Thirteen

'What do you suppose he meant by that?' asked Neville, as the door closed behind Baker, ushering Superintendent Hannasyde out.

'Trying to rattle you,' replied Sally briefly.

'Well, he's succeeded,' said Neville. 'I'm glad I ate that handsome breakfast before he came, for I certainly couldn't face up to it now.'

'Talking of breakfast –' began North.

'How insensate of you, if you are!' said Neville. 'Helen, darling, you have such a fertile imagination: are you quite sure you really saw Ernie showing his strange visitor out?'

'Of course I'm sure! What would be the point of making up such a tale?'

'If it comes to that, what was the point of deceiving John all this time?' said Neville reasonably. 'Irrational lunacy – that's tautology, but let it stand – peculiar to females.'

She smiled, but replied defensively: 'It wasn't irrational. I know now it was silly, but I – I had a definite reason.'

'It would be nice to know what that was,' he remarked.

'Or no, on second thoughts, it would probably tax my belief too far. Only inference left to John was that you had committed what the legal profession so coyly calls misconduct with Ernie. Sally and I nearly wrote him an anonymous letter, divulging the whole truth.'

'In some ways, I wish you had,' said North. 'If you will allow me to say so, it would have been far more helpful than your efforts to get your uncle to give back those IOUs. I've no doubt your spirit was willing, but –'

'Then you know very little about me,' interrupted Neville. 'My spirit was not in the least willing. I was hounded into it, and just look at the result! Being regarded as a sort of good Samaritan, which in itself is likely to lead to hideous consequences, is the least of the ills likely to befall me.'

'I'm terribly sorry,' sighed Helen, 'but even though you didn't get my notes back, and we did land ourselves in a mess, my bringing you into it did lead to good. If I hadn't, John and I might never have come together again.'

Neville closed his eyes, an expression on his face of acute anguish. 'What a thought! How beautifully put! I shall not have died in vain. Ought I to be glad?'

'Look here!' Sally interposed. 'It's no use regretting what you've done. You've got to think about what you're going to do next. It's obvious that the police suspect you pretty hotly. On the other hand, it's equally obvious that they haven't got enough evidence against you to allow of their applying for a warrant for your arrest. The question is: can they collect that evidence?'

Neville opened his eyes, and looked at her in undisguised horror. 'Oh, my God, the girl thinks I did it!'

'No, I don't, I've got an open mind on the subject,' said Sally bluntly. 'If you did it, you must have had a darned good reason, and you have my vote.'

'Have I?' Neville said, awed. 'And what about my second victim?'

'As I see it,' replied Sally, 'the second victim – we won't call him yours just yet – knew too much about the first murder, and had to be disposed of. Unfortunate, of course, but, given the first murder, I quite see it was inevitable.'

Neville drew a deep breath. 'The weaker sex!' he said. 'When I recall the rubbish that has been written about women all through the ages, it makes me feel physically unwell. Relentless, primitive savagery! Inability to embrace abstract ideas of right and wrong utterly disruptive to society. Preoccupation with human passions nauseating and terrifying.'

Sally replied calmly: 'I think you're probably right. When it comes to the point we chuck all the rules overboard. Abstractions don't appeal to us much. We're more practical than you, and – yes, I suppose more ruthless. I don't mean that I *approve* of murder, and I daresay if I read about these two in the papers I should have thought them a trifle thick. But it makes a difference when you know the possible murderer. You'd think me pretty rotten if I shunned you just because you'd killed one man I loathed, and another whom I didn't even know existed.'

'I'm afraid, Sally, you're proving Neville's point for him,' said North, faintly smiling. 'The fact that he is a friend of yours should not influence your judgment.'

'Oh, that's absolute rot!' said Sally. 'You might just as

well expect Helen to have hated you when she thought you were the murderer.'

'So I might,' he agreed, apparently still more amused.

'Well, we've wandered from the point, anyway,' she said. 'I want to know whether the police can possibly discover more evidence against you, Neville.'

'There isn't any evidence! I keep on telling you I had nothing to do with it!' he said.

'Who had, then?' she demanded. 'Who *could* have had?'

'Oh, the mystery man!' he said airily.

'With what motive?'

'Same as John's. *Crime passionnel.*'

'What, *more* IOUs?'

'No. Jealousy. Revenge. All the hall-marks of a passionate murder, don't you think?'

'It's an idea,' she said, knitting her brows. 'Do you happen to know if he'd done the dirty on anyone?'

'Naturally I don't. I should have spilt the whole story, dear idiot. But lots of pretty ladies in Ernie's life.'

'You think some unknown man murdered him because of a woman? It sounds quite plausible, but how on earth did he manage to do it in the time?'

'Not having been there, I can't say. You work it out.'

'The point is, will the Superintendent be able to work it out?' she said.

'A much more important point to me is, will he be able to work out how I could have committed both murders?' retorted Neville.

Both points were exercising the Superintendent's mind at that moment. Having told PC Glass in a few well-chosen words what he thought of his conduct in condemning the morals of his betters, he set off with him towards the police station.

'The Lord,' announced Glass severely, 'said unto Moses, say unto the children of Israel, Ye are a stiff-necked people: I will come up into the midst of thee in a moment, and consume thee.'

'Very possibly,' replied Hannasyde. 'But you are not Moses, neither are these people the children of Israel.'

'Nevertheless, the haughtiness of men shall be bowed down. They are sinners before the Lord.'

'That again is possible, but it is no concern of yours,' said Hannasyde. 'If you would pay more attention to this case, and less to other people's shortcomings, I should be the better pleased.'

Glass sighed. 'I have thought deeply. All is vanity and vexation of the spirit.'

'There I agree with you,' said Hannasyde tartly. 'With the elimination of both Mr and Mrs North, nearly everything points now to Neville Fletcher. And yet – and yet I don't like it.'

'He is not guilty,' Glass said positively.

'I wonder? How do you arrive at that conclusion?'

'He has not seen the light; he has a naughty tongue, and by his scorning will bring a city into a snare; yet I do not think him a man of violence.'

'No, he doesn't give me that impression either, but I've been wrong in my summing up of men too often to set much store by that. But whoever murdered Fletcher must also have murdered Carpenter. Perhaps it was young Fletcher – but I'd give a year's pension to know what he did with the weapon!'

'Is it so certain that the same weapon was used?' asked Glass in his painstaking way.

'It seems extremely probable, from the surgeon's reports on the injuries in each case.'

'What of the man whom I saw? He was not Neville Fletcher.'

'Perhaps Carpenter.'

Glass frowned. 'Who then was the man seen by Mrs North?'

'I can't tell you, unless again it was Carpenter.'

'You would say that he returned, having been sent away? For what purpose?'

'Only he could have answered that, I'm afraid.'

'But it seems to me that the matter is thus made darker. Why should he return, unless to do Fletcher a mischief? Yet, since he himself is dead, that was not so. I think the man Fletcher had many enemies.'

'That theory is not borne out by what we know of him. There was always the possibility that North might have been the murderer, but no one else, except Budd, who does not correspond with the description of the man in evening dress seen last night, has come into the case. And we've been into Fletcher's past fairly thoroughly. A nasty case. The Sergeant said so at the start.'

'The unholy,' said Glass, his eye kindling, 'are like the chaff which the wind driveth away!'

'That'll do,' said Hannasyde coldly, terminating the conversation.

When the Sergeant heard, later, that North's innocence was established, he spoke bitterly of resigning from the Force. 'The hottest suspect we had, and he must needs go and clear himself!' he said. 'I suppose there's no chance his alibis were faked?'

'I'm afraid not, Skipper. They're sound enough. I've been into them. We seem to be left with Neville Fletcher only. He has no alibi for last night. He admits, in fact, that he was in London.'

'Well,' said the Sergeant judicially, 'if it weren't for his work on Ichabod, I'd as soon pinch him as anybody.'

'I know you would, but unfortunately there's a snag – two snags. He stated, quite frankly, that he was wearing a dinner-jacket suit last night. But he also said that his hat was a black felt. The man we want wore an opera hat.'

'That's nothing,' said the Sergeant. 'He probably made that up.'

'I don't think so. No flies on that young man. He said it was the only hat he possessed. I could so easily disprove that, if it weren't true, that I haven't even tried to. What is more, he is either a magnificent actor, or he really didn't know what I was driving at when I questioned him on his movements last night.'

'All the same,' said the Sergeant, 'if North's out, young Neville's the only one who could have done it in the time.'

'What time?'

The Sergeant answered with a touch of impatience: 'Why, between Mrs North's leaving and Ichabod's arrival, Chief!'

'Less time than that,' corrected Hannasyde. 'The murder must have been committed after 10.01 and before 10.02.'

'Well, if that's so there hasn't been a murder,' said the Sergeant despairingly. 'It isn't possible.'

'But there has been a murder. Two of them.'

The Sergeant scratched his chin. 'It's my belief Carpenter didn't see it done. If he left at 10.02, he couldn't have. Stands to reason.'

'Then why was he killed too?'

'That's what I haven't worked out yet,' admitted the Sergeant. 'But it seems to me as though he knew something which would have told him who must have committed the murder. Wonder if Angela Angel had any other boy-friends?' He paused, his intelligent eyes more bird-like than ever. 'Suppose he was shown out at 9.58? And suppose, when he was walking off, he caught sight of a chap he knew, sneaking in at that side gate? Think that might put ideas into his head? Seems to me he'd add two and two together and make 'em four when he read about the late Ernie's being found with his head bashed in.'

'Yes, quite reasonable except for one detail you've forgotten. You're assuming that the man Glass saw at 10.02 was not Carpenter, but the murderer, and we're agreed that whenever that man may have entered the garden he cannot have murdered Fletcher until after 10.01. And that won't do.'

'Nor it will,' said the Sergeant, discomfited. After a moment's thought, he perked up again. 'All right! Say Carpenter went back, to see what this other chap was up to. He saw the murder done, and he legged it for the gate as hard as he could.'

'And the other man?'

'Like I said before. He heard Ichabod's fairy footfall, and hid himself in the garden, and slipped out as soon as Ichabod reached the study. The more I think of it, Chief, the more I see it must have been like that.'

'It does sound plausible,' Hannasyde conceded. 'What was the unknown man's motive? Angela?'

'Yes, I think we'll have to say it was Angela, on account of Charlie's being linked up with him.'

'Yet her friend – what was her name? Lily! – whom you questioned didn't mention any man but Carpenter and Fletcher in connection with Angela, did she?'

'Not what you might call specifically. She said there were plenty hanging round the poor girl.'

'Doesn't seem likely that an apparently unsuccessful admirer would go to the lengths of killing Fletcher, does it?'

'If it comes to that, nothing seems likely about this case, except that we'll never get to the bottom of it!' said the Sergeant crossly.

Hannasyde smiled. 'Cheer up! We've not done with it yet. What did you manage to find out today?'

'Nothing that looks like being of any use,' the Sergeant replied. 'We've got hold of one of Carpenter's relations, but he couldn't tell us much. Wait a bit: I've got it all here, for what it's worth.' He picked up a folder, and opened it. 'Carpenter, Alfred. Occupation, Clerk. Aged 34 years. Brother to the deceased. Has not set eyes on deceased since 1935.'

'Did he know anything about Angela Angel?'

'No, only hearsay. According to him, Charlie was never what you'd call the hope of the family. Sort of kid who pinched the other kids' belongings at school. He started life in the drapery business, and got the sack for putting the petty cash in the wrong place. No prosecution; old Carpenter – he's dead now – paid up. After that, our hero joined a concert-party. Seems he could sing a bit, as well as look pansy. He stuck to that for a bit, and then he got a job on the stage proper – male chorus. By that time what with one thing and another, his family had got a bit tired of him, and they gave him order of the boot from home, and no mistake. Then he went and got married to an actress. Name of Peggy Robinson. The next thing the family knew was that he'd waltzed off into the blue, and his wife was on their doorstep, calling out for his blood. Alfred didn't take to her. Said that was one thing he didn't blame brother Charlie for, leaving a wife that was more like a raging tigress than a decent woman. They managed to get rid of her, but not for long. Oh no!! She went off on tour, and though Alfred says they had news that she was properly off with another fellow, that didn't stop her coming back to tell Charlie's people how she'd heard that he was in town again, and living with a girl he'd picked up somewhere in the Midlands. Seems he'd been on tour likewise. What the rights of it was I don't know, and nor does Alfred, but there doesn't seem to be much doubt about it that the girl was none other than Angela Angel.'

'Where is the wife now?' interrupted Hannasyde.

'Pushing up daisies,' replied the Sergeant. 'Died of pneumonia following influenza, a couple of years ago. Alfred knew Charlie had been to gaol, but he hadn't had word of him since he came out, and didn't want to. He never saw Angela, but he says he was pretty sure she wasn't on the stage when Charlie picked her up. From what the wife told him, he gathered it was a regular village-maiden story. You know the sort of thing. Romantic girl, brought up very strict, falls for wavy-haired tenor, and elopes with him. Well, poor soul, she paid for it in the end, didn't she?'

'Did Alfred Carpenter remember what her real name was?'

'No, because he never knew it. But taking one thing with another, it looks to me as though one mystery's solved at least, which is why no one ever turned up to claim Angela when she did herself in. If she came from a strait-laced sort of home you may bet your life she was cast off, same as Charlie was. I've known people like that.'

Hannasyde nodded. 'Yes, but it doesn't help us much. Did you dig anything out of Carpenter's landlady, or the proprietor of the restaurant he worked at?'

'What I dug out of Giuseppe,' replied the Sergeant acidly, 'was a highly talented performance, but no good to me. How these foreigners can keep it up and not get tired out beats me! He put on a one-man show all for my benefit, hair-tearing, dio-mios, corpo-di-baccos, and the rest of it. I had to buy myself a drink to help me get over it, but he was as fresh as a daisy when he got through, and starting a row with his wife. At least, that's the way it looked to me, but I daresay it was only his way of carrying on a quiet chat. Anyhow, he doesn't know anything about Charlie.'

'And the landlady?'

'She doesn't know anything either. Says she's one for keeping herself to herself. That doesn't surprise me, either. She's not my idea of a comfortable body anyone would confide in. And there we are. It's Neville or no one, Chief. And if you want to know what he did with his weapon, how about him having slid a stout stick up his sleeve?'

'Have you ever tried sliding a club up your sleeve?' inquired Hannasyde.

'Not a club. Call it a malacca cane.'

'A malacca cane would not have caused those head injuries. The weapon was heavy, if a stick a very thick one, more like a cudgel.'

The Sergeant pursed his lips. 'If it's Neville we don't have to worry about the weapon he used to do in his uncle. He had plenty of time to get rid of that, or clean it, or whatever he did do with it. As far as the second murder's concerned – I suppose he couldn't have got that paper-weight into his pocket, could he?'

'Not without its being very noticeable. The head of the statue on top must have stuck out.'

'Might not have been noticed in the bad light. I'll get on to Brown again – he's the chap with the coffee-wagon – and that taxi-driver. Not but what I'm bound to say we questioned them pretty closely before. Still, you never know.'

'And the hat?'

'The hat's a nuisance,' declared the Sergeant. 'If he hasn't got an opera hat, perhaps he borrowed the late Ernie's, just because he knew no one would expect him to wear one. He could have carried it shut up under his arm without the butler's noticing it when he left the house. When he changed hats, he must have stuffed his own into his pocket.'

'Two bulging pockets now,' observed Hannasyde dryly. 'Yet two witnesses – we won't commit the girl; she was too vague – said there was nothing out of the ordinary about him. And that raises another point. The taxi-driver, who seemed to me quite an intelligent chap, described his fare's appearance as that of an ordinary, nice-looking man. He didn't think he would know him again if confronted with him. When pressed, he could only repeat that he looked like dozens of other men of between thirty and forty. Now, if you met Neville Fletcher, do you think you'd recognise him again?'

'Yes,' said the Sergeant reluctantly. 'I would. No mistaking him. For one thing he's darker than most, and not what I'd call a usual type. He's got those silly long eyelashes too, and that smile which gets my goat. No: no one in their senses would say he's like dozens of others. Besides, he's younger than thirty, and looks it. Well, what do we do now?'

Hannasyde drummed his fingers lightly on the desk, considering. The Sergeant watched him sympathetically. Presently he said in his decided way: 'Angela Angel. It comes back to her. It may sound far-fetched to you, Skipper, but I have an odd conviction that if only we knew more about her we should see what is so obstinately hidden now.'

The Sergeant nodded. 'Sort of a hunch. I'm a great believer in hunches myself. What'll we do? Advertise?'

Hannasyde thought it over. 'No. Better not.'

'I must say, I'm not keen on that method. What's more, if her people didn't come forward at the time of her death it isn't likely they will now.'

'I don't want to precipitate another tragedy,' Hannasyde said grimly.

The Sergeant sat up with a jerk. 'What, more headbashings? You don't think that, do you?'

'I don't know. Someone is pretty determined that we shan't penetrate this fog we're groping in. Everything about the two murders suggests a very ruthless brain at work.'

'Maniacal, I call it,' said the Sergeant. 'I mean, just think of it! You can understand a chap cracking open another chap's head if he was worked up into a white-hot rage. At the same time you'd expect him to feel a bit jolted by what he'd done, wouldn't you? I don't reckon to be squeamish, but I wouldn't like to have done the job myself, no, nor to have seen it done. Nasty, messy murder, I call it. But our bird isn't upset. Not he! He waltzes off and repeats the act – in cold blood, mind you! Think that's sane? I'm damned if I do!'

'All the more reason for being careful not to hand him a motive for killing someone else.'

'That's true enough. But if we are dealing with a lunatic, Super, it's worse than I thought. You can catch up on a sane man. His mind works reasonably, same as your own; and, what's more important, he always has a motive for having committed his murder, which again is helpful. But when you come to a madman's brain you're properly in the soup, because you can't follow the way it works. And ten to one he hasn't got a motive for murder – not what a sane person would consider a motive, that is.'

'Yes, there's a lot in what you say, but I don't think our man's as mad as that. We've a shrewd idea of what his motive was for killing Carpenter, and presumably he had one for killing Fletcher.'

The Sergeant hunted amongst the papers before him on the desk, and selected one covered with his own handwriting. 'Well, Super, I don't mind telling you that I've had a shot at working the thing out for myself. And the only conclusion I've come to is that the whole thing's impossible from start to finish. Once you start putting all the evidence down on paper you can't help but see that the late Ernest wasn't murdered at all. Couldn't have been.'

'Oh don't be absurd!' said Hannasyde rather impatiently.

'I'm not being absurd, Chief. If you could chuck Mrs North's evidence overboard, all well and good. But, setting aside the fact that she's got no reason to tell lies now she knows that precious husband of hers isn't implicated in the crime, we have the postman's word for it that a woman dressed like her came out of Greystones at just after 10.00 p.m. on the 17th. So that fixes her. If it weren't for his having compared his watch with the clock in the late Ernest's study, I'd say old Ichabod was mistaken in the time he saw a chap coming out of the side gate. But he's a conscientious, painstaking officer, is Ichabod, and he's not the sort to state positively that it was 10.02 if it wasn't. I mean to say, you ought to hear him on the subject of false witnesses. Ticked me off properly, when I tried to shake his evidence a bit. But if you can make his evidence fit Mrs North's, all I can say is you're cleverer than I am. It wasn't so bad when the only fixed times we had were 10.02, when Ichabod saw the unknown, and 10.05 when he discovered the body of the late Ernest. But the moment we began to collect more fixed times the whole case got so cock-eyed there was no doing anything with it. We're now faced with four highly incompatible times, unless you assume young Neville murdered his uncle, and Carpenter saw it, and bolted for his life. We've got 9.58, or thereabouts, when

Ernest saw Mrs North's man off; 10.01, when Mrs North left; 10.02 when Ichabod's man left by the side gate; and 10.05 when Ernest was found dead. Well, it just doesn't add up, and that's all there is to it. Unless you think Neville did it, and Mrs North's covering him up?'

'No, not a chance. Mrs North isn't interested in anyone except her husband. But I think the man she saw and the man Glass saw were one and the same. It's by no means conclusive, but we did find a pale grey felt hat amongst Carpenter's belongings.'

'All right, we'll say they were the same. Now, we don't know what Carpenter went back for, having been shown out, but there might be scores of reasons, setting aside any violent ones. Suppose he saw young Neville in the study with his uncle, and decided it was no use waiting? Quite reasonable, isn't it? Well, he goes off. The fact that he hurried away doesn't prove a thing. He wasn't up to any good anyway, and he naturally wouldn't want to be questioned by a policeman. All this time Carpenter doesn't know Neville from Adam. But here's where we have the brainwave of the century, Chief! Do you remember young Neville getting his photo in one of the daily picture papers?'

'I do – as the Boots, and under the name of Samuel Crippen,' said Hannasyde grimly.

'That wouldn't matter. Suppose Carpenter saw the paper? Stands to reason he'd be following the case fairly closely. He'd recognise Neville straight off. And if he'd seen him in evening dress on the night of the murder he'd know there was something phoney about that story of Neville's being employed as the Boots. My idea is that he saw his way to make a bit of easy money, and sneaked down to make a contact with Neville. No difficulty about that. Only Neville's too sharp to allow anyone to share a secret that would put a rope round his neck, and he proceeded to eliminate Carpenter double-quick. How's that?'

'It's perfectly plausible up to a point, Skipper. But it falls down as soon as it reaches the time of Carpenter's death, for reasons already stated.'

'Then Carpenter was murdered by someone else altogether,' said the Sergeant despairingly.

'Where's the data you collected about that murder?' Hannasyde asked suddenly. 'Let me have a look at it.'

The Sergeant handed him some typewritten notes. 'Not that you'll be able to make much of it,' he remarked pessimistically.

Hannasyde ran his eye down the notes. 'Yes, I thought so. Landlady stated Carpenter was alive at 9.30. Dora Jenkins said that the man in evening dress passed by on the other side of the road just before the policeman appeared, coming from the other direction.'

'Yes, and if you read on a bit further you'll see that her boy-friend said the policeman came by ages before the man in evening dress. Of the two, I'd sooner believe him. She was simply trying to spin a good tale.'

'She was, but surely – yes, I thought so. Brown put the time he saw the policeman at about 9.40, and stated that as far as he could remember the man in evening dress passed a minute or two later. That seems to tally more or less with the girl's story. Did we ascertain from the Constable what time it was when he entered Barnsley Street?'

'No,' admitted the Sergeant. 'As he didn't see any man

in evening dress, or notice anything wrong at No. 43, I didn't think that it was important.'

'I wonder?' Hannasyde was frowning at the opposite wall.

'Got an idea, Chief?' the Sergeant asked, his interest reviving.

Hannasyde glanced at him. 'No. But I think we'll find out just when the Constable did pass up the street.'

The Sergeant said briefly: 'Sorry, Chief!' and picked up the telephone-receiver.

'My own fault. I didn't see that it might be important either. It may not be. Can but try.'

While the Sergeant waited to be connected with the Glassmere Road Police Station, Hannasyde sat reading the notes on both cases, his brows knit. The Sergeant, having exchanged a few words with the official on duty at the police station, lowered the receiver, and said: 'Just come on duty, Super. Will you speak to him?'

'Yes, tell them to bring him to the phone,' said Hannasyde absently.

The Sergeant relayed this message, and while Constable Mather was being summoned, sat watching his superior with a puzzled but alert expression on his face. A voice speaking in his ear distracted his attention. 'Hullo! Is that Mather? Hold on! Detective-Superintendent Hannasyde wants a word with you. Here you are, Chief.'

Hannasyde took the instrument from him. 'Hullo! This is with reference to last night, Mather. I want you to clear up a point which seems to have been left in the air.'

'Yes, sir,' said PC Mather dutifully.

'Do you remember at what hour you reached Barnsley Street on your beat?'

There was a slight pause; then the Constable said rather anxiously: 'I don't know to the minute, sir.'

'No, never mind that. As near as possible, please.'

'Well, sir, when I passed the post office in Glassmere Road the clock there said 9.10, so by my reckoning it would be just about 9.15 when I got to Barnsley Street.'

'What?' Hannasyde said. 'Did you say 9.15?'

'Yes, sir. But I wouldn't want to mislead you. It might have been a minute or so more or less.'

'Are you quite certain that it wasn't after 9.30?'

'Yes, sir. Quite. It wouldn't take me all that time to get to Barnsley Street from the post office. There's another thing, too, sir. Brown – the man with the coffee-stall – hadn't taken up his pitch when I passed.'

'But Brown stated when questioned that he had seen you shortly after he arrived at 9.30!'

'Said he saw me last night?' repeated Mather.

'Yes, quite definitely.'

'Well, sir,' said Mather, in a voice of slowly kindling suspicion, 'I don't know what little game he thinks he's playing, but if he says he saw me last night he's made a mistake. If I may say what I think, sir –'

'Yes, go on!'

'Well, sir, I suppose for a matter of six or seven days he *has* seen me, for I've been down Barnsley Street, sometimes at one time, and sometimes at another, each evening, but always after 9.30. Only, as it so happens, I took Barnsley Street and Letchley Gardens early last night. It seems to me Brown was making that up, sir, kind of banking on what he thought probably did happen. If I may say so.'

'All right: thanks! That's all.'

Hannasyde replaced the instrument on its rest, and turned to find the Sergeant regarding him with newly awakened interest.

'You needn't tell me, Super! I gathered it all right. Mather passed up the street at 9.15, and Brown never saw him at all. Well, well, well! Now we do look like getting somewhere, don't we? What you might call opening up a new avenue. Who is Mr Brown, and what has he got to do with the case? Come to think of it, he did answer me remarkably pat. But what he's playing at – unless he killed Carpenter – I *don't* see.'

'Alfred Carpenter,' said Hannasyde, disregarding these remarks. 'What's his address? I want the name of that travelling company Carpenter joined.'

'Back on to Angela?' said the Sergeant, handing over Alfred Carpenter's deposition. 'She wasn't one of the members of the company, if that's what you're thinking.'

'No, I'm not thinking that. What I want is a list of the towns visited by that company.'

'Holy Moses!' gasped the Sergeant. 'You're never going to comb the Midlands for a girl whose name you don't even know?'

Hannasyde looked up, a sudden twinkle in his deep-set eyes. 'No, I'm not as insane as that – quite.'

The Sergeant said suspiciously, 'What do you mean by that, Chief? Pulling my leg?'

'No. And if the notion that has occurred to me turns out to be as far-fetched as I fear it is, I'm not going to give you a chance to pull mine either,' replied Hannasyde. 'Yes, I see Alfred Carpenter's on the telephone. Get his house, will you, and ask if he knows the name of that company or, failing that, a possible agent's name. He ought to be home by now.'

The Sergeant shook his head in a somewhat dubious manner, but once more picked up the telephone. After a few minutes, he was able to inform his superior that Mr Carpenter, denying all knowledge of the companies his brother had toured with, did seem to remember hearing him speak of an agent.

'It might have been Johnson, or Jackson, or even Jamieson,' said the Sergeant sarcastically. 'Anyway, he feels sure the name began with a J. Isn't that nice?'

'Good enough,' Hannasyde replied. 'I'll go into that in the morning.'

'And what do you want me to do?' the Sergeant inquired. 'Ask Mr Brown a few searching questions?'

'Yes, by all means. Get hold of the girl again as well, and see if she sticks to her original story. And look here, Hemingway! Don't mention any of this to anyone at all. When you've interviewed Brown and Dora Jenkins, go down to Marley. I'll either join you there, or send a message through to you.'

'What do I do there?' asked the Sergeant, staring. 'Hold a prayer meeting with Ichabod?'

'You can check up on your own theory about Neville Fletcher's hat. You can take another careful look at the paper-weight, too.'

'Oh, so now we go all out for young Neville, do we?' said the Sergeant, his gaze fixed on the Superintendent's face. 'Are you trying to link *him* up with Angela, Chief? What have you suddenly spotted, if I may make so bold as to ask? Twenty minutes ago we had two highly insoluble murder cases in front of us. It doesn't seem to me as though you're particularly interested in Brown, so what is it you're after?'

'The common factor,' answered Hannasyde. 'It only dawned on me twenty minutes ago, and may very possibly be a mare's nest.'

'Common factor?' repeated the Sergeant. 'Well, that's the weapon, and I thought we'd been after that ever since the start.'

'I wasn't thinking of that,' said Hannasyde, and left him gaping.

Fourteen

The following morning was considerably advanced when Sergeant Hemingway was at last free to journey down on the Underground Railway to Marley. His two interviews had not been very successful. Miss Jenkins, vacillating between instinctive fear of the police and a delightful feeling of importance, screwed the corner of her apron into a knot, giggled, patted her frizzy curls, and didn't know what to say, she was sure. She hoped no one thought she had had anything to do with the murder, because you could have knocked her down with a feather when she read about it in the paper, and realised why she had been questioned. Under the Sergeant's expert handling she gradually abandoned her ejaculatory and evasive method of conversation, and reiterated her conviction that the gentleman in evening dress had passed only a minute or two before the policeman, and had certainly been wearing an opera hat, ever so smart.

From what he had seen of the erratic young man, Sergeant could not believe that this rider could be applied with any degree of appositeness to Neville Fletcher. He left Miss Jenkins, and went in search of Mr Brown.

This quest led him to Balham, where Brown lived, and was peacefully sleeping after his night's work. His wife, alarmed, like Miss Jenkins, by the sight of the Sergeant's official card, volunteered to go and waken him at once, and in due course Mr Brown came downstairs, bleary-eyed and morose. He looked the Sergeant over with acute dislike, and demanded to know why a man was never allowed to have his sleep out in peace. The Sergeant, who felt a certain amount of sympathy for him, disregarded this question, and propounded a counter one. But Mr Brown replied testily that if the police thought they could wake a working-man up just to ask him what he'd already told them they were wrong. What he had said he was prepared to stand by. Confronted with PC Mather's own statement, he stared, yawned, shrugged, and said: 'All right: have it your own way. It's all the same to me.'

'So you didn't see the Constable, eh?' said the Sergeant.

'No,' retorted Mr Brown. 'The street's haunted. What I saw was a ghost.'

'Don't try and get funny with me, my lad!' the Sergeant warned him. 'What were you doing at 9.40?'

'Cutting sandwiches. What else would I be doing?'

'That's for you to say. Ever met a chap called Charlie Carpenter?'

Mr Brown, recognising the name, turned a dark beet-root colour, and invited the Sergeant to get out before he was put out. Rebuked, he defied the whole of Scotland Yard to prove he had ever laid eyes on Carpenter, or had left his coffee-stall for as much as a minute the whole evening.

There was little more to be elicited from him. The Sergeant presently departed, and made his way down to Marley. Finding Glass awaiting his orders at the police station, he said somewhat snappishly that he wondered he could find nothing better to do than hang about looking like something out of a bad dream.

Glass replied stiffly: 'He that uttereth slander is a fool. I have held myself in readiness to do the bidding of those set over me. Wherein I have erred?'

'Oh, all right, let it go!' said the exasperated Sergeant. 'You haven't erred.'

'I thank you. I see that your spirit is troubled and ill at ease. Are you no nearer the end of your labour on this case?'

'No, I'm not. It's a mess,' said the Sergeant. 'When I've had my lunch, I'm going up to make a few inquiries about Master Neville's doings. He's about the only candidate for the central role we've got left. I don't say it was easy when North was a hot favourite, but what I do say is that it's a lot worse now he's out of it. When I think of the way he and that silly wife of his have been playing us up, I'd as soon arrest him for the murders as not.'

'They have told lies, and it is true that lying lips are an abomination to the Lord, but it is also written that love covereth all sins.'

The Sergeant was quite surprised. 'Whatever's come over you?' he demanded. 'You'd better be careful: if you go on like that you'll find yourself growing into a human being.'

'I, too, am troubled and sore-broken. But if you go to seek out that froward young man, Neville Fletcher, you will waste your time. He is a scorner, caring for nothing, neither persons nor worldly goods. Why, then, should he slay a man?'

'There's a lot in what you say,' agreed the Sergeant. 'But, all the same, his latest story will bear sifting. You go and get your dinner: I shan't be wanting you up at Greystones.'

An hour later he presented himself at the back door of Greystones, and after an exchange of compliments with Mrs Simmons, a plump lady who begged him to get along, do, retired with her somewhat disapproving husband into the butler's pantry.

'Tell me this, now!' he said. 'How many hats has young Fletcher got?'

'I beg pardon?' said Simmons blankly.

The Sergeant repeated his question.

'I regret to say, Sergeant, that Mr Neville possesses only one hat.'

'Is that so? And not much of a hat either, from the look on your face.'

'It is shabbier than one cares to see upon a gentleman's head,' replied Simmons, but added rather hastily: 'For man looketh on the outward appearance, but the Lord looketh on the heart.'

'Here!' said the Sergeant dangerously. 'You can drop that right away! I hear quite enough of that sort of talk from your friend Glass. Let's stick to hats. I suppose your late master had any number of them?'

'Mr Fletcher was always very well dressed.'

'What's been done with his hats? Packed up, or given away, or something?'

'No,' replied Simmons, staring. 'They are in his dressing-room.'

'Under lock and key?'

'No, indeed. There is no need to lock things up in *this* house, Sergeant!'

'All right,' said the Sergeant. 'Just take me along to the billiard-room, will you?'

The butler looked a little mystified, but raised no objection, merely opening the pantry door for the Sergeant to pass through into the passage.

A writing-table set in one of the windows in the billiard-room bore upon it a leather blotter, a cut-glass inkstand, and a bronze paper-weight, surmounted by the nude figure of a woman. The Sergeant had seen the paper-weight before, but he picked it up now, and inspected it with more interest than he had displayed when Neville Fletcher had first handed it to him.

The butler coughed. 'Mr Neville will have his joke, Sergeant.'

'Oh, so you heard about that joke, did you?'

'Yes, Sergeant. Very remiss of Mr Neville. He is a light-hearted gentleman, I am afraid.'

The Sergeant grunted, and began to coax the paper-weight into his pocket. He was interrupted in his somewhat difficult task by a soft, slurred voice from the window, which said: 'But you mustn't play with that, you know. Now they'll find nothing but your finger-prints on it, and that might turn out to be very awkward for you.'

The Sergeant jumped, and turned to find Neville Fletcher lounging outside one of the open windows, and regarding him with the smile he so much disliked.

'Oh!' said the Sergeant. 'So it's you, is it, sir?'

Neville stepped over the low window-sill into the

room. 'Oh, didn't you want it to be? Are you looking for incriminating evidence?'

'The Sergeant, sir,' said Simmons woodenly, 'wishes to know whether the master's hats are kept under lock and key.'

'What funny things policemen are interested in,' remarked Neville. 'Are they, Simmons?'

'No, sir – as I informed the Sergeant.'

'I don't immediately see why, but I daresay you have put a rope round my neck,' said Neville. 'Do go away, Simmons! I'll take care of the Sergeant. I like him.'

The Sergeant felt quite uncomfortable. He did not demur at being left with his persecutor, but said defensively: 'Soft soap's no good to me, sir.'

'Oh, I wouldn't dare! Malachi told me what happens to flatterers. I do wish you had been here yesterday. I found such a good bit in Isaiah, all about Malachi.'

'What was that?' asked the Sergeant, diverted in spite of himself.

'Overflowing scourge. I do think the Superintendent ought to have told you.'

The Sergeant thought so too, but remarked repressively that the Superintendent had something better to think about.

'Not something better. His mind was preoccupied with my possible but improbable guilt. I think yours is too, which upsets me rather, because I thought we were practically blood-brothers. On account of Malachi. Why hats?' His sleepy eyes scanned the Sergeant's face. 'Tell me when I'm getting warm. My ill-fated journey to London. Black felt. And Ernie's collection. Oh, did I borrow one of Ernie's hats?'

The Sergeant thought it best to meet frankness with frankness. 'Well, did you, sir?'

Neville gave a joyous gurgle, and took the Sergeant by the hand. 'Come with me. Do policemen lead drab lives? I will lighten yours, at least.'

'Here, sir, what's all this about?' protested the Sergeant, dragged irresistibly to the door.

'Establishing my innocence. You may not want me to, but you oughtn't to let that appear.'

'It's a great mistake to get any silly idea into your head that the police want to arrest an innocent man,' said the Sergeant severely. He found himself being conducted up the shallow stairs, and protested: 'I don't know what you're playing at, but you might remember I've got work to do, sir.'

Neville opened the door into an apartment furnished in heavy mahogany. 'My uncle's dressing-room. Not, so far, haunted, so don't be frightened.'

'To my way of thinking,' said the Sergeant, 'the things you say aren't decent.'

Neville opened a large wardrobe, disclosing a view of a shelf of hats, ranged neatly in a line. 'Very often not,' he agreed. 'These are my uncle's hats. Theoretically, do you feel that private possession is all wrong? What sort of a hat was I wearing?'

'According to you, sir, you were wearing a black felt.'

'Oh, don't let's be realistic! Realism has been the curse of art. That's what upset the Superintendent. He is very orthodox, and he felt my hat was an anachronism. Of course, I must have been wearing one of those that go pop. Irresistible to children, and other creatures of simple intellect, but too reminiscent of patent cigarette-boxes, and other vulgarities. Now tell me, Sergeant, do you think I borrowed my uncle's hat?'

The Sergeant, gazing at the spectacle of Mr Neville Fletcher in an opera hat quite three sizes too small for him, fought with himself for a moment, and replied in choked accents: 'No sir, I'm bound to say I do not. You'd – you'd have to have a nerve to go about in that!'

'Yes, that's what I thought,' said Neville. 'I like comedy, but not farce – I can see by your disgruntled expression that the hat lets me out. I hope it never again falls to my lot to be suspected of murder. Nerve-racking, and rather distasteful.'

'I hope so too, sir,' replied the Sergeant. 'But if I were you I wouldn't jump to conclusions too hastily.'

'You're bound to say that, of course,' said Neville, returning his uncle's hat to its place on the shelf. 'You can't imagine who the murderer can be if not me.'

'Well, since you put it like that, who can it be?' demanded the Sergeant.

'I don't know, but as I don't care either, it doesn't worry me nearly as much as it worries you.'

'Mr Fletcher was your uncle, sir.'

'He was, and if I'd been asked I should have voted against his death. But I wasn't, and if there's one occupation that seems more maudlin to me than any other it's crying over spilt milk. Besides, you can have too much of a good thing. I'd had enough of this mystery after the second day. Interest – but painful – revived when I stepped into the rôle of chief suspect. I must celebrate my reprieve from the gallows. How do you ask a girl if she'd like to marry you?'

'How do you do what?' repeated the Sergeant, faint but pursuing.

'Don't you know? I made sure you would.'

'Are you – are you thinking of getting married, sir?' asked the Sergeant, amazed.

'Yes, but don't tell me I'm making a mistake, because I know that already. I expect it will ruin my entire life.'

'Then what are you going to do it for?' said the Sergeant reasonably.

Neville made one of his vague gestures. 'My changed circumstances. I shall be hunted for my money. Besides, I can't think of any other way to get rid of it.'

'Well,' said the Sergeant dryly, 'you won't find any difficulty about that if you *do* get married, that's one thing.'

'Oh, do you really think so? Then I'll go and propose at once, before I have time to think better of it. Goodbye!'

The Sergeant called after him: 'Here, sir, don't you run away with the idea I said you were cleared of suspicion, because I didn't say any such thing!'

Neville waved an airy farewell, and disappeared down the stairs. Ten minutes later he entered the drawing-room of the Norths' house through the long window. Helen was writing a letter at her desk, and her sister was sitting on the floor, correcting four typescripts at once.

'Hullo!' she said, glancing up. 'You still at large?'

'Oh, I'm practically cleared! I say, will you come to Bulgaria with me?'

Sally groped for her monocle, screwed it into her eye, and looked at him. Then she put down the typescript she was holding, and replied matter-of-factly: 'Yes, rather. When?'

'Oh, as soon as possible, don't you think?'

Helen twisted round in her chair. 'Sally, what on earth do you mean? You can't possibly go away with Neville like that!'

'Why not?' asked Neville interestedly.

'Don't be absurd! You know perfectly well it wouldn't be proper.'

'Oh no, it probably won't. That's the charm of travel in the Balkans. But she's very broadminded, really.'

'But –'

'Wake up, darling!' advised Sally. 'You don't seem to realise that I've just received a proposal of marriage.'

'A . . . ?' Helen sprang up. 'You mean to tell me that was a proposal?'

'Oh, I do hate pure women: they have the filthiest minds!' said Neville.

'Sally, you're *not* going to marry a – a hopeless creature like Neville?'

'Yes, I am. Look at the wealth he's rolling in! I'd be a fool if I turned him down.'

'*Sally!*'

'Besides, he's not bossy, which is more than can be said for most men.'

'You don't love him!'

'Who says I don't?' retorted Sally, blushing faintly.

Helen looked helplessly from one to the other. 'Well, all I can say is I think you're mad.'

'Oh, I am glad!' said Neville. 'I was beginning to feel frightfully embarrassed. If you haven't got anything more to say it would be rather nice if you went away.'

Helen walked to the door, remarking, as she opened it: 'You might have waited till I'd gone before you proposed – if that extraordinary invitation was really a proposal.'

'But you showed no signs of going, and it would have made me feel very self-conscious to have said: "Oh, Helen, do you mind going, because I want to propose to Sally?"'

'You're both mad!' declared Helen, and went out.

Sally rose to her feet. 'Neville, are you sure you won't regret this?' she asked anxiously.

He put his arms round her. 'No, of course I'm not: are you?'

She gave one of her sudden smiles. 'Well, yes – pretty sure!'

'Darling, that's handsome of you, but deluded. *I'm* only sure that I shall regret it awfully if I don't take this plunge. I think it must be your nose. Are your eyes blue or grey?'

She looked up. He kissed her promptly; she felt his arms harden round her, and emerged from this unexpectedly rough embrace gasping for breath, and considerably shaken.

'Ruse,' said Neville. 'Grey with yellow flecks. I knew it all along.'

She put her head on his shoulder. 'Gosh, Neville, I – I wasn't sure – you really meant it till now! I say, is it going to be a walking tour, or something equally uncomfortable?'

'Oh no! But I thought we might do some canal work, and we're practically bound to spend a good many nights in peasants' huts. Can you eat goat?'

'Yes,' said Sally. 'What's it like?'

'Rather foul. Are you busy this week, or can you spare the time to get married?'

'Oh, I should think so, but it'll mean a special licence, and you can't touch Ernie's money till you've got probate.'

'Can't I? I shall have to borrow some, then.'

'You'd better leave it to me,' said Sally, her natural competence asserting itself. 'You'd come back with a dog-licence, or something. By the way, are you certain you won't be arrested for these tiresome murders?'

'Oh yes, because Ernie's hat doesn't fit!' he replied.

'I suppose that's a good reason?'

'Yes, even the Sergeant thought so,' he said happily.

The Sergeant did think so, but being unwilling to let his last suspect go, he kept his conviction to himself. On his way downstairs from Ernest Fletcher's dressing-room, he encountered Miss Fletcher, who looked surprised to see him, but accepted quite placidly his explanation that Neville had invited him. She said vaguely: 'Dear boy! So thoughtless! But men very often are, aren't they? I hope you don't think he had anything to do with this dreadful tragedy, because I'm sure he would never do anything really wicked. One always knows, doesn't one?'

The Sergeant made a non-committal sound.

'Yes, exactly,' said Miss Fletcher. 'Now, what can have become of Neville? He ought not to have left you alone upstairs. Not that I mean – because, of course, that would be absurd.'

'Well, madam,' said the Sergeant. 'I don't know whether I'm supposed to mention it, but I fancy Mr Fletcher has gone off to get engaged to be married.'

'Oh, I'm so glad!' she said, a beaming smile sweeping over her face. 'I feel he ought to be married, don't you?'

'Well, I'm bound to say it looks to me as though he needs someone to keep him in order,' replied the Sergeant.

'You're so sensible,' she told him. 'But how remiss of me! Would you care for some tea? Such a dusty walk from the police station!'

He declined the offer, and succeeded bit by bit in escaping from her. He walked back to the police station in a mood of profound gloom, which was not alleviated, on his arrival there, by the sight of Constable Glass, still awaiting his pleasure. He went into a small private office, and once more spread his notes on the case before him, and cudgelled his brain over them.

Glass, following him, closed the door, and regarded him in a melancholy fashion, saying presently: 'Fret not thyself because of evil-doers. They shall soon be cut down like the grass, and wither as the green herb.'

'A fat lot of withering they'll do if I *don't* fret over them!' said the Sergeant crossly.

'Thou shalt grope at noonday as the blind gropeth in the darkness.'

'I wish you'd shut up!' snapped the Sergeant, exasperated by the truth of this observation.

The cold blue eyes flashed. 'I am full of the fury of the Lord,' announced Glass. 'I am weary of holding-in!'

'I haven't noticed you doing much holding-in so far, my lad. You go and spout your recitations somewhere else. If I have to see much more of you I'll end up a downright atheist.'

'I will not go. I have communed with my own soul.

There is a way which seemeth right to a man, but the end thereof are the ways of death.'

The Sergeant turned over a page of his typescript. 'Well, there's no need to get worked up about it,' he said. 'If you take sin as hard as all that, you'll never do for a policeman. And if you're going to stay here, for goodness' sake sit down, and don't stand there staring at me!'

Glass moved to a chair, but still kept his stern gaze upon the Sergeant's face. 'What said Neville Fletcher?' he asked.

'He talked me nearly as silly as you do.'

'He is not the man.'

'Well, if he isn't he may have a bit of a job proving it, that's all I can say,' retorted the Sergeant. 'Hat or no hat, he was in London the night Carpenter was done in, and he was the only one of the whole boiling who had motive *and* opportunity to kill the late Ernest. I grant you, he isn't the sort you'd expect to go around murdering people, but you've got to remember he's no fool, and is very likely taking us all in. I don't know whether he did in Carpenter, but the more I look at the evidence, the more I'm convinced he's the one man who *could* have done his uncle in.'

'Yet he is not arrested.'

'No, he's not, but it's my belief that when the Superintendent thinks it over he will be.'

'The Superintendent is a just man, according to his lights. Where is he?'

'I don't know. He'll be down here soon, I daresay.'

'There shall be no more persecution of those that are innocent. My soul is tossed with a tempest, but it is written, yea, and in letters of fire! Whoso sheddeth a man's blood by man shall his blood be shed!'

'That's the idea,' agreed the Sergeant. 'But as for persecuting the innocent –'

'Forsake the foolish and live!' Glass interrupted, a grim, mirthless smile twisting his lips. 'Woe to them that are wise in their own eyes! Know that judgments are prepared for scorners, and stripes for the back of fools!'

'All right!' said the Sergeant, nettled. 'If you're so clever, perhaps you know who really is the murderer?'

Glass's eyes stared into his, queerly glowing. 'I alone know who is the murderer!'

The Sergeant blinked at him. Neither he nor Glass had noticed the opening of the door. Hannasyde's quiet voice made them both jump. 'No, Glass. Not you alone,' he said.

Fifteen

The Sergeant, who had been looking at Glass in utter incredulity, glanced quickly towards the door and got up. 'What the – What *is* all this, Chief?' he demanded.

Glass turned his head, regarding Hannasyde sombrely. 'Is the truth known, then, to you?' he asked. 'If it be so, I am content, for my soul is weary of my life. I am as Job; my days are swifter than a post: they flee away, they see no good.'

'Good Lord, he's mad!' exclaimed the Sergeant.

Glass smiled contemptuously. 'The foolishness of fools is folly. I am not mad. To me belongeth vengeance and recompense. I tell you, the wicked shall be turned into hell!'

'Yes, all right!' said the Sergeant, keeping a wary eye on him. 'Don't let's have a song and dance about it!'

'That'll do, Hemingway,' said Hannasyde. 'You were wrong, Glass. You know that you were wrong.'

'Though hand join in hand the wicked shall not be unpunished!'

'No. But it was not for you to punish.'

Glass gave a sigh like a groan. 'I know not. Yet the

283

thoughts of the righteous are right. I was filled with the fury of the Lord.'

The Sergeant grasped the edge of the desk for support. 'Holy Moses, you're not going to tell me *Ichabod* did it?' he gasped.

'Yes, Glass killed both Fletcher and Carpenter,' replied Hannasyde.

Glass looked at him with a kind of impersonal interest. 'Do you know all, then?'

'Not all, no. Was Angela Angel your sister?'

Glass stiffened, and said in a hard voice: 'I had a sister once who was named Rachel. But she is dead, yea, and to the godly dead long before her sinful spirit left her body! I will not speak of her. But to him who led her into evil, and to him who caused her to slay herself I will be as a glittering sword that shall devour flesh!'

'Oh, my God!' muttered the Sergeant.

The blazing eyes swept his face. 'Who are you to call upon God, who mock at righteousness? Take up that pencil, and write what I shall tell you, that all may be in order. Do you think I fear you? I do not, nor all the might of man's law! I have chosen the way of truth.'

The Sergeant sank back into his chair, and picked up the pencil. 'All right,' he said somewhat thickly. 'Go on.'

Glass addressed Hannasyde. 'Is it not enough that I say it was by my hand that these men died?'

'No. You know that's not enough. You must tell the whole truth.' Hannasyde scanned the Constable's face, and added: 'I don't think your sister's name need be made public, Glass. But I must know all the facts. She met Carpenter when he was touring the Midlands, and played for a week at Leicester, didn't she?'

'It is so. He seduced her with fair words and a liar's tongue. But she was a wanton at heart. She went willingly with that man of Belial, giving herself to a life of sin. From that day she was as one dead to us, her own people. Even her name shall be forgotten, for it is written that the wicked shall be silent in darkness. When she slew herself I rejoiced, for the flesh is weak, and the thought of her, yea, and her image, was as a sharp thorn.'

'Yes,' Hannasyde said gently. 'Did you know that Fletcher was the man she loved?'

'No. I knew nothing. The Lord sent me to his place where he dwelt. And still I did not know.' His hands clenched on his knees till the fingers whitened. 'When I have met him he has smiled upon me, with his false lips, and has bidden me good-evening. And I have answered him civilly!'

The Sergeant gave an involuntary shiver. Hannasyde said: 'When did you discover the truth?'

'Is it not plain to you? Upon the night that I killed him! When I told you that at 10.02 I saw the figure of a man coming from the side gate at Greystones I lied.' His lip curled scornfully; he said: 'The simple believeth every word: but the prudent man looketh well to his going.'

'You were an officer of the Law,' Hannasyde said sternly. 'Your word was considered to be above suspicion.'

'It is so, and in that I acknowledge that I sinned. Yet what I did was laid upon me to do, for none other might wreak vengeance upon Ernest Fletcher. My sister took her own life, but I tell you he was stained with her blood! Would the Law have avenged her? He knew himself to be safe from the Law, but me he did not know!'

'We won't argue about that,' Hannasyde said. 'What happened on the evening of the 17th?'

'Not at 10.02, but some minutes earlier did I see Carpenter. At the corner of Maple Grove did I encounter him, face to face.'

'Carpenter was the man Mrs North saw?'

'Yes. She was not lying when she told of his visit to Fletcher, for he recounted all to me, while my hand was still upon his throat.'

'What was his object in going to see Fletcher? Blackmail?'

'Even so. He too had been in ignorance, but once, before he served his time, he saw Fletcher at that gilded den of iniquity where my sister displayed her limbs to all men's gaze, in lewd dancing. And when he was released from prison, and my sister was dead, there was none to tell him who her lover was, except only one girl who recalled to his memory the man he had once seen. He remembered, but he could not discover the man's name until he saw a portrait of him one day in a newspaper. Then, finding that Ernest Fletcher was rich in this world's goods, he planned in his evil brain to extort money from him by threats of scandal and exposure. To this end, he came to Marley, not once but several times, at first seeking to enter by the front door, but being repulsed by Joseph Simmons who, when he would not state his business with Fletcher, shut the door upon him. It was for that reason that he entered by the side gate on the night of the 17th. But Fletcher laughed at him, and mocked him for a fool, and took him to the gate, and drove him forth. He went away, not towards the Arden Road, but to Vale Avenue. And there I met him.'

He paused. Hannasyde said: 'You recognised him?'

'I recognised him. But he knew not me until my hand was at his throat, and I spake my name in his ear. I would have slain him then, so great was the just rage consuming me, but he gasped to me to stay my hand, for my sister's death lay not at his door. I would not heed, but in his terror he cried out, choking, that he could divulge the name of the guilty man. I hearkened to him. Still holding him, I bade him tell what he knew. He was afraid with the fear of death. He confessed everything, even his own evil designs. When I knew the name of the man who had caused my sister's death, and remembered his false smile and his pleasant words to me, a greater rage entered into my soul, so that it shook. I let Carpenter go. My hand fell from his throat, for I was amazed. He vanished swiftly, I knew not whither. I cared nothing for him, for at that moment I knew what I must do. There was none to see. My mind, which had been set whirling, grew calm, yea, calm with the knowledge of righteousness! I went to that gate, and up the path to the open window that led into Fletcher's study. He sat at his desk, writing. When my shadow fell across the floor, he looked up. He was not afraid; he saw only an officer of the Law before him. He was surprised, but even as he spoke to me the smile was on his lips. Through a mist of red I saw that smile, and I struck him with my truncheon so that he died.'

The Sergeant looked up from his shorthand notes. 'Your truncheon!' he ejaculated. 'Oh, my Lord!'

'The time?' Hannasyde asked.

'When I looked at the clock, the hands stood at seven minutes past ten. I thought what I should do, and it seemed to me that I saw my path clear before me. I picked up the telephone that stood upon the desk, and reported the death to my sergeant. But that which is crooked cannot be made straight. I was a false witness that speaketh lies, and through my testimony came darkness and perplexity, and the innocent was brought into tribulation. Yea, though they are enclosed in their own fat, though they are sinners in the sight of the Lord, every one, it was not just that they should suffer for my deed. I was troubled, and sore-broken, and my heart misgave me. Yet it seemed to me that all might remain hidden, for you who sought to unravel the mystery were astonished, and knew not which way to turn. But when the finger-prints were discovered to be those of Carpenter's hand, I saw that my feet had been led into a deep pit from which there could be no escape. When it was divulged to the Sergeant where Carpenter abode, I was standing at his elbow. I heard all, even that he dwelt in a basement room, and was become a waiter in an eating-house. The Sergeant gave me leave to go off duty, and I departed, wrestling with my own soul. I hearkened to the voice of the tempter, but a man shall not be established by wickedness. Carpenter was evil, but though he deserved to die, it was not for that reason that I killed him.'

'You were the Constable the coffee-stall owner saw!' the Sergeant said.

'There was such a stall; I doubt not that the man saw me. I passed him as though upon my beat; I came to the house wherein Carpenter dwelt; I saw the light shining through the blind in the basement. I went down the area steps. The door at the bottom was not locked. I entered softly. When I walked into his room Carpenter was standing with his back to me. He turned, but he had no time to utter the scream I saw rising to his lips. Yet again I had his throat in my hands, and he could not prevail against me. I slew him as I slew Fletcher, and departed as I had come. But Fletcher I slew righteously. When I killed Carpenter I knew that I had committed the sin of murder, and my heart was heavy in me. Now you would arrest Neville Fletcher in my stead, but he is innocent, and it is time that the lip of truth be established.' He turned towards the Sergeant, saying harshly: 'Have you set down faithfully what I have recounted? Let it be copied out, and I will set my name to it.'

'Yes, that will be done,' Hannasyde said. 'Meanwhile, Glass, you are under arrest.'

He stepped back a pace to the door, and opened it. 'All right, Inspector.'

'Do you think I fear you?' Glass said, standing up. 'You are puny men, both. I could slay you as I slew the others. I will not do it, for I have no quarrel with you, but set no handcuffs about my wrists! I will be free.'

A couple of men who had come in at Hannasyde's call took him firmly by the arms. 'You come along quiet, Glass,' said Sergeant Cross gruffly. 'Take it easy now!'

Sergeant Hemingway watched Glass go out between the two policemen, heard him begin to declaim from the Old Testament in a fanatical sing-song, and mopped his brow with his handkerchief, bereft for once of all power of speech.

'Mad,' Hannasyde said briefly. 'I thought he was verging on it.'

The Sergeant found his voice. 'Mad? A raving

homicidal lunatic, and I've been trotting around with him as trusting as you please! My God, it gave me goose-flesh just to sit there listening to him telling his story!'

'Poor devil!'

'Well, that's one way of looking at it,' said the Sergeant. 'What about the late Ernest and Charlie Carpenter? Seems to me they got a pretty raw deal. And all for what? Just because a silly bit of fluff who was no better than she should be ran off with one of them, and was fool enough to kill herself because of the other! I don't see what you've got to pity Ichabod for. All that'll happen to him is that he'll be sent to Broadmoor, an expense to everybody, and have a high old time preaching death and destruction to the other loonies.'

'And you call yourself a psychologist!' said Hannasyde.

'I call myself a flatfoot with a sense of justice, Super,' replied the Sergeant firmly. 'When I think of the trouble we've been put to, and that maniac ticking us off right and left for being ungodly – well, I daren't let myself think of it for fear I'll go and burst a blood-vessel. What was it first put you on to it?'

'Constable Mather's saying that Brown hadn't taken up his pitch when he passed up Barnsley Street. That, coupled with the conflicting evidence of the pair at the other end of the street, made me suddenly suspicious. The presence of a policeman on the occasions of both murders was the common factor I spoke of. But I admit it did seem to me in the wildest degree improbable. Which is why I didn't tell you anything about it until I'd worked it out a bit more thoroughly. As soon as I began to think it over, all sorts of little points cropped up. For instance, there was the letter from Angela Angel which we found in Carpenter's room. Do you remember the quotations from the Bible in it? Do you remember when we discovered Angela's photograph in Fletcher's drawer that Glass wouldn't look at it, but said something in rather an agitated way about her end being as bitter as wormwood? The more I thought about it the more certain I felt that I'd hit on the solution. When I traced Carpenter's old agent this morning, and got a list of the towns Carpenter visited on that tour his brother spoke of, all I did was to inquire of the police at each one whether a family of the name of Glass lived, or had ever lived, there. As soon as I discovered some Glasses living at Leicester, and heard from the local Superintendent that there had been a girl attached to the family who had run off with an actor some years ago, I knew I was right on to it. All things considered, I thought it wisest to come straight down here and confront Glass with what I knew – before he took it into his head to murder you,' he added, twinkling.

'Well, that *was* nice of you, Chief,' said the Sergeant, with exaggerated gratitude. 'And what about me getting myself disliked by Brown, and wasting my time watching young Neville try on his uncle's hats?'

'Sorry, but I didn't dare let Glass suspect I might be getting on to his trail. I must notify Neville Fletcher that the mystery is cleared up.'

'You needn't bother,' replied the Sergeant. 'He's lost interest in it.'

Hannasyde smiled, but said: 'All the same, he must be told what's happened.'

'I wouldn't mind betting he'll think it's a funny story. He hasn't got any decency at all, let alone proper feelings. However, I won't deny he dealt with Ichabod better than any of us. You tell him I'm expecting a bit of wedding-cake.'

'Whose wedding-cake?' demanded Hannasyde. 'Not his own?'

'Yes,' said the Sergeant. 'Unless that girl with the eyeglass has got more sense than I give her credit for.'

He was interrupted by the entrance into the room of the Constable on duty, who announced that Mr Neville Fletcher wanted to speak to him.

'Talk of the devil!' exclaimed the Sergeant.

'Show him in,' said Hannasyde.

'He's on the phone, sir.'

'All right, put the call through.'

The Constable withdrew, Hannasyde picked up the receiver, and waited. In a few moments Neville's voice was wafted to him. 'Is that Superintendent Hannasyde? How lovely! Where can I buy a special licence? Have you got any?'

'No,' replied Hannasyde. 'Not our department. I was just coming up to see you, Mr Fletcher.'

'What, again? But I can't be bothered with murder cases now. I'm going to get married.'

'You aren't going to be bothered any more. The case is over, Mr Fletcher.'

'Oh, that's a good thing! We've really had quite enough of it. Where did you say I can buy a special licence?'

'I didn't. Do you want to know who murdered your uncle?'

'No, I want to know who keeps special licences!'

'The Archbishop of Canterbury.'

'No, does he really? What fun for me! Thanks so much! Goodbye!'

Hannasyde laid down the instrument, a laugh in his eyes.

'Well?' demanded the Sergeant.

'Not interested,' Hannasyde replied.

Behold, Here's Poison

Georgette Heyer

When Gregory Matthews, patriarch of the Poplars, is found dead one morning, imperious Aunt Harriet blames it on the roast duck he ate for supper, after all, she had warned him about his blood pressure. But a post-mortem determines that the cause of death is much more sinister. Murder. By poison.

Suspicion falls immediately amongst his bitter, quarrelsome family. Each has a motive; each, opportunity. It falls to Superintendent Hannasyde to sift through all the secrets and lies and discover just who killed Gregory Matthews, before the killer strikes again . . .

arrow books